Minimum Wage

Magic

DFZ Book 1 of 3

RACHEL AARON

SERIES INFORMATION

Minimum Wage Magic

Part-Time Gods

Night Shift Dragons

COPYRIGHT AND PUBLISHING INFO

ISBN Paperback: 978-1-952367-00-7
ASIN eBook: B07JWFDM2F

Cover Illustration by Tia Rambaran
Cover Design by Rachel Aaron
Editing provided by Red Adept Editing

Author's Note: *This is the first in a new series set in the same universe as my Heartstrikers books, but you don't need to have read those stories to enjoy this one.*

Minimum Wage Magic *was written to stand by itself, so if you haven't read the others, don't worry! I wrote this book with you in mind.*

Thank you so much for reading!
- Rachel

CHAPTER 1

The apartment looked like a fallout shelter.

It was in a sub-subbasement, twenty feet below street level down a wobbly flight of metal stairs so steep they were practically a ladder. The light at the bottom was burned out, of course, so the landing was pitch black. Also mysteriously wet. No idea how, since we hadn't had any rain in Detroit for a month, but these are the sort of lovely things you discover when you win a cheap bid.

"Gonna be one of *those* jobs, I see," I said, pulling my rubber gloves out of my bag.

"At least it's not big," Sibyl chirped in my ear, her computerized voice cheerful as always. "The building's custodian AI says the apartment's a one bedroom. I bet we can fit the whole thing in one truck."

"That's good," I said. "'Cause one truck is all I have."

I dug out my poncho next, grimacing as I pulled the slick, protective material over my sweat-dampened ponytail. Even down in the Underground where the sun never shone, the temperature was already in the upper eighties, and it wasn't even 9 a.m. Not good weather for covering yourself in plastic. But unlike my jeans and long-sleeved work shirt, my poncho was warded, and I'd learned the hard way that drowning in sweat was preferable to walking into someone's No Trespassing curse without protection.

"All right," I said, cinching the hood of my poncho tight under my chin so that I was draped head to toe in spellworked plastic. "Light 'er up."

The words were barely out of my mouth when the LEDs on the side of my AR goggles lit up like miniature suns, filling the dank stairwell with blazing white light. It was so bright that I missed the little red recording icon that came on next in the corner of my augmented-reality vision. Thankfully, AIs never forgot protocol.

"This is the video log for Unit 4B, Building 92, Detroit Free Zone Underground Block 14," Sibyl recited. "Purchase Date: Monday, July 22, 2115. Receipt #144528. Cleaner ID: Opal Yong-ae. Do you verify?"

"This is Opal Yong-ae, and I verify," I replied dutifully, hitting the button to flip to my interior camera for a shot of my sweat-streaked face beneath my protective gear. "Proceeding with occupant notification."

CYA out of the way, I slung my work bag around to my back and reached out to knock on the door, trying not to think too hard about the way the furry black spots on the paint squished under my gloves. "Cleaner," I announced loudly, thanking my lucky stars that I'd had the presence of mind to put on my rebreather *before* I'd climbed down into all this mold. "If you're inside, open up."

There was no reply. There was *never* a reply, but I always asked, because the one time I didn't, I just knew I'd open the door and find some junkie staring me down with a shotgun. Speaking of, I grabbed a fistful of local magic from the air and slapped it against my poncho to activate the antibullet wards. Just in case.

"Unit has no reply," I told my recorder. "Proceeding with reclamation."

"Ready when you are," Sibyl said, flagging the point in the video so that if someone tried to contest this job in arbitration later, I could point to the exact moment at which I stated my intent.

"This is Opal Yong-ae," I told the almost certainly empty apartment. "Subcontractor for Detroit Free Zone Habitation Management. You're thirty days behind on your rent and have not responded to multiple contact attempts from Collections. Therefore, by the terms of your rental agreement with the city, this apartment and all possessions therein are now property of the DFZ."

By which I meant property of *me*. When people skip town without paying their rent, the city takes their stuff to pay the bill. No bureaucrat wants to deal with sorting through someone else's abandoned junk, though, so they send the unit to auction, where it's bought by someone like me. I'm a Cleaner. I buy delinquent apartments in the hopes of selling what's inside for a profit. Sometimes I scored big. Other times—almost every time, recently—I paid for the privilege of shoveling trash.

Thankfully, on this particular unit, the bar for profit was practically on the ground. I'd gotten the whole thing for three hundred bucks, basically free, and despite the mold, I already had a good feeling about it. Just as in the picture that had convinced me to bid on the place, I could see the telltale marks of a ward beneath the dirt on the scuffed edges of the front door's frame. Wards were expensive, and expensive security meant good stuff.

"All right," I said when the silence on the other side of the door had stretched longer than the required thirty seconds. "Let's crack it open and see what we've got."

The red light vanished from my heads-up display as Sibyl stopped recording. I gave it a few seconds to be sure, and then I dug my gloved hand into the neck of my poncho to pull out the key I wore around my neck like a crucifix. The Master Key was a sacred object and a Cleaner's only real identification. It had been made for me by the Spirit of the City, and it could open any door in the DFZ if the city believed you had a right to be there.

That last bit was the tricky part. Unlike every other city in the world, the Detroit Free Zone was alive. *Literally* alive, with her own soul, mind, opinions, and, occasionally, off-the-books real estate deals. Collections tried their best to keep up, but they were only human. Sometimes rent was paid in ways that simply couldn't be reported. When that happened, it didn't matter how long a unit had been in collections. It would never open up.

In the one and a half years that I'd been Cleaning, I'd gotten a locked unit only once, but you didn't forget getting stiffed for two grand by the living goddess of your city. Thankfully, this was not going to be one of those days. The moment I touched my master key to the lock, the bright silver teeth rearranged themselves like water and slid right in, popping the deadbolt with a satisfying *click*.

The rest of the locks were another matter.

"Wow, this guy was paranoid," Sibyl said, bringing up density scanner results at the corner of my right eye. "I'm seeing four more deadbolts, two chains inside, and a rod in the floor."

"Don't forget the ward," I added, poking at the spellwork I could just barely see painted across the rusted metal doorjamb with the steel toe of my boot. "Not that I blame him. Look at where he lived."

The cheap apartment block this unit was at the bottom of was located in one of the lowest points of the DFZ Underground, almost a hundred feet below the elevated bridges of the Skyways that divided the top half of the city—the part with sunlight, superscrapers, trendy restaurants, and luxury housing—from the Underground, a cavelike world of underpasses, neon, and cheap rent. Parts of the Underground were nicer than others. I, for example, lived in a perfectly respectable walk-up over in Hamtramck, or what had been Hamtramck before Detroit had been destroyed, rebuilt, destroyed again, and then rebuilt again. This wasn't one of the nice bits, though. It wasn't the *worst*, but it was as bad as I went voluntarily. I didn't have crime stats for the place, so maybe I was prejudging it, but in my experience, anywhere that had more vending machines for guns than for soda wasn't winning any safe-neighborhood awards.

"These should crack easy enough, though," I said, shining my lights into the gap between the door and the frame to get a better look at the locks. "The ward's the real problem. If we don't get rid of that, we'll be fried chicken."

"*You'll* be fried chicken," Sibyl said smugly. "I'm backed up to the cloud."

I rolled my eyes and crouched down, pressing my plastic-covered head against the door so the cameras in my goggles could get a good shot of the spellwork at my feet. "Any clue what it does?"

"Nope," she said after the picture scanned. "Zero matches returned from all spellwork libraries. Looks like a custom job."

I grinned inside my mask. Custom spellwork was the hallmark of a serious mage. Probably an unsavory one since he was hiding down here, but unsavory magic sold even better than legitimate stuff, and Cleaners couldn't afford to be picky.

"I bet he's got something *good* in there. Mages are always loaded."

"Not always," Sibyl said. "I mean, you're a mage, and you're broke."

"Leave me my hope," I begged as I rose to my feet. "It's been a *really* bad couple of months, so let's just assume this apartment is piled high with priceless magical objects of high resale value."

"Whatever you need to tell yourself," Sibyl said. "But what do you want to do about the ward? This door's the only way in according to the blueprints."

I frowned at the symbols by my feet. Deciphering spellwork had never been my strong suit, but this stuff looked like arcane chicken scratch. I couldn't even spot the variables that would tell me if this was just an alarm ward or something that would cut your head off if you crossed it. It *felt* strong, though. Now that I was standing right next to it, I could feel the ward's magic humming even through the soupy ambient power of the DFZ. Whatever this thing did, it did it *hard*, which meant my best move was to avoid it entirely.

"Right," I said, stepping back. "Let's try the crowbar."

The crowbar was a spell of my own invention. Unlike the deadbeat owner of the apartment I was attempting to loot, I wasn't a Thaumaturge who treated magic like a mathematical equation to be solved. I knew enough spellwork to get by—since it followed logical rules that could be written down, Thaumaturgy was the easiest form of magic to teach, which meant it was the one that every mage learned in school—but I could never wrap my head around the higher logic needed to be actually good.

For me, magic had always been a feeling, a physical sensation I could trace with my fingers, like dipping my hand into a stream of water. If

Thaumaturges used spellwork to build complex logic-gated irrigation systems, then I cast by splashing. As my tutors had lectured me countless times, it was a fast, reckless way to use magic (or, if they were being less polite, lazy and dangerous). To me, though, it had always been the only way that felt right. I still appreciated quality Thaumaturgy—my poncho was proof of that; the thing was covered in top-tier corporate spellwork—but when it came to casting for myself, all those rules and variables just got in the way. It was a lot simpler to do everything freehand, which was what I did right now, reaching out to grab two big fistfuls of the DFZ's ambient magic.

As always, touching the city's magic in the Underground felt like dipping my fingers into oil-slicked water. *Noisy* water. The magic down here was full of car horns and voices and the rumble of engines mixed with the smell of greasy street food and wet pavement. Even the texture was different than the magic up on the Skyways: syrupy and thick, like trying to hold motor oil between your fingers.

Such thick, slippery power would have been a nightmare to push through spellwork, but when it came to my slapdash casting, the viscosity actually made things easier. I didn't even bother with a casting circle. I just kept pouring the power back and forth between my cupped hands, adding to it in fistfuls until the magic in my hands felt greater than the magic radiating from the ward on the door.

This turned out to be slightly more than I could safely hold, so I picked up the pace, squeezing the oozing magic between my hands until it was more or less the shape I wanted: a dense bar with a hook at one end, exactly like a real crowbar. The form was entirely for me. Magic didn't follow actual physics any more than dreams did, but casting was all about understanding. The whole point of spellwork equations was to prove to yourself logically *why* something would work. Since I'd never fully understood any spellwork, that method had never worked for me, but I knew what a crowbar did. I knew how to jam one into a door and wedge it open, so that was what I did now, jamming my magic between the ward and the door frame until the whole thing snapped with an explosive *crack.*

"Whoa!" Sibyl said as I jumped away from the splintering wood. "That's one way to do it."

"At least we don't have to worry about the other locks now," I said, nodding at the door, which had snapped in half from the pressure.

"I know, right?" my AI agreed. "Who needs proper casting? Brute force wins again!"

"Hey, I do better when I stick to what I'm good at," I said defensively. Then my face split into a grin as I turned the laserlike beams of my headlamps toward the room I'd just revealed. "Let's see what we've got!"

Being a Cleaner is all about being an optimist. No matter how many apartments full of dirty clothes and rat droppings you cleaned out, there was always that chance that the next one would be a treasure trove, and like I said, I had a good feeling about this place. I dove at what was left of the door like a kid jumping into a pool on the first day of summer, knocking the broken wood out of my way as if it were brittle glass. The more I cleared out, the more excited I became, because the ward on the doorframe was even better than I'd expected. I couldn't see the individual markings anymore now that I'd broken them, but I knew from the burn mark they'd left in the wood that that thing had been seriously powerful. I'd popped it fairly easily, but I broke into apartments (legally) for a living. A more standard mage, one who cared about fancy stuff like preserving spellwork or being quiet, would have tried to unlock it and probably gotten themselves fried as a result.

Fried *and* recorded. Now that the door was gone, I could see all kinds of wires running along the ceiling behind it. The entire front foyer of the apartment was rigged with cameras, sensors, and a tripwire leading to a bucket of cement that had been rigged to drop from the top of the coat closet door. If I'd come in normally, that thing would have crushed my head, which only made me more excited. Whoever had lived down here had clearly been hiding something *good*. The only question was had he taken it with him when he'd skipped town without paying his rent?

Going by what I could see from the doorway, my guess was no. It didn't look like anyone had ever taken *anything* out of here. Once you got past the traps at the front, the entire apartment was stacked floor to ceiling with boxes. There were a few canyonlike paths that ran between the stacks, but otherwise the whole place appeared to be little more than a glorified storage locker.

My heart began to flutter at the sight. Other than actually scoring a major find, this was my favorite part of being a Cleaner. Pulling out my wire cutters, I disarmed the entryway, cutting the tripwires and the power feeds to the sensors. When I was certain I wouldn't get crushed, shot, or garroted by anything automated, I crept inside, stepping into the canyon of boxes like an explorer entering a pharaoh's tomb. That was exactly how I felt, too. Like I was Indiana Jones—the *good* one from the original classic movies, not the ghastly seventeen-film reboot they did in the 2040s. I was about to dig into the first pile to see what I'd scored when the smell hit me.

"Ugh," I said, stumbling back. "What *is* that?"

It smelled like rotting meat left out on a hot day. Given that the temperature inside the apartment was over ninety (the AC was the first thing Collections cut off when an account went delinquent), my guess was that something had crawled in and died, but this didn't smell like sewer rat or mana vole or any of the other usual suspects. It was also strong enough to get through my rebreather, which meant it was *rank*. A person without protective gear would probably have been gagging from the moment the door opened. Even with my mask, my stomach was still doing the twist as I swung my light around to find the source.

"Is there a kitchen?" I asked Sibyl. "Maybe the previous occupant abandoned twenty pounds of bacon in the fridge."

"No kitchen," my AI replied. "According to the blueprints, it's just this room, the bedroom, and the bathroom."

"Well, it's gotta be coming from somewhere," I said, breathing through my mouth, which actually made it worse since I could taste the stench now instead of just smelling it. "Let's check the bedroom."

According to Sibyl, the bedroom was to my left, but there were so many boxes in my way that I couldn't even see the door. After much pushing and one really awful encounter with a spider web that I don't want to talk about, I eventually spotted my target: a flimsy wooden door with yet another ward etched into its pressboard frame. Unlike the ward on the front door, though, this one was dark. No magic answered me when I poked it, which meant it was either not active or someone wanted me to *think* it wasn't active so I'd go through and get fried.

Hoping it was the former rather than the latter, I squeezed through the last of the boxes and grabbed the doorknob, which turned easily. But while the door opened, it didn't go more than a foot before hitting something. The obvious guess was more boxes, but this didn't feel like a box. It had too much give, and it made a strange *clunk* when the door hit it. Curious, I pushed harder, shoving whatever it was back until the crack in the door was wide enough for me to squeeze my head through…

And see what was left of the dead body lying face down on the carpet.

✳✳✳

"God dammit, Broker!" I yelled into my phone. I was stalking back and forth in the mysteriously wet stairwell, too mad to care that my boots were splashing the unknown liquid up onto my legs. "You sold me a coffin!"

"Calm down, Opal," Broker said, his drawling voice soothing, like a rancher trying to sweet-talk a sheep off a cliff. "It's not that big a deal."

"Not a big deal? There's a *dead guy* rotting in my unit! Collections is supposed to check for this sort of thing!"

"They did check," Broker said. "It says right here on the unit's record that they tried multiple times to contact the occupant. They even sent someone over to check in person, but he didn't answer."

"Of course he didn't answer," I snapped. "He's dead! From the smell, I'd say he's been dead the whole thirty days his account's been delinquent. But that's not my problem. *My* problem is that you sold me a unit full of stuff that I can't sell. The DFZ might not have much in the way of laws, but inheritance is still a thing. I bid on that unit because it was small and I needed the money *today*. Now I can't touch anything until the city makes three good-faith attempts to contact dead dude's next of kin, which will take another month at least. Meanwhile, I'm stuck with a unit I can't use, and it's *your* fault!"

"No need to get snippy," Broker grumbled. "We'll refund your bid, of course. Just give it a week to get through accounting and another fifteen business days for processing, and the full amount will be transferred back to your bank account, no problem."

My scowl deepened. "How is it that you can take my payment instantly, but when I need it back, it suddenly takes fifteen business days?"

"Hey, I just work here, sweetheart. I don't make the rules. But if you don't want to wait, you can go ahead and take your payment out of what's in the apartment."

I frowned. "Is that legal?"

"It's legal-ish," Broker said slyly. "Dead or not, he's still delinquent on his rent. The city has a right to that money whatever his next of kin says, and since we already recouped it when we sold the unit to you, I don't see why you couldn't take your share of the debt out of his heir's inheritance. We'll just write the whole thing up as a property lien. It's not like anyone's going to challenge it. I mean, the guy's been dead for a month and no one noticed. If he does have an heir, they clearly don't care. The unit will probably be put right back up for sale next month when Collections fails to find the next of kin, so think of this as your chance to get the good stuff early. Or wait for the refund. Makes no difference to me."

From the tone of his voice, it clearly made a *huge* difference to Broker which one I picked. Approving a refund meant formally admitting that someone had messed up. Collection officers were supposed to verify if a unit was still occupied—or had a dead body in it—before putting it up for auction. Obviously, whoever had checked this unit had dropped the ball, which meant Broker had dropped the ball since it was his job as auctioneer to guarantee the units he sold.

Sweeping those failures under the rug was undoubtedly why he was so willing to bend the usually intractable Cleaning rules into origami for me. A properly ruthless Cleaner would have held that over his head, but I had a debt payment due at the end of the week, and I needed my money. If Broker was going to let me pillage the best parts out of this unit without actually cleaning it for resale—the only work Cleaners were legally obligated to do after they won a unit—I was happy to oblige. I just hoped there was something in all those boxes that was worth the three hundred bucks I'd paid for the privilege of walking in on that horror show.

"All right," I grumbled. "I'll take the unit."

"Glad you see it my way," Broker said cheerfully. "I'm sending someone over to take care of the body right now. Go ahead and start digging through his stuff. Just do me a favor and don't touch anything that looks personal. You know, just in case they do manage to find someone who cares."

I shrugged. "Fine with me. Not like there's a market for family photos."

"You're a gem, Opal. See you at the next auction."

I rolled my eyes at the tired old "gem" compliment and hit the End Call button.

"So what now?" Sibyl asked as I lifted my poncho to slip my phone back into my jeans pocket. "Wait for the disposal team to come for the body?"

"That could take hours," I said, walking back through the door I'd blown off on my way in. "If I had that kind of time to waste, I'd have made Broker give me a legit refund. No." I pulled my gloves back on. "We're going to get to work."

Technically, AIs don't have actual emotions, but Sibyl was a top-of-the-line social companion bot, and she did a good job of sounding legitimately horrified. "You can't start digging through a dead guy's stuff while he's still lying on the floor!"

"Why not?" I asked. "It's not as if he's going to complain, and I have a deadline."

A hard one. I owed a very nasty individual a lot of money, and he wasn't flexible about payments. If I didn't have the cash by Friday, bad things were going to happen.

"At least we have a lot to work with," I said, pointing at the wall of boxes. "There's so much here, some of it *has* to be good."

"By what logic?" Sibyl asked.

None, I admitted silently, but my AI already knew she was right, so I didn't bother bumming myself out by admitting the truth aloud. I just grabbed a box off the top of the pile and started ripping it open, peeling off the packing tape with a silent prayer to the living soul of the DFZ that something good was going to come out.

***

Suffice it to say, my prayers were not answered. Two hours later—a hundred and twenty disgusting, sweaty, putrid minutes of digging through dusty boxes in a dead man's living room while said corpse was rotting not ten feet away—I had exactly zero to show for it. The best I could say was that at least it was interesting. Most of the boxes turned out to be full of scholarly books about ancient magical methodologies. Primarily different styles of alchemy, but there were several boxes on ancient Egyptian sorcery, plus a whole stack of books about extinct magical animals. Clearly, whoever our dead man had been, he'd been a fan of historical magic.

I could relate. Before my life had gone to hell, I'd gotten my master's degree in magical art history and anthropology, which was a long-winded way of saying I studied old magical stuff left behind by ancient cultures. There was a surprising amount of it. In ancient times, the world had been *very* magical, even more magical than it was now. Then, for reasons only the Merlins knew, all that power had vanished.

For nearly eleven centuries, roughly 1000 to 2035 CE, the world had been completely unmagical, a period we now called the Drought. During that dark time, all of those magical treasures—the enchanted swords and religious relics and other venerated items of power crafted by ancient sorcerers and priests using techniques modern magic still didn't fully understand—lost their power and became merely pretty things. Some were preserved, coveted by various cultures and collectors as sacred objects even if they didn't actually work anymore, but countless more were lost to time.

Time and *ignorance*. We'd never know how many precious treasures had been destroyed by people who couldn't tell the difference between an enchanted hammer of the gods and a hammer you used to build houses. Those objects that did survive regained their power just like everything else when magic had suddenly returned eighty years ago, but so many more were gone forever.

Clearly, I wasn't the only one who found that heartbreaking. Our dead guy didn't have any actual relics, much to my dismay, but he had a truly impressive collection of archival photo prints. There were some very detailed pictures of ancient Persian alchemical tools in the boxes that even I hadn't seen before. They were all mass-produced prints, which meant they weren't worth the paper they were printed on, but it was still a lovely collection, and I ended up slipping several photos into my bag for myself.

But while I couldn't fault the dead man's taste, books and photos didn't sell. After opening every single one of the three hundred and twenty boxes crammed into the basement apartment's tiny living room, I estimated the entire collection at around a hundred bucks, which was two hundred short of what I needed just to break even. There was nothing in the bathroom, either, so I was forced to move on to the only room I hadn't touched yet.

The bedroom.

"Excuse me," I said to the dead man as I squeezed inside. "Just here to look around."

It was a stupid thing to say and more than a bit macabre, but dead or not, barging into someone's bedroom felt unspeakably rude. Rude and cold, because after two hours of digging through his collection, I felt like I knew the guy. He was a fellow historian, or at least an enthusiastic collector, and that deserved respect. Not "I'm not going to dig through your drawers looking for hidden lockboxes" levels of respect, but I felt I should acknowledge his presence at least.

"What do you think he died of?" I asked Sibyl as I started going through the stuff on top of his bureau. "The front door was intact, so I don't think he was killed in a robbery."

"I bet it was something internal," my AI replied, zooming my cameras in on the corpse's face, which was black and sunken with decomposition. "There's no obvious evidence of—"

"Could you not?" I snapped, yanking the cameras back. "This is creepy enough without you going for the close-up!"

"I was just answering your question," Sibyl said defensively. "As I was *trying* to say, there's no obvious evidence of violence. No blood splatters or bullet holes or anything like that. Add in the way he collapsed face forward on the ground, and a health crisis seem most likely. Stroke, heart attack, aneurysm, something like that."

I glanced at the mini fridge in the corner, which was sitting with its door wide open to reveal the melted—but otherwise completely undecayed—stack of microwave burritos inside. "Going by what he ate, my money's on heart attack." I shook my head. "Poor bastard."

"At least this room's not filled with boxes," Sybil said cheerfully. "If I have to look up resale prices for one more stack of dusty old books that don't have proper QR codes, I'm going to log myself out."

I was likewise sick of digging through outdated scholarly paperbacks, but the relative emptiness of this room meant that my chances of earning out on this unit were lower than they'd ever been. Biting my lip, I glanced over my shoulder at the dead guy. It was hard to tell since his clothes were so stained with decomposition, but he didn't look rich. He had none of the flashy jewelry or talismans you normally saw on underworld mages. He wasn't even wearing warded clothes. Other than being dead, the only actually remarkable thing about him was the fact that he had a cybernetic hand.

That wasn't unusual in the DFZ. Unlike other countries with their pesky safety regulations, anything you wanted to do to your body was perfectly legal here, even the really crazy stuff. Implants were cheap, too, since the DFZ also didn't require a medical license to install or build cybernetics. Hell, I'd seen homeless guys with camera eyes, but you didn't usually see augs on mages since cybernetics interfered with the flow of magic through the body.

Given the custom wards on his door and his obsession with ancient magic, I would've thought this guy would rather go handless than give up some of his magic to a machine, but clearly that wasn't the case. Who knew? Maybe he liked having a piece of him that was better than human more than he cared about absolute magical efficiency. Either way, that hand was worth a pretty penny. It didn't look like a high-end model, but you could always sell cybernetics. That said, Broker had only okayed me to loot the unit. He hadn't given me *carte blanche* to steal from the dead. No one could, not anymore.

Since the return of magic, the world had filled with gods. The first to rise had been Algonquin, Lady of the Great Lakes. The very night magic returned, she'd come out of her lakes in a tidal wave to punish humanity for polluting her waters. The resulting flood had devastated the entire

Great Lakes region, but nowhere was hit harder than Detroit. Since it had been one of the greatest polluters, Algonquin's hatred for the Motor City was special, and her wave had wiped it off the map. When she'd finished hammering it into the ground, Algonquin built a new city on Detroit's ruins—the first Detroit Free Zone—and claimed it for herself. The United States of America didn't even fight her over it. They were too busy dealing with the sudden return of mages and dragons and everything else to care about losing a troublesome, bankrupt city.

For the next sixty years, Algonquin had ruled the DFZ like an empress, forging it into a magical nexus of unbridled human greed. But the magic wasn't done coming back. The first night had been the most explosive, but the background magic kept creeping up slowly as the decades rolled on. Eventually, the ambient power got so high that it birthed a new god: the Spirit of the DFZ itself.

The ensuing battle for control of the city had leveled Detroit yet again. In the end, Algonquin got booted back to her lakes, and the new goddess claimed control. That was twenty years ago. The DFZ had rebuilt herself bigger than ever in the years since, and she wasn't alone. The tipping point of rising power that had created her—now known as the Second Crash—brought many other gods as well. Some were old, like Algonquin, and some were new, like the DFZ, but they were all powerful, and an inordinate number of them were gods of death.

No one knew how many death gods there were exactly, but their presence meant that doing anything disrespectful to a dead body, *especially* stealing, was a very bad idea. Death gods weren't forgiving as a rule, and here in the DFZ, the most magical city in the world, they were at their strongest. That cybernetic hand might be worth a thousand at auction, but the curse I'd get for taking it would cost me a lot more, so I left the hand where it lay and focused on digging through the dead man's underwear drawer, hoping against hope that he'd hidden something of value beneath all his tighty whities. I'd just moved on to his shirts when I heard someone say my name.

I nearly jumped out of my skin. Thankfully, Sibyl was on it, swirling my cameras to give me eyes in the back of my head just in time to see a young black man with a rather sketchy-looking tomcat on his shoulder walk through the bedroom door.

"Peter!" I gasped, clutching my poor chest. "Don't do that to me!"

"Sorry, Opal," he said apologetically. "I tried to knock, but the front door was gone." A smirk spread over his face. "Not that I should have expected anything less, seeing it was you."

"Hey, I don't *always* take the door off," I said grumpily, eyeing the folding stretcher he was carrying under his left arm. "But what are you doing here? Broker said he was sending a disposal detail."

"He called in for one," Peter said. "But when I heard that the victim had been dead in his apartment for a month and no one noticed, I volunteered to take care of him." He reached up to pet his rangy cat. "He seemed like our kind of fellow."

When he put it that way, it made sense. Peter was a priest for one of those new death gods. Specifically, he'd dedicated himself to the Empty Wind, Spirit of the Forgotten Dead, which definitely included our guy.

"Do you need help getting him out?"

"I can manage, thanks," Peter said, leaning over to let his cat jump down. "Once we commit the body, he'll get a lot easier to move. The Empty Wind takes care of his own."

From anyone else, that would have been a cryptic thing to say, but Peter made it sound like a blessing. That was how he always talked, though. He came to the Cleaner auctions sometimes to buy up units he claimed belonged to the Forgotten Dead. Auctions were always a circus, but even when everyone else was shouting, Peter never raised his voice. He didn't have to. The moment he bid, everyone else shut up. Broker claimed it was all superstition and rallied us to bid higher, but he made his living taking a cut off the top of our auctions. He also didn't understand. I hadn't either before I'd started Cleaning. I'd thought the DFZ was just a crazy city with a mind of its own, but get down in the Underground where people are really desperate, and you see things. I didn't worship the Empty Wind like Peter did, but I didn't doubt for a moment that he was real, and spooky as that was, I was happy our dead guy had a god to care about him, since no one else seemed to.

"I'll just keep going, then," I said, turning back to the drawers. "Let me know if you need help."

"I will," Peter said. "Thank you, Opal."

There was power in those words. Gods had long memories, which meant being nice to priests was always a good idea. I would have helped him anyway, though, because I liked Peter. Priesthood aside, he was a genuinely good guy. Those were a rare commodity anywhere, but they were nigh unheard of in the DFZ. That made me eager to stay in his good graces, even if it meant hauling a dead guy up two flights of stairs.

Thankfully, it didn't come to that. Peter didn't ask for anything. He just knelt beside the dead man, whispering promises of eternal remembrance in his calm, deep voice while I dug through the drawers. It was so peaceful, I didn't even flinch when a grave-cold wind rose from nowhere, sweeping the heavy, putrid air out of the apartment. I was still appreciating the cool when I heard Peter unfold his stretcher and start loading the body.

That broke the spell real quick. Turns out, month-old corpses make *horrible* noises when you move them. Frantic to distract myself from the nightmare soundtrack going on behind me, I picked up the pace, shoving my hand below the bed, the only place in the apartment I hadn't searched yet. I was groping blindly through the dust bunnies when something sharp stabbed into my finger.

"*Ow!*"

"What?" Peter said, stretcher clattering to the ground.

"Nothing, nothing," I said, yanking my arm back to cradle my smarting fingers. "Just being an idiot."

A *total* idiot. I'd been so eager to take my mind off the goopy biology behind me that I'd broken the number-one rule of Cleaning: never put your hand where you can't see it. Luckily, I still had all my fingers, but the first two were burning like they'd been bitten by a wasp rat. If my gloves hadn't been so thick, I would have suspected there was an actual critter under there, but not only was the rubber still whole, my skin looked fine when I yanked my glove off, which meant it wasn't an animal that had bitten me.

It was a spell.

My face split into an enormous grin. Moving at the speed of greed, I dropped to my stomach and wiggled under the bed, using my headlamps to spot the culprit: a warded box tucked into the gap where the bed's leg met the wall. Not stupid enough to get bitten a second time, I reached into my bag and pulled out my tongs, using the rubber-coated grips to grab the box and ease it out into the light.

What came out was a metal container slightly larger than a shoebox and absolutely covered in the same bizarre chicken-scratch custom spellwork as the front door. Some of the markings were still glowing from where the spell had zapped me, but unlike the ward on the front door, which could have done who knew what, even I could see this was a security spell. Complicated, powerful, but still just a safe at the end of the day, and if there was anything I'd learned from a year and a half in this business, it was how to crack a safe.

"Oh, yeah!" I said as I pulled magic into my hands. "Come on, loot box!"

Since Peter was here, I had to keep my magic toned down, which meant it took me five minutes to crush the first lock and a full ten to crack the next. By the time I reached the final one, Peter had our dead guy wrapped in a dignified sheet on the stretcher. He was clearing a path through the living room to the front door when the warded box in my lap finally clicked open.

Completely forgetting my earlier lesson about sticking parts of myself where they shouldn't be, I tore the lid open and shoved my hand inside, grabbing for whatever magical treasure *had* to be in there. Given this guy's obsession with ancient magic, I was hoping for something really good: a legit alchemical relic, ancient spellwork tablets, old enchanted glass.

What I got was a stack of paper.

"What?!" I cried, turning the box upside down to dump the pile of perfectly normal, not-even-ancient paper into my lap. "You've to be kidding me!"

They were notes. Notes for *what* I couldn't say since they were written in the same gobbledygook custom spellwork as everything else, but they looked like plans for something complicated. There were tons of size and time calculations written in the margins, along with dollar amounts that made my eyes go wide. I was trying to figure out if they were costs or expected earnings when I found the stack of receipts.

I didn't actually recognize what they were at first. I mean, who still used physical receipts? But our dead guy's love of paper must have extended beyond books, because he'd printed and kept hundreds of receipts going back more than a year. Some were for startling amounts, and even more interesting, they were all for magical reagents.

In the old days, back when the local ambient power had been too thin to just pull whatever magic you needed out of the air, mages had been forced to use external sources to power their spells, usually the body parts of magical animals. These days, there was so much magic floating around that that sort of thing wasn't necessary unless you were after a very specific magical flavor or property, but this mage must have been doing something crazy, because he had receipts for stuff I hadn't even heard of. Very *expensive* stuff.

"Sibyl," I said quietly, fanning the stack of receipts in front of my cameras. "What's the total on these?"

"Two hundred eighty-three thousand nine hundred and forty dollars and twenty-seven cents," my AI replied immediately. "It would have been less, but he got rush shipping on a lot of stuff."

That was a number to make my eyes go wide. "What was he doing with it all?" I whispered. "I mean, why pay this much for power when you live in a city that's drowning in free magic?"

"No clue," Sibyl said. "But if he'd done it anywhere else, it would have been illegal." She placed a red arrow on my heads-up display, drawing my attention to a receipt in the middle of the pile. "This one's for a unicorn horn, which only comes off with the unicorn's head. I don't have to tell you how heavily protected unicorns are. They're not even endangered, but humans go crazy anytime one gets hurt. If we weren't in the DFZ, just having this paper could get you in trouble."

"Maybe that's why he was here," I said thoughtfully. The current DFZ wasn't quite as *laissez-faire* as it had been under Algonquin's rule—the spirit of the lakes had famously cared more for fish than for people, and her lack of laws had shown it—but the modern Detroit Free Zone still lived up to its name. Practically everything short of murder, theft, and slavery was legal here, including, apparently, unicorn poaching. Still. "This has to be worth something," I said firmly. "You don't spend this much on reagents and not get something good out of the spell."

"Well, whatever he was doing, he didn't do it here," Sibyl pointed out. "There isn't enough room in this apartment for even the starting ritual circle he drew on page one."

That was a good point. "You know," I said, looking around the tiny bedroom, which was well stocked with general supplies like clothes but curiously light on personal items. "I don't think he actually lived here. I think this was a place he ran to in emergencies. You know, like a safe house."

"That would explain all of the security," Sibyl agreed. "And the cruddy location. No one ever seems to hide in nice places."

I nodded, paging through the spell notes again. Even accounting for my terrible skill at reading spellwork, they still looked depressingly like a madman's manifesto. Every page was written out to the margins, and there were doodles of weird creatures with chicken heads and snake tails surrounded by arrows and exclamation points. But nutty as the notes looked, they were all I had. There was no way I was hauling a thousand pounds of books up those slimy, mold-covered stairs for a measly hundred bucks. If the spell laid out on these pages wasn't worth money, I'd wasted my entire morning and three hundred bucks on this hole.

"Sibyl, does Heidi Varner still work at the Institute for Magical Arts?"

"According to her social media, she does," my AI replied. "Do you want me to send her a message?"

"No," I said quickly. I hadn't used any of my social media accounts in a year, and I wasn't about to reopen that can of worms for a long shot like this. But where I'd focused primarily on the art and history parts of my magical art history degree, Heidi was a trained Thaumaturge with a specialization in ancient alchemy. She also owed me for not telling her boyfriend about the time she got drunk and kissed another guy in college.

"I'll just pay her a visit," I said. "Are her office hours still the same?"

"Same as when you left, according to IMA's website," Sibyl reported. "But are you sure you want to go? Not that I'd ever read your private mail, but the subject lines of the messages she's sent you over the last year and a half seem pretty angry."

I was sure they did, which was why I'd never looked at them. But desperate times, desperate measures. If there was a chance the spell outlined in these notes was worth anything close to the cost of its reagents, then visiting Heidi was a risk I was willing to take. I was overdue for a change of luck. Maybe our mage had ordered all that stuff but died before he'd gotten the chance to actually cast the spell. For all I knew, there was $283,940.27 worth of reagents just sitting in a warehouse somewhere, waiting for me to come and pick it up.

"I guess it could happen," Sibyl said when I mentioned this. "It's not *likely*, but—"

"I know, I know," I said as I tucked the pages into my bag. "Just pull the truck around, would you?"

My AI heaved a long, recorded sigh. "Calling it now."

"Thank you, Sibyl," I said, walking down the path Peter had cleared through the living room to see if he needed any help getting the dead body up to the street.

CHAPTER 2

Most established Cleaners owned their own trucks, which made sense when you considered that we basically moved houses for a living. But owning a vehicle of any sort was stupid expensive in the DFZ, so I'd opted for the much cheaper route of leasing from one of the car subscription services. Better still, in a rare stroke of foresight, I'd prepaid for the entire year back in January when I'd had money to burn. I'd also bought a fancy intelligent rice maker and an augmented-reality TV, both of which I'd had to turn around and sell months ago to make my rent.

But the car thing at least I'd gotten right. Subscription vehicles weren't fancy, fast, or particularly safe—the small pickup I'd been given this time was missing its bumper and looked like it was made entirely from recycled plastic—but it cost less than half what owning my own vehicle would have, and I got to use it for up to two hundred hours a month. Sometimes more if no one else had it booked.

I didn't even have to drive. Once Sibyl activated it, the truck's AI piloted itself. The cab didn't even have a steering console, just a flat plastic dash with a cheap touch screen featuring a badly animated dog asking where I wanted to go in a cheerful, childish voice.

"Institute for Magical Arts," I said as I shut the chintzy door.

"Right away, Miss Yong-ae," the truck replied. "Would you like to upgrade your ride today? We have over five hundred entertainment options from the hottest new—"

"No," I said, cutting off the upsell. "Also: No. No. No. I decline the insurance option. And No."

"Yes ma'am," the vehicle said when its cheap AI finally finished processing all of my answers. "We should reach your destination in thirty-nine minutes. Until then, please enjoy these messages from our corporate partners!"

I scrambled for the volume, frantically mashing my finger against the down arrow on the touch screen as ads started blasting at deafening levels from the tinny speakers.

"You know, you really should just pay the extra ten dollars a month for the ad-free service," Sibyl said when I'd gotten the cheerful jingles down to a not hearing-destroying level. "It would improve your mental state."

"If I could afford an extra ten bucks a month, my mental state wouldn't need improving," I reminded her, flopping into the cheap plastic seat as the truck backed itself out of the alley. "But why did it say it's going to be forty minutes? It shouldn't take more than twenty to get to the IMA campus from here."

"There's a lot of activity in our way," Sibyl said, bringing up a map of the city, which was covered in bright-red warning icons. "Looks like the DFZ's doing some moving of her own."

That turned out to be a very accurate description. Everything looked relatively normal in the Underground—just the usual cheap apartment blocks, discount stores, and neon-lit vending machine bars selling the standard assortment of canned liquor—but when we turned up the ramp to the Skyways, it was like entering a whole other world.

The first thing that hit me was the sunlight. I cringed like a bad movie vampire when we came out of the tunnel into the upper city. Even through the smog, the summer afternoon was so blue and bright it scarcely looked real. I was so used to being under bridges that I'd almost forgotten how big the summer clouds could be, but even they were dwarfed by the city's superscrapers.

I grew up moving between Seoul, LA, and Hong Kong, so I was used to giant buildings, but the ones in the DFZ were on an entirely different level. Some of the glass and steel spires were a full quarter mile around at the base, with peaks so tall they created their own rain shadows. Even modern steel-strengthening spellwork couldn't account for how enormous they were, because these buildings hadn't been built by human hands. They were the product of the spirit of the city, sprouted from the ground like trees by the DFZ herself. And apparently she wasn't done.

"Wow," I breathed, pressing my face against the scratched-up window.

Ahead of us to the left, on the route we normally would have taken, an entire section of the New I-75 flyover had lifted from its support beams and was slowly moving to the north, much to the fury of the cars stuck on top of it. The angry blaring of horns was even louder than the advertisements still yakking through my speakers, but they were still nothing compared to the stomach-churning scrape of steel on stone from the new building that was rising from the ground where the highway had been.

Even after three and a half years in the DFZ, the sight was a shock. I gawked like a tourist, watching wide-eyed as ribbons of steel rebar shot up from the exposed Underground like seedlings racing toward the sunlight. Cement followed more slowly, creeping up the metal as the new building constructed itself in front of my eyes. Given that the top of it was already visible above the Skyways, there had to be multiple floors already constructed in the Underground below that I wasn't seeing, not to mention foundations. I hadn't noticed a thing when I'd driven through that area this morning, though, which meant the DFZ had done all of that during the time I'd been stuck in the dead guy's apartment. God or no, that struck me as quite impressive, and I whistled in appreciation.

"I wonder what kind of building it'll be."

"Given the area of the base, it's either another superscraper or a stadium," Sibyl replied. "Not that we need either. This area's too crowded as it is."

I chuckled. "I think the city knows what she's doing."

"Well, I just wish she'd wait until after rush hour to do it," my AI grumped, bringing up the map again, which was updated in real time by the DFZ City Council, the only municipal service the city provided for free. "Look at this mess!"

It *was* pretty dire. According to the warnings, I-75 had been on the move for the last forty-five minutes. All the side streets near the new building had been cut off as well on both the Skyways and Underground levels, and the resulting chaos had turned this entire section of the city into a parking lot.

"Good thing we're going south," I said, looking sympathetically at the cars stranded on top of the moving bridge. "That thing doesn't look like it's coming down anytime soon."

"There's no estimated end time listed on the traffic report," Sibyl confirmed, her voice disgusted. "What is the DFZ thinking? She's not exactly known for taking her citizens' convenience into account, but moving a major commuter highway on a Monday just feels like bad planning."

I shrugged. "Spirits move in mysterious ways. I mean, for all we know, the delays are the point. She *is* the living incarnation of the city, and what's more citylike than a traffic jam?" I smiled at the interstate, which was now a good fifty feet above the already elevated Skyways and still rising. "I'm just glad the truck's AI was smart enough to route us around."

"Hooray for minimal competency," Sibyl said dryly. "On the bright side, though, this means there should be a lot of Cleaning jobs coming up in the next few months. Historical data shows that there's always a surge in vacancies after the DFZ does something big like this."

"It's never comfortable to be reminded that you're an ant in a god's world," I agreed, staring up at the two enormous superscrapers that were tilting sideways to make way for the new building, sending entire floors full of office furniture sliding in the process. "I just hope I'm still around to take advantage of it."

Normally, this was where Sibyl would insist things weren't *that* bad, but her protocol against lying was stronger than her directive to cheer me up, and we both knew the truth. It was right there on the wallet icon at the top of my heads-up AR display. After a year of doing really well as a Cleaner, I'd hit a dry streak nothing seemed able to break. Today's fiasco was just the latest in a long line of absolutely horrid luck. If I hadn't been a mage and able to check these things for myself, I'd have sworn that I was cursed. Every time I looked, though, there was nothing. It was just plain old bad luck, statistical clustering, which meant it *had* to break soon. No one could be this unlucky forever. Whether I could hold out long enough to reach the other side, though, was another issue entirely.

"Maybe we'll get lucky and these'll turn out to be a brilliant translation of some lost alchemical text," I said, pulling the dead mage's mysterious notes out of my bag. "Heidi's a sucker for that stuff, and her department has serious corporate funding. We could still make bank."

"If that mage was capable of anything worth 'bank,' he wouldn't have been living on frozen burritos in a basement apartment," my AI pointed out.

I rolled my eyes. "Thanks for the vote of confidence."

"I just don't want you getting your hopes too high," Sibyl said. "As a social support AI, it's my job to assist in your mental health, and these fits of wild optimism that crumble into crushing despair when they run into reality are *not* good for you. I think it would be much healthier for you to drop the notes in Heidi's box and go home for a shower before the evening auction. I don't have a nose, but I'm pretty sure you smell like dead guy."

That was undoubtedly true, but the thought of abandoning the notes—my *only* score from today's disgusting, backbreaking work—in a cubby at the history department's unorganized office was too much to bear. "Not a chance," I said firmly. "We're going inside. If these notes are worth something, I want to know today."

"Suit yourself," Sibyl said. "I'm just saying there's a strong likelihood this whole thing is a waste of time."

"Better to waste time than money," I said stubbornly. "Time I've got." Until Friday, at least.

We spent the rest of the ride in silence. Thankfully, the traffic disruption from the moving highway was mostly confined to the northern half of downtown. Midtown, where the IMA campus was, was moving just fine. Once we got out of the glut, we made good time, cruising down the cheap toll lanes until we reached the turnoff for the institute just as the ride meter ticked to thirty-nine minutes, exactly as predicted.

"Haven't been here in a while," I said, self-consciously brushing the grime off my warded poncho as I stepped onto the pristine white cement of IMA's new visitor pavilion. "I like the new duck pond."

"I think it's supposed to be a reflecting pool," Sibyl said. "The ducks are just swimming in it."

"Then I hope they're ready to sell their souls to pay tuition," I joked, looking around at the perfect green lawn and artistically scattered white buildings that made up IMA's main campus. "You go into debt just for breathing around here."

Like everything else that was worth real money, IMA was up on the Skyways. It had a *nice* location, too, taking up several elevated blocks just half a mile south of the Dragon Consulate where the Peacemaker, the dragon who claimed the DFZ as his territory, kept his lair. I wasn't sure why the DFZ allowed any dragon, particularly one as famously eccentric as the Peacemaker, to claim her as his land, but there must have been some kind of history there, because she *loved* him. Her buildings were forever shifting around the multilevel Dragon Consulate to make sure the dragons had a clear flight path coming in.

And they were *always* coming in. Thanks to the Peacemaker's Edict, which declared that no dragon could attack another within the city without facing the Peacemaker's wrath, the DFZ had turned into a sort of dragon Switzerland. Clans that would kill each other on sight anywhere else in the world routinely met in the DFZ to talk. Not about peace—normal dragons never talked peace—but they talked a lot of business, which was probably why the DFZ gave them so much leeway. No one loved capitalism more than she did, and when you considered how much wealth the average dragon accumulated over their immortal life, courting them was just good sense.

It was also good for IMA. Being so close to the Dragon Consulate, and the spectacle of the giant dragons that constantly flew through the sky surrounding it, gave the school an edge that other magical arts universities simply could not top. Add in the fact that they'd converted their entire Skyway campus into a lavish park complete with water features, semi-tropical gardens, and buildings that looked like modern art installations, and the whole place just reeked of exclusivity and money.

Of the three major magical colleges in the DFZ, the Institute for Magical Arts was the most expensive by an order of magnitude. While MIT-Thaumaturgical and the New Wayne College of Magic had to pour their efforts into industrial spellwork research to court corporate funding, IMA dedicated itself to the "art" part of magical arts with graduate programs in expressive casting, illusionary sculpture, magical theatre, and, my specialty, magical art history. It was the best magic-focused liberal arts school in the world, which meant it was trust fund kids all the way down. I'd fit right in when I'd first arrived almost four years ago. Now I felt like a homeless bum who'd wondered onto campus by accident.

At least I could still look like I knew where I was going. The campus had changed a lot since I'd finished my master's degree a year and a half ago, but the path to the art history department was still drilled into my memory. Once I figured out how to get out of the fancy new visitor's area, I walked straight there, ordering my truck to circle the block a few times so I wouldn't have to pay for parking while I cut across the bright-green grass lawn toward the perfect white cube that was IMA's historical arts building.

As a lowly doctoral student, Heidi's office was in the basement. It was a very nice basement with reactive lighting and fake LED windows displaying real-time footage of famous landscapes, but it was still a bunch of closet-sized offices crammed into an underground hallway. I didn't remember which one was Heidi's anymore—it *had* been more than a year—but I didn't need to. Her door was still covered in the same history jokes and pictures of her and her golden retriever as I remembered. It opened the moment I knocked, revealing a startlingly tall blond woman with tanned skin, a healthy, athletic glow, and cheekbones that could cut glass.

"*Opal!*" Heidi cried, rushing forward to hug me before I could warn her about my wards. "*Ugh,*" she said a moment later, snatching her arms back. "What are you wearing? It feels like a trash bag."

"Anti-dirt wards," I explained, pointing at my poncho. "And anti a lot of other stuff, which is why it feels so slippery. That and the fact that it is actually made of plastic."

Heidi looked horrified. "Why are you wearing that horrible thing?" she asked, stepping back to let me inside. "You're not still working as a Cleaner, are you?"

I shrugged and took a seat on the minimalist metal stool in front of her neatly organized desk. "It's not so bad."

"Really?" she asked, shutting the door behind me. "Because you look terrible."

I rolled my eyes. "Thanks."

"I'm serious," Heidi snapped, walking back to her desk. "You're thin, and I don't mean that as a compliment."

"It's been a rough few months," I admitted, reaching into my bag. "But I'm working on turning it around. That's why I'm here, actually. I need a favor. I found these on a job, and—"

"Stop," Heidi said angrily. "Just stop right there. What do you think you're doing?"

I blinked at her. "Asking for help?"

"Help?" she said, her perfect face growing furious. "Opal, you *vanished!* You got your degree, and then you disappeared!"

"I didn't disappear," I said defensively. "I was still here in the DFZ. I just needed a change of—"

"You moved out of our apartment in the middle of the night!" she yelled at me. "The only reason I knew you were working as a Cleaner is because your mother called to see if I could talk you out of it. Which I *couldn't* because you never answered any of my messages!"

I winced. Maybe coming back here hadn't been such a good idea after all. "I'm sorry, I just—"

"Sorry?" Heidi yelled, slamming her hands on her desk. "It's a little late for *sorry!*"

The raw anger in her voice was a shock. I'd known Heidi for years, but I'd never seen her get this emotional. To be honest, I hadn't realized she'd cared so much, which made me feel like a jerk. In my defense, I'd had a lot going on at the time, but that didn't take the sting out of seeing her stare at me like I'd stabbed her in the back.

"Why, Opal?" she said, her voice cracking. "I was your roommate. I *thought* I was your friend. Why did you leave without saying goodbye?"

"I wasn't doing it to be mean," I said, pulling off my goggles so that I could look at her properly. "And you are my friend, I just…I needed a clean break, that's all."

"A clean break from what?" Heidi demanded. "Were you in trouble?"

I'd actually done it to get myself *out* of trouble, but I couldn't tell Heidi that. I'd lied to her enough back when we'd been roommates, which was one of the main reasons I'd left. I was tired of lying all the time. Tired of doing the dance that was necessary to keep everyone else safe. Tired of being me.

A pretty gem of little value.

"I had to go," I said, hardening my voice. "I can't tell you more than that, but trust me when I say that it was for the best. I wouldn't have bothered you now, but I really need to know what this spellwork—"

"*Please,* bother me!" Heidi begged, reaching out to grab my dirty hands. "What part of 'I am your friend' do you not understand? If you're in trouble, let me help. I'm still living in our old apartment. You can move back in anytime you want. Or don't, I don't care, just *please* let me help you! I can't stand to see you like this. You look homeless and you smell like death."

"Told you," Sibyl whispered in my earpiece.

I muted her with a flick of my finger and focused on Heidi. "Thank you for the offer. It means a lot to me, it really does, but I can't."

Heidi's brown eyes narrowed. "It's your dad, isn't it?"

I stopped cold. "No," I said after way too long.

"You're not nearly as good a liar as you think you are," she said, crossing her arms. "Look, I know you and your dad don't get along. Given the way you used to yell into your phone, I'm pretty sure the whole building knew. But if he's the reason you ran away, I swear I won't tell him you're back. Just come home. Whatever you're running from, we'll work it out together. I can even give you a job. There's an opening right now in my department. I can get you set up today if you want. For the love of God, Opal, you have a graduate degree from the best magical arts institute in the world! You don't have to dig through other people's trash to make a living!"

I'd be lying if I said I wasn't tempted. After my last five months, moving back into Heidi's sun-drenched apartment on the Skyways sounded like paradise. But if she knew about my dad, then she was already in too deep. I'd left precisely so he couldn't use people like her against me. If I took her offer now, I'd be playing right into his hands.

"I can't."

"Opal!"

"*No*," I said, clenching my hands into fists. "I'm sorry about the way I left. I didn't mean to make you worry. I just had a lot of stuff I had to deal with on my own, and this was the only way I could do it."

"By becoming a Cleaner?" she cried. "How does that help anything?"

It had helped a lot, actually. Unlike respectable art historians, no one cared what Cleaners did. They came and went as they pleased, and they made their own money. Much better money than an entry-level job at IMA paid, current bad luck notwithstanding. It wasn't neat or respectable, but I needed money more than I needed my pride right now. And anyway, I *liked* Cleaning. It was surprisingly fun digging through people's lives, and sometimes I found great stuff. Heidi wouldn't understand that, though. From the look on her face, she clearly thought I was little better than a rag picker, and the fact that I looked the part certainly wasn't helping matters.

"I appreciate the job offer. Really, I do, but I'm not coming back." I held up my dirty poncho. "It's not pretty, but this is my life now, and I'm happy with that. Honest."

Heidi did not look convinced, but at least she didn't keep arguing. "So does that mean you'll answer when I message you now?"

"Sure," I lied. There was no way I could stay in contact with her. Not until my debt was paid and I was in the clear. But for all her talk about me being a bad liar, she must have bought it, because for the first time since I'd come in, Heidi smiled at me.

"How are you so stubborn?" she muttered, sinking into her office chair.

"Talent," I said, smiling back. "So can you help me or not?"

She sighed. "What do you need?"

I pulled out the folded notes I'd found in the warded box under the mage's bed. "Can you look at these and tell me what they are? The forms look alchemical to me, but deciphering ancient spellwork is your area of expertise, not mine."

"You always were more of a brute-force-o-mancer," Heidi agreed, wrinkling her nose as she plucked the papers from my hand. "Do I want to know why these smell like dead animal?"

I shook my head, and she sighed, thumbing through the sheets as if she was grading papers. "They're plans for a ritual," she said after a few minutes.

I nodded excitedly. "A ritual for what?"

"Something big," she said, sounding interested now despite herself. "The main structure involves multiple overlapping circles, which is an influence of modern Thaumaturgy, but the core spellwork is absolutely alchemical. Primarily the Islamic forms, but there's lots of stuff stolen from the Ancient Greeks as well." She glanced at me. "Where did you find these again?"

"In an amateur historian's apartment," I said, tactfully leaving out the bit where said amateur historian had been lying dead right next to them. "I'm trying to determine if they're valuable."

"They're certainly unique," Heidi said, laying the pages out on her desk in a grid so she could see all of them at once. "Historically, alchemy was all about transformation—turning one thing into another. Usually lead into gold, but there's no mention of gold here."

That was disappointing. Gold always sold. "So what was he trying to do?"

"I'm not sure," Heidi said, squinting at the papers. "It looks as though he's using the transformational nature of alchemy as a tool to make something, but I can't see…Ah ha!" She stabbed her finger down on a particularly doodle-covered page. "Here it is. I had to find the central variable. This is a ritual to make a cockatrice egg."

"You can make those?" I asked. Cockatrices were one of the many mythical animals that had reappeared when the magic came back. I didn't know much about them, but it seemed to me that cockatrice eggs would come from other cockatrices, not from alchemy.

"Cockatrice eggs were a vital ingredient in many Indo-European alchemy transformations," Heidi explained. "You see them mentioned all the time in historical texts, but due to their organic nature, very few are still in existence. Other than the ones laid by actual cockatrices, of course. But it takes an egg laid by a rooster and incubated by a toad to make a cockatrice naturally, which obviously doesn't happen very often, so most ancient alchemists just made their own. Unfortunately, the process for creating them was either so secret or so obvious, no one wrote it down. At least, we've never found a recipe."

My heart began to beat faster. "Does that mean these notes are valuable?"

"Not to my department," Heidi said. "I'm a magical *historian*, and while this little project is interesting, it's not historical. It also doesn't look very practical. I don't know how much a cockatrice egg costs these days, but this spell requires over two hundred thousand dollars in reagents, some of which are extremely morally questionable." She shrugged. "I'm sorry, Opal. It's an interesting piece of spellwork, but it's not valuable. It's not old enough or groundbreaking enough to be academically relevant, and I can't believe anyone would go through the trouble of gathering this many reagents just to make a cockatrice egg."

My soaring hopes fell with every word she spoke, but I wasn't ready to give up yet. "But do you think it would work?" I pressed. "If all the reagents were present and the spell was cast as written, do you think it would actually make an egg?"

Heidi shrugged. "Probably? I mean, I don't see any reason it *wouldn't* work, but you can never tell with a spell until you actually cast it. Just speaking for myself, though, if I had those reagents sitting around, I'd sell them. Or turn them in to the proper authorities. Or even keep them for my own experiments. I certainly wouldn't waste them on *this*. Even if you love cockatrices, this spell is simply too expensive to be practical."

I heaved a long sigh. "Well, I guess that's that," I said, standing up. "Thanks for looking at least."

"Any time," Heidi said, scraping the notes back into a neat stack and handing them to me. "But do think about my offer. I'm sure Cleaning isn't actually as dangerous as the TV shows make it look, but you graduated with honors from IMA. You're better than this. Your skills are being wasted on this garbage. *You* are being wasted, and I hate seeing that." She gave me a plaintive look. "Can I have your new number at least? Just in case I find a job that can tempt you away from Cleaning?"

I *really* didn't want to. What was the point of sucking up the pain of cutting everyone out of your life if you were just going to let them back in? But I couldn't take the way Heidi was staring at me, especially not after she'd helped me when I'd done nothing to deserve it. I could always change my number again later, so I wrote it down for her, lying through my teeth when she made me swear to answer her calls.

By the time I finally left her office, I felt utterly defeated. Not only were the notes I'd pinned my hopes on apparently worthless, I'd been thoroughly reminded of my status as the world's worst friend. Definitely not my best day, and for all her claims of being a socially sensitive AI, Sibyl wasn't helping.

"I *told* you this was a waste of time," she said as we climbed the stark white modern stairs back to the ground floor. "You should toss those stupid notes in the trash before they cost us any more."

"Not yet," I said stubbornly. "Some of those reagent receipts were dated less than a week before he went delinquent on his rent." I put up my hand to shield my eyes as we emerged from the basement into the late-afternoon sunlight. "That means he had to have bought them right before he died. You don't pay that much for a spell without trying it. I bet he'd either just cast it or was about to when he died. Either way, somewhere in this city, there's an unclaimed magical circle with a cockatrice egg or two hundred thousand in reagents inside it, and we're the only ones who know. That's worth keeping a line on, don't you think?"

"No I do not," Sibyl snapped. "*I* think you're letting your optimism run away with you again. Even if you're right, and there *is* a pot of gold at the end of this wild goose chase, the DFZ is a hundred and ninety-four square miles that *move around*. The chance of you finding one mage's circle in all of that is practically zero, and we don't have the resources to waste trying. Need I remind you that if you don't have ten thousand dollars by midnight on Friday, you're going to be screwed? You bought me to give you good advice, so listen for once: forget this and let's get back to the Cleaner office. If we hustle, we can still make it in time for the evening auction. There's always more stuff up for sale at night. We'll get a good unit, clean it fast, and turn a nice profit in time to go back tomorrow and do it all again. That's how we're going to make enough money to get through this. Not chasing wild cockatrices."

She was right, of course. Sibyl was *always* right, which was why I'd downloaded her. But as sensible as her advice was, throwing away the notes felt too much like tossing a lotto ticket before the numbers were announced. I just couldn't bring myself to do it, so I tucked them back into my bag instead, ordering my AI to recall our truck before she could pull up a picture of eyes to roll at me.

***

One of the hazards of living in a sentient city was that things were constantly moving around on you. It wasn't quite as bad as they made it seem in the movies where characters went to sleep in one part of the city and woke up somewhere else entirely, but it wasn't uncommon for blocks to relocate themselves every couple of months. Being a municipal building, the Cleaner's Office moved more than most. The DFZ loved reshuffling buildings that were entirely hers, so it wasn't uncommon to have to drive to a different part of town every day just to go to the same place you always did.

Thankfully, the office was still in the same place it had been this morning: taking up the lion's share of an Underground block a mile west of the big casinos by the river. The building was actually an old elementary school, one of those indestructible brick monsters from the 1950s that had survived two magical apocalypses. I had no idea why the DFZ had chosen something so old to be one of her personal buildings. She was relentlessly modern in everything else: demanding that all civic business be conducted online via smartphone and rebuilding Town Hall every six months so that it was always on the cutting edge of architecture. Whatever the reason, though, I liked it. The old school had a gravitas that the rest of the eternally moving city did not. I also found the fact that it still had all of its original fixtures *hilarious*. You have not lived until you've watched a tricked-out chromehead with leg extenders trying to drink from a water fountain built for kindergarteners. Of course, this also meant I had to put up with tiny toilets, but still: totally worth it.

The auctions were held in the old school auditorium. There were two per day: one at six a.m. and one at six p.m. Which one I went to depended on my schedule, but I almost never attended both. Hitting two auctions in one day was for volume buyers and crazy people, but apparently I fit the latter today, because here I was, and I could already tell it was going to be bad.

The room was packed. All the big Cleaners were here, including DeSantos, which *sucked*, because I'd thought he was still on vacation. DeSantos was the current king of the Cleaners. He had a ten-man team and a chain of secondhand stores to sell all the stuff they salvaged. He normally went for the big prizes: abandoned warehouses, closed shops, places with enough stuff to justify sending over a truck full of guys. This meant our interests didn't usually overlap, but that didn't matter. I didn't hate going up against DeSantos because he was competition. I hated being in auctions with him because DeSantos was a born troll who loved to bid people up. It didn't matter if he wanted a unit or not. If he thought *you* wanted it, he'd bid against you just for the pleasure of watching you squirm.

Thankfully, he seemed distracted tonight, sitting in the front row and waving his hands through an AR interface I couldn't see like he was conducting an invisible orchestra. I took the seat directly behind him, hoping that if he couldn't see me, he'd find someone else to pick on. I was arranging my goggles on top of my head so that Sibyl's best camera was pointed at the stage when someone sat down in the folding chair next to mine.

My head whipped around, and I froze, stomach curling into a knot. Great. Just *great.* The one night I really needed to win something decent, and Nikola Kos was sitting next to me.

Other than DeSantos's bullying, Nik was my biggest roadblock at auctions. He was a solo operator just like I was, which meant we tended to go for the same jobs: small units we could clean for good profit in a reasonable amount of time. Unlike me, though, Nik didn't have five months of horrendous bad luck dragging him down, which meant if we ended up going head to head on an auction tonight, he was going to win. But while I resented his presence on a business level, what made me flinch away was simple self-preservation.

After three and a half years in the DFZ, I was used to scary people, but Nik was a special kind of intimidating. It was hard to say why, exactly. He wasn't particularly tall or big, especially not compared to some of the other Cleaners who'd gone so overboard on the cyberwear and body augs they couldn't sit in the folding chairs without crushing them. But while he didn't have any obvious modifications or weapons I could see, there was something about Nik that put me on edge. Maybe it was the way his gray eyes never stopped moving, sizing up each person as they sat down like he expected to be attacked at any moment. Or maybe it was the way he always sat on the edge of his seat with his hands in the pockets of his black leather bomber jacket, despite the fact that it had to be ninety degrees in here.

Not that I could talk, of course. I was still wearing my warded poncho and sweating like a sponge because of it. But I'd rather faint from dehydration than take off my protections anywhere close to Nik Kos. Other than winning units I wanted, he'd never actually done anything to me, but I'd lived among predators long enough to recognize danger when it sat down next to me. I was about to move to another seat, DeSantos be damned, when Nik's roving gray eyes landed on me.

"Look who's back for more," he said, glancing down to where my hands were clutching my bag, then to my goggles, then to my filthy boots before finally returning to my face. "I heard you got sold a coffin."

"How'd you hear that?" I asked, because I hadn't told anyone except Broker and Peter.

Nik shrugged. "Did you get your money back, or did Broker cut you a deal to preserve his 'no refunds' streak?"

"Why do you want to know?" I asked suspiciously.

He shrugged again. "Just trying to determine if you already picked the place over so I know not to bid on it when it comes back up for auction." He flashed me a sharp smile. "So did you find anything good?"

Now it was my turn to shrug. "You think I'd be back here if I did?"

"Yes," he said without hesitation. "Cleaning a unit takes no time if you don't have to actually clean. You can grab the good stuff, auction it, have a nap, and come back for another round. That's what I'd do."

I sighed. That's what I would've *liked* to do, but there was no way I was telling Nik about my day of failure, so I changed the subject instead. "Why are *you* back? Didn't you win two jobs this morning?"

"I did," he said. "But they were both evictions in closet communities. You know, the apartment buildings where all the units are six-by-six-foot boxes stacked on top of each other? Those things take no time to clean. I had everything wrapped up before lunch, so now I'm back for more."

He said this as if it were a good day's work, but the more he talked, the more I pulled back into my chair. This was the *real* reason I didn't like Nik. Cleaning wasn't exactly a noble calling—we were scavengers who paid for the privilege of digging through other people's trash in the hopes of finding enough treasure to make it worth the effort—but at least I didn't kick people out of their homes for profit.

A very good profit, admittedly. Unlike Cleaning, you didn't have to bid on eviction jobs. The city paid a flat rate to clean out delinquent tenants, *and* you got to keep all their stuff in return for cleaning the apartment so it could be rented again. It was the best money you could make in this business hands down, but desperate as I was for cash, there were some lines you just didn't cross, and apparently terrifying broke people out of their tiny closet homes was mine. I was trying to think up an excuse to get away from this conversation when Broker walked into the room.

I should point out that "Broker" was not Broker's real name. No one who made his money selling people's abandoned apartments to scavengers was stupid enough to give out anything that could be traced back to his real life. Even his face was anonymous, so perfected by plastic surgery that he looked more like a photo collage of menswear models than an actual person. He was the only full-time member of the Collections or Cleaning offices that any of us ever saw, and he made sure even that was a professional mask.

"Settle down, children, settle down," he said as he hopped up onto the stage. "We've got a lot of units to get through tonight, so we're going to do this fast. First up are evictions. I've got seven. Who wants them?"

I glanced hopefully at Nik. If he took another eviction job, that would remove my main competition. But my bad-luck streak must have still been running hot, because his hand stayed down. There were plenty of other heartless thugs who loved cash in the room, though, and the evictions went quick, moving us on to the real show: the Cleaner Auction.

Auctions were a pretty simple affair. Every unit up for bid had an address, square footage, and usually a picture taken from just outside the front door. Sometimes, if it was a really big place, you'd get a second picture from the back for scale, but normally those three bits were all the information you got. The trick to being a good Cleaner was knowing how to use them.

For example, tonight's first auction was for a five-room penthouse in the Financial District. The posh address was enough to get the new guys salivating, but I wasn't even tempted, because while the picture showed a lot of fancy-looking furniture, the paintings above them were mass-produced reproductions of the same ten super-famous modern works every wanna-look-rich jerk in the DFZ hung on his walls.

They weren't even *good* reproductions. The printing on the copy of Fowley's abstract masterpiece *New Spirits* hanging over the white leather sofa was so bad that I could see the artifacting from here. If the previous owner had been that sloppy about his art picks, the rest of his stuff was sure to be just as tacky and fake. I knew without even seeing them that the other four rooms would be packed with the same sort of cheaply made, overpriced junk, and while the downtown boutiques made bank selling that garbage to rich idiots who didn't know better, it was hell to move, and you couldn't resell it to save your life, which meant it was worthless. I wouldn't have paid five hundred for that unit, much less the thousands the idiots in the back were shouting out. Nik and DeSantos kept their hands down as well, happy to let the competition waste their money.

After that was when things got really interesting. Broker hadn't been kidding when he'd said it was a big list tonight. There was a whole slew of top-ticket items on the block, including an entire abandoned auto mechanic's shop complete with equipment. DeSantos was the only bidder in the room with enough people to handle something that size, and he ended up winning it for a song, the lucky bastard. He lost the next big offering, a boarded-up shoe shop, to Melly, an eccentric old lady who was always snapping bulk cloth and clothing lots to fuel her upcycled fashion business, but not before bidding her right to the edge of profitability.

Thankfully, he seemed to calm down once we got to the midrange auctions. Given how nice the list had been so far, my hopes were sky high, but though there were a lot of units to choose from, I couldn't find one I wanted. Everything in my price range was too old, too risky, too boring, too damaged, too *something*, and when I *did* spot something promising, it quickly got bid out of my reach. Then, when we were getting close to the end and the auditorium was starting to empty out as winners left to claim their units, a picture flashed up on the screen that made me sit bolt upright.

It was a townhouse in Magic Heights, one of the quiet little neighborhoods that moved around between the city's three major magical universities. I'd lived there myself during my first year at IMA, before I'd moved in with Heidi, and it was one of my favorite places to Clean. It wasn't as rich as the big developments by the river where all the corporate mages lived, but what it lacked in money, Magic Heights made up in good taste and eccentricity. I'd scored some of my best finds there, so I would have been interested no matter what, but what *really* caught my attention now was the complicated spellwork painted on the front door frame.

Spellwork I immediately recognized.

It took every bit of self-control I had not to leap out of my seat. The burned-out ward in the picture in front of me had the same spellwork as the notes in my bag. The DFZ was a huge city full of mages, but the chances of there being two who used the same eccentric mishmash of modern Thaumaturgy and ancient Alchemy seemed impossible. It *had* to be the same guy.

"Opal," Sibyl whispered warningly. "Don't."

I ignored her, lifting my finger to tap my wallet icon. My AR wasn't nearly as robust when I wore my goggles pushed up in my hair rather than properly seated on my face, but so long as the mana contacts inside the band were touching my body, I could still access the basics. Including my bank account, which was what I checked now, wincing when the number flashed up.

$2016.32

That was not a lot of money, especially not for a unit in Magic Heights. But through the haze of my excitement, I could vaguely hear Broker explaining that this was a smashed unit, which meant it had been robbed. That caught me by surprise. I'd been so focused on the spellwork, I hadn't even noticed that the front door wasn't just open, it was missing entirely, the wood kicked in until it had splintered into kindling. The rest of the place was similarly trashed. How trashed was impossible to say without seeing more, but every piece of furniture in the picture was broken.

That made my heart beat faster than ever. We didn't get units until they'd been in Collections for at least thirty days. Robbers were far less patient, so we saw smashed places a lot. They always went for peanuts since presumably the thieves had already taken everything of value. But robbers didn't pay attention to spellwork unless it was in their way, like a ward. Other circles, especially ones full of custom, esoteric spellwork they couldn't read, might go unnoticed, which meant the circle from the notes in my bag—or, even better, the stuff used to power it—might still be there.

"Opal," my AI growled. "Don't you dare."

But my hand was already in the air. "Two hundred."

Broker looked at me like I was nuts. The rest of the room did too, and I started to sweat. Two hundred was my usual opening bid, so I'd said it out of habit, which was a very stupid thing to do in hindsight. Bids on smashed units usually started in the tens. By bidding in the hundreds, I'd just tipped my entire hand, and from the way he was smirking at me over his shoulder like a hyena, DeSantos knew it.

"Three hundred," he called.

I clenched my fists. "Three fifty."

"*What are you doing?*" Sibyl yelled in my ear. "The place is smashed! If anything was there, it's long gone. You don't have money to waste on this!"

"We have three fifty," Broker said. "Do I hear three seventy-five?"

Still grinning at me, DeSantos raised his hand.

I glared back. "Four hundred."

"Five hundred," DeSantos said before I'd even finished.

"Six."

"Seven."

"One thousand!" I snarled, hoping that would cut him off. DeSantos might love trolling, but there was no way messing with me was fun enough to risk wasting a thousand dollars on a robbed unit. Sure enough, the older man blew me a kiss and turned back around in his seat. It was just starting to hit me that I'd won when a new voice spoke from my left.

"Eleven hundred," said Nik.

I whirled in my chair. "*What?*"

Nik's sharp gray eyes met mine. "Eleven hundred," he repeated calmly.

"Eleven hundred from Mr. Kos," Broker said, getting excited at the prospect of a real bidding war. "Do I hear twelve?"

"Let him have it," Sibyl whispered fiercely. "I swear, Opal, I will cut you off from your bank account if you say one more—"

I reached up and stabbed my finger through her mute button. "Twelve hundred."

"Thirteen," Nik said, leaning back in his chair.

"Fourteen."

"Fifteen."

"*Two thousand!*" I yelled, breath coming fast.

Even as I said it, I knew I was making a huge mistake. The chances of there being anything worth two grand in that apartment were slim to none. Even if they couldn't read the spellwork, there was no way any self-respecting robber would miss two hundred thousand in casting reagents, or a cockatrice egg. This was stupid. I should have shut up and let Nik have the damn thing. At least that way I could've claimed I was just bleeding my competition. But I couldn't. From the moment I'd seen the spellwork, I'd known—*known*—there was something good inside. It was the same instinct that had led me to all the treasures I'd ever found. It had also lost me tens of thousands of dollars over the last few months. As always, though, I couldn't let it go. I was already bracing myself to go even higher when Nik shrugged in surrender.

"Two thousand going once," Broker said. "Going twice." There was a long pause, and then he clapped his hands together. "*Sold* to Miss Yong-ac for two thousand dollars!"

The words echoed in my ears as I watched the money vanish from my account. Broker had already moved on to the next auction, but I didn't stick around to hear it. Whatever it was, I couldn't afford it. But done was done, so I hauled myself out of my seat and slipped past Nik toward the door to go see what I'd just spent all my money on.

CHAPTER 3

I didn't unmute Sibyl until I reached Magic Heights.

"Do I even need to say anything?" she said as I parked my truck across the street from my new unit.

I sighed and stepped out onto the sidewalk, which was lined with flowering dogwood trees despite the fact that it was the middle of July and the cement ceiling of the Skyways overhead blocked every photon of sunlight. Ah, the perks of living in a magical neighborhood. I missed them.

"You have to know how stupid that was," my AI went on. "We're supposed to be earning money, not wasting it!"

"I thought you said you weren't going to say anything," I grumbled, scanning the row of brick townhouses to find the one I'd won. "And it was a calculated risk."

"There was nothing calculated about it!" she shouted, making my ears ring. "You got carried away, just like you *always* do, and now you're screwed again. Just. Like. *Always.*"

"I don't need this right now," I said, reaching for her mute button again only to discover that it had vanished from my interface. "*Sibyl!*"

"No," she said sharply. "You told me two weeks ago that if you didn't get it together by this Friday, you were done for. You *ordered* me to make sure you didn't go off track! But then, when I try to do my job, you go and mute me! How am I supposed to help you if you won't help yourself?"

"I *am* helping myself!" I yelled, drawing strange looks from the pack of university students walking on the other side of the road. "You saw the other auctions. There was nothing! This is the best lead I've had in months. If I can get my hands on even a quarter of those reagents, I'll have enough to make my debt payments *and* cover rent for the rest of the summer! That's worth a gamble."

"On a hundred, maybe," Sibyl said. "But two *thousand?* That's all the money you had left!"

"I know, I know, I *know*," I said, scrubbing my hands through my sweaty hair. "I get it, okay? But done is done. The money's gone, and I can't bid on another auction until tomorrow morning. There's no turning things around tonight, so let's just go inside and see if we can make my money back."

Sibyl made a sound so frustrated it would have made her emotional-development programmer cry, but she didn't say another word. When I was certain she was done, I reached into the neck of my poncho and pulled out my master key, scurrying across the quiet street to the townhouse at the end of the row, my target.

It was a lot nicer than I'd anticipated. From the picture, I'd expected another basement apartment, but the address was for the entire townhouse. It was a corner unit, too. Sure, the western wall was built right up against the massive cement cliff of a Skyway support beam, which meant the whole place rattled whenever a big truck drove overhead, but it only had neighbors on one side. The street was quiet and tree-lined, too, all huge luxuries in the Underground. The pale-pink paint job on the brick exterior was a little odd, but overall it was a charming little house, which made no sense given everything else I'd seen today.

"I don't get it," I said, pushing open the chain-link gate that separated the townhouse's postage-stamp yard from the sidewalk. "If he had a place like this, why did he die locked in that hole?"

"You said yourself that the subbasement was probably a safe house," Sibyl reminded me. "If that's right, then it makes total sense that he'd run there after his door was kicked in."

I shook my head. "We don't know if this happened before or after his death. Seeing how both of his units came up for auction on the same day, though, I bet the timing was close."

More than close. I was already putting the timeline together in my head. Something had made this man feel threatened, so he'd fled to his safe house. When the people who'd made him afraid realized he was gone, they'd smashed up his home. The only question left was why.

"I bet it was money," Sibyl said when I mentioned it. "Someone had to foot the bill for all those reagents, and kicking in doors is classic loan shark behavior."

As usual, my AI had a good point, but as we climbed the cement steps to the townhome's tiny porch, I couldn't shake the feeling that there was more to it. I'd Cleaned abandoned apartments for plenty of loan shark victims, and in my experience, debt collectors broke bones, not stuff. Stuff could be sold to pay back the loan, but whoever had broken into this place didn't seem to care about stuff at all. A suspicion that became cold, hard fact when we reached the unit's door.

"Wow," I said.

The front door wasn't just kicked off its hinges, it had been annihilated. There wasn't even a splinter left for my master key to unlock. Just a few lines of yellow caution tape Collections had placed over the empty doorway to keep random people from wandering in. The spellwork I'd spotted on the door frame was still there, but now that I was standing on top of it, I could see that huge portions were burned black, probably from trying to stop whoever had busted their way in here. And then busted their way through everything else, if the living room was any indication.

"Were they getting paid by the piece?" I asked, looking around at the furniture, or what was left of it.

The living room had looked plain old trashed in the picture, but now that I was actually here, I could see that every stick of furniture had been carefully and methodically broken into segments no longer than an inch. The sofa looked like a pile of cotton confetti, and the glass coffee table had been smashed back into sand. The pictures on the walls—more museum photos of ancient alchemical artifacts, though much higher-quality ones than what I'd found in the basement apartment—had been bashed out of their frames and shredded into streamers. Even the built-in bookcases had been pried out of their nooks, the books methodically ripped in half, which was just obscene. Unlike the collection I'd gone through this morning, there'd been some nice stuff in here, and it was all ruined.

"I don't understand," Sibyl said, turning my cameras slowly to get a panorama of the destruction. "What kind of robber kicks in a door and then sits around breaking valuables into tiny pieces?"

"None," I said, pulling a fistful of magic into my hand and slapping it against my poncho to activate all of my personal wards. "This wasn't a robbery. They were looking for something." And I bet I knew what.

I reached into my bag for the notes I was still carrying. Of everything in that basement apartment, these were what our poor dead mage had chosen to hide, which meant they were probably what the people who'd broken in here had been looking for. I had them now, though, and if there was something worth finding here, I was certain these notes were the key to it.

"All right, Sibyl," I said, pointing at the line of chicken scratch Heidi had identified as the spell's main variable. "Add this to your photo recognition library, and let's see if we can't find something interesting."

"Or we could leave," Sibyl suggested. "There's still time to cut our losses and bail."

"Why would we do that?" I demanded. "We just got a hint that this gamble might actually pay out! What happened to 'Oh, Opal, we need to make money'?"

"It got preempted by 'Oh, Opal, we need to stay alive,'" my AI said nervously, darting my cameras toward the other rooms, which were also filled with meticulously broken furniture. "Does nothing about this make you think that perhaps we're stepping into something we shouldn't? People who do this to furniture are also capable of doing it to human bodies, and I'm pretty sure I'll be deleted if you get yourself killed."

"It'll be fine," I assured her, scraping my boot across the floor. "Look at the dust. No one's been here in weeks. Even if someone *was* watching, I'm just a Cleaner doing my job. Nothing suspicious at all. Now are you going to help me or not?"

Sibyl heaved a recorded sigh. "Hold it up."

I fanned the pages of spellwork out in front of me and then held still while Sibyl took her pictures. When she'd finished scanning all the parts I wanted for photo recognition, I stuck the notes back into my bag and pulled my hood up so my wards protected my head. "I want all cameras on lookout," I ordered, pulling on my rubber gloves. "I'll do the Cleaning, you keep your eyes open."

"Yes ma'am," she said, turning my cameras to get a 360-degree view of the room. "But what are we looking for, exactly?"

I took a deep breath as I stared at the remains of the destroyed life I'd bought for two thousand bucks.

"Anything."

***

"Anything" turned out to be not as much as I thought. The townhouse was smaller than it had looked from the outside—just two floors, and both of them were busted. Even the brooms in the pantry had been broken in half. I grabbed one anyway, using the bristles like a shovel to push the pulverized furniture into a pile while my cameras searched for some sign there'd ever been anything interesting here. But while our mage had clearly been a huge fan of putting spellwork on things, it was all basic utility stuff: an anti-mildew ward in the bathroom, a heating spell for his chair, that sort of thing. There was definitely no giant magical circle full of cockatrice eggs or giant treasure chest full of reagents. I didn't let that get me down, though, because I'd seen the receipts. I *knew* he'd already bought everything he'd needed for that spell, which meant it had to be somewhere. If it wasn't here in his smashed house, that greatly increased the odds of it being whole and together somewhere else. I just had to find out where.

"Is there anything left in the house's computer?" I asked Sibyl when we'd turned over every bit of wreckage. "A saved locations file, rent payments for another address, anything like that?"

"Nada," my AI said. "I got into the home network while you were still climbing the front steps, but everything was already wiped. That's typical, though. I mean, when have we ever Cleaned a place that's had old data lying around?"

"Fair point," I said grumpily, leaning against the kitchen wall, which for some inexplicable reason was painted bright canary yellow.

"We could try asking the neighbors," Sibyl suggested. "This much destruction must have been loud. I bet someone heard it."

I snorted. "This is the DFZ Underground. No one hears anything." At least not for free. If I'd had cash to spare, I probably could have gotten someone to talk, but I'd spent too much on this already, and I was beginning to worry I'd never get it back. I was wracking my brain to think of a new angle when something made me freeze.

It was hard to say what. I hadn't seen or heard anything specific, but something had caught my body's attention, and I'd learned to pay attention to things like that.

"What's wrong?" Sibyl asked.

I waved my hand to bring up my AR keyboard. *Not sure,* I typed.

What do you want to do? she typed back, which I appreciated even though no one could hear her voice but me.

I moved closer to the kitchen window, pulling magic into my hands as I went, just in case. *Get me a shot of the street.*

My cameras whirred in reply, and I leaned forward just enough to slip the lens mounted on the edge of my goggles past the window frame. Even with my night-vision filter, though, I didn't see anything. Just the tree-lined street out front, which was just as picturesque as it had been when I'd come in, though a bit rowdier since this was a college neighborhood and it was closing in on nine o'clock, prime party time.

Releasing the magic I'd gathered, I stepped away from the window, careful to stay out of line of sight. It was probably nothing, but I'd come by my paranoia honestly, and I'd learned to trust it. If I felt like something was wrong, something almost always was, which meant it was time to pick up the pace.

"Change of plans," I said, kneeling on the floor. "We're going to try some magic."

"Are you sure?" Sibyl asked nervously. "Not to bring you down, but your spellwork is…not the best. Not that you're not fantastic when it comes to blowing stuff up on the fly, but—"

"It's okay, you don't have to sweet-talk me," I said, digging around in my bag for the tiny nubbin of casting chalk I carried specifically for times like this. "I've had twenty years of the best experts money can buy telling me in excruciating detail exactly how much my spellwork sucks. I *know* it's not my strong suit, but there are some things you just can't do by throwing a bunch of magic around. It's all right, though. Even I can manage something like this." Especially if the alternative was leaving empty-handed. "Just go online and look me up a tracing spell. A simple one, please."

Sibyl had a whole list up before I'd finished my request, which would have been impressive if I hadn't known how easy they were to find. Tracing spells were grade school-level magic. All you needed was a piece of whatever you were looking for—a splinter, a crumb, a hair—and the spell would do the rest. There were limits, of course. Distance, importance of the object being used as a link, and whether the thing you were looking for was inside a ward or not were all factors. But finding spells were famously flexible and, most importantly for me, forgiving. I just hoped there was something here for me to find.

"All right," I said, tapping on the spell whose description looked the closest to what I wanted to do. "Let's give this a try."

I swept my arm across the kitchen floor to create a clean spot and drew a circle on the tile with my chalk. I hadn't done this in a while, so my first few were more like ovals, but that was why I used casting chalk and not markers. Every time it came out wrong, I just erased the line and tried again, drawing and redrawing until, at last, I had a more or less perfect circle.

I copied the spellwork next, blatantly stealing from the example spell Sibyl had looked up for me. But while that covered the basics, nothing could help with the hardest part: modifying the spellwork to fit my custom search parameters.

"What are you even going to search for?" Sibyl asked.

I rustled the stack of notes at her, and my AI made a choking sound. "That's *not* going to work."

"Why not?" I asked, dropping the pages into the middle of the circle I'd just drawn. "He wrote all this stuff himself. Why can't I use it to find more?"

"That's not the problem," she said. "I'm sure you'll find *tons* of custom spellwork, because this house is filled with the stuff. But unless you're looking for his anti-soap scum charm, it's not going to do you any good."

"Ah," I said with a grin. "But all of those charms are broken. I'm going to use this to find something that *isn't*."

"And do what with it?"

I hadn't figured that part out yet, but I was getting desperate. If I couldn't turn up something good here, then I'd spent all of my money on nothing. That was enough to inspire some serious creative thinking, and soon I had the spell modified for what I *thought* would lead to what I wanted. The only way to know for sure was to test it, though, so I reached out and grabbed the ambient magic floating through the house, shoving power by the fistful into the circle I'd drawn on the kitchen floor until the spellwork was glowing like phosphorus. When I couldn't push any more in, I took a deep breath and removed my gloves, placing my bare fingers on the chalk circle that was now vibrating with magic.

"Please work," I whispered, closing my eyes. "Please—"

The circle pulsed with enough power to knock me on my ass. When I scrambled up again, every bit of still-functional spellwork in the house was glowing like neon.

"Huh," I said, grinning at the lights that now surrounded me on all sides. "What do you know? It worked!"

"Only because the spellwork you stole was foolproof," Sibyl chided, her voice staticky thanks to the mud-thick magic that now filled the house. "You always put too much power in!"

I shrugged. "Go big or go home."

"You're lucky you didn't blow the whole place sky high," my AI went on. "It's a good thing you're used to a lot of magic, or you'd be bleeding like a stuck pig right now."

I *was* bleeding a little from my nose, but Sibyl hadn't noticed yet, so I saw no reason to tell her. I was too busy scouring the house for any spellwork I hadn't noticed earlier.

As Sibyl had predicted, there were a lot of false positives. Pretty much everywhere you could put spellwork, our mage had crammed it in. But I'd combed through the house pretty thoroughly by this point, so I was able to quickly dismiss the stuff I'd already seen. I was looking for something new, something I hadn't seen in my earlier searching, and a few minutes later, I found it.

"Gotcha!"

It was in the pantry, buried under a bunch of boxes of instant potatoes the people who'd been through this place had torn apart and left in a pile. But underneath the white flakes and green flecks of freeze-dried parsley, something was shining. A *lot* of something, and that gave me hope.

I grabbed my broom, sweeping the potato flakes out into the kitchen to reveal the pantry's floor. But the glowing spellwork wasn't on the tiles. It was *under* them, the blaze of my finding spell shining up through the cracks in the mortar.

"That's what I'm talking about!" I said excitedly, reaching for my pocketknife. I was grinning so hard my face hurt when the blade slid easily between the clay tiles, popping one up to reveal a hidden space below the floor. And shoved into that space was a warded box exactly like the one I'd found under the dead mage's bed.

"Huh," Sibyl said. "I guess I owe you an apology."

"You owe me a lot more than that," I said joyfully as I grabbed my tongs out of my bag, because I was *not* going to get bitten this time. "I want to hear you saying I was right for a week when I pay off all my…"

My voice trailed off. When the rubber-tipped tongs had closed around the box, the ward on its surface had vanished. There was no crack, no snap of power. It just stopped glowing, as if it had turned itself off.

Scowling, I set the tongs on the floor and grabbed the box with my gloved hands, bracing for the bite, but nothing happened. It was just a box. An *actual* shoebox this time for a pair of faux-leather loafers in men's size ten. Hopes sinking, I pulled off the lid, and then I groaned aloud.

"Oh, come *on*."

It was full of papers. Yellow legal-pad papers this time, all folded in half and covered in the same janky, chicken-scratch handwriting I was starting to loathe.

"This guy really needs a better filing system," Sibyl said as I dumped the papers out into my lap. "So what is it? More spellwork?"

It wasn't, actually. When I spread the papers out flat in the light from my headlamp, I saw that the writing was plain old-fashioned English. There was still a good bit of spellwork notation in the margins, but most of the pages were just long columns of short sentences that said things like "Confirm stabilization at 9.4" and "Double-check for containments RE transmorph vivication."

"Great," my AI said. "You found his to-do list."

"That's still something," I said stubbornly, thumbing through the pages. "He wouldn't have hidden it if it wasn't important."

There *had* to be something here. I read each page all the way through, but they were all just more of the same lists and notes that meant nothing without context. The only really remarkable thing I found was an old staff ID from MIT Thaumaturgical with a picture of a stately-looking gentleman in his fifties that vaguely matched the decaying corpse I'd found this morning. There was also a name.

"Dr. Theodore Lyle," I read. "Huh. Looks like our guy was a professor."

"That's not surprising," Sibyl said. "This *is* Magic Heights. And he's a *former* professor. According to the MIT's online staff directory, Dr. Theodore Lyle retired two years ago."

I sat back on my heels to think that through. This was a pretty nice house by Underground standards. *Too* nice to afford on a university pension. Add in the rent on his basement bolt-hole and two hundred grand he'd spent on reagents, and it was obvious someone was providing Dr. Lyle with supplemental funding. Probably someone not very nice given the state of his house and how he'd died, but that actually worked out in my favor. I would have felt bad taking the life's work of a poor dead mage from his next of kin, but I was totally fine with ripping off house-smashing sleazebags. It wouldn't even be stealing. By the law of the DFZ, everything in here belonged to me now, including any clues to potential giant payoffs. I just had to figure out where it was, because I didn't see anything like the big circle from Dr. Lyle's ritual notes glowing through my finding spell. It had to be *somewhere*, though.

Frowning, I turned back to the pile of paper in my lap, paging through the lists for an address or coordinates, anything that might tell me where he'd actually done all the magical minutiae he'd written these lists to remind himself to do. But while I didn't find anything actually useful, I did notice on my second time through that the pages were dated at the top. The latest was just over a month ago, probably only a few days before he'd died. It was also the messiest, the lined paper crinkled and torn at the top as though it had been ripped out in a hurry. I was scanning the list to see

why this one was special when I saw something at the bottom that made
me freeze.

> ~~Burn material links~~
> ~~Stock food (sixty days)~~
> ~~Move final reagents to ritual location~~
> ~~parse coords to VCI~~

They were all crossed out, but that only made me more excited,
because this proved I was right. There *was* a separate ritual location! All
the materials had already been moved there, too, which meant that
somewhere—presumably wherever VCI was—there was a ritual worth two
hundred grand just waiting to be scooped up.

"Sybil," I said, shoving the new notes into my bag next to the old
ones. "What does VCI mean?"

"A lot of stuff," my AI said, bringing up a depressingly long list of
acronyms. "Venture Capital Investments, Vital Communications
Infrastructure, Veterinary Council of Indiana. Take your pick."

With a huff of frustration, I started reading, flicking my finger to
scroll the list as I searched for the combination V, C, and I words that
would make sense in this context. I was still looking when I got that
watched feeling again.

It was a *lot* stronger this time. I'd been focusing on my AR display,
so again, I couldn't say what had caused it, but my whole body was on
alert. I was about to ask Sibyl to play back the last thirty seconds of
ambient audio when something slammed into my head.

The first thing I felt was pressure. The impact was hard enough to
send me flying back into the pantry, but banging my elbows on the shelves
when I caught myself hurt a lot more than my head did. I was scrambling
to figure out how that could be when I saw the flattened bullet hit the floor
beside my feet with a musical *ping*.

The world slowed to a crawl. Gasping for breath, I grabbed my
warded poncho, which was no longer glowing with the magic I'd put into

it. That had all been burned up when my ward against bullets had done its job and stopped the slug on the floor from entering my brain. The pressure I'd felt had been the counterforce of the spell blocking the shot and sending me flying as a result. But while I was definitely going to leave a glowing review for my store-bought wards the next time I was online, I now had a huge problem, because that ward had a one-time use, and I still didn't know who was shooting at me.

"Duck!"

I hit the ground before Sibyl finished her warning, getting out of the way just in time as the second shot landed in the drywall behind me. My new position had me prone and cornered in the pantry, but at least I could see the shooter.

It was a man. More than that was hard to say since he was wearing baggy black clothes and AR goggles very similar to my own. He must have been in good shape, though, because he was perched in the crown of the dogwood tree just outside the open kitchen window, the one that had given me the creeps before. He was already moving his pistol to adjust for my new position, and I cursed myself for an idiot. I should have listened to my instincts earlier. I should have listened to Sibyl and never bid in the first place. Now I was going to die on the floor of Dr. Lyle's filthy townhouse, and I wasn't even getting paid for it.

But then, just as I was pulling magic into my hands for a desperate attack I knew perfectly well I'd never get off in time, something incredible happened. A man wearing a black leather bomber jacket and the same knee-high, everything-proof Cleaner boots that I used walked calmly into my tunneled vision and reached through the window with both arms to shove the shooter out of the tree.

It happened so fast, I wasn't sure it had actually happened at all until the strange man turned around and grabbed my arm, lifting me off the floor as if I weighed nothing.

"You okay?" he asked in Nik Kos's voice.

I couldn't answer. The fight or flight was pounding in me so hard my whole body was vibrating. If he hadn't had my arm locked in a grip of iron, I would have already been sprinting for the exit. But he did, which turned out to be a very good thing when another man dressed in the same dark clothes and goggles as the shooter, who was now cursing up a storm at the base of the dogwood tree, walked through the kitchen door.

I heard the shot before I saw the gun. The crack went off like a firework in my ear, but the bullet didn't touch me, because at the last second, the man holding my arm leaned in to block the shot with his shoulder.

It was at this point that my poor, reeling brain seized onto two very important facts. One, it *was* Nikola Kos who'd come to my rescue, and two, the black bomber jacket he always wore no matter the weather was armored. I saw the ballistics inside it ripple right in front of my nose when the bullet bounced off Nik's shoulder. He didn't even stagger, just took the shot like a wall. I was still staring in wonder when I saw the man who'd fired at us cock his gun to shoot again.

As he re-aimed the barrel at my face, the fight-or-flight instinct that had been warring inside me suddenly and definitively pinned itself on fight. "You *asshole!*" I screamed, lobbing the magic I'd pulled into my hand earlier over Nik's shoulder at the shooter. I didn't even bother to shape it into anything. I just threw the raw power as hard as I could, creating a shockwave that exploded against the man's chest, flinging him backward into the living room. "*Do you know how much I paid for this place?*"

I might not have been the best at spellwork, but when it came to fast reactions, no one had me beat. I had the next handful of magic ready before my assailant hit the ground, and I was about to shove it in his face when Nik let go of my arm and pulled a gun of his own.

He moved so fast, I didn't even see where the weapon came from. The sleek black pistol just appeared in his hand and fired, sinking a bullet deep into the right calf of the man I'd just knocked to the floor. The scream wasn't even out of his mouth before Nik was on top of him, kicking the dropped gun away and planting his steel-toed Cleaning boot on the man's chest.

The guy started thrashing when Nik's weight landed, his wounded leg getting blood all over the floor I'd just swept up. I was worried he was going to kick his way to freedom by pure panicked accident when Nik calmly reached down and ripped the AR goggles off the terrified man's face before pointing his gun at the spot where they'd been. He was tightening his finger on the trigger when I finally realized what was happening.

"Hey, whoa!" I said, running forward to grab Nik's elbow before he executed a man in front of me. "Don't kill him!"

Nik's gray eyes flicked back toward me. "I wasn't going to," he said. "Not yet, anyway. But why do you care? He was going to kill you."

That was a good point. But while I'd been totally okay with crushing him to death myself not ten seconds ago, that had been in self-defense. This was just murder, and despite what some people assumed about me, I was not okay with that.

"Well, he's not killing me now," I said, glancing out the kitchen window where I could see the first guy, the one Nik had pushed out of the tree, sprinting down the street as fast as his legs could carry him. "Crisis has been averted, so let's take it down a notch."

"Yeah, man," the guy on the floor said in a panicked voice. "Listen to the lady and take it down a—"

He cut off when Nik's eyes flicked back to him, his arms shooting up over his head in surrender. "Good," Nik said, though he didn't lower his gun. "Now, who hired you to watch this building?"

"We weren't watching nothing," the man said in a panicked rush. "We were just scoping the neighborhood when we saw the Cleaner go in, and we thought—"

He cut off with a curse when Nik fired a shot into the floor beside his head. I jumped, too, flinging up my hands to protect my face from the wood the shot sent flying. "Who hired you?" Nik asked again in the same calm voice he'd used when he'd asked me about being sold a coffin.

"No one!" the man cried. "Who'd hire guys to watch a house that's already been robbed?"

That struck me as a sensible question, but Nik didn't even blink. "If you knew it had already been robbed, why would you set a trap for the Cleaner?" he asked, pointing his pistol dead between the man's eyes. "You knew she wouldn't have anything. But your partner was already in that tree when she arrived, so clearly something else was going on. Why don't you stop lying and tell me what it was?"

"Wait," I said, frowning at Nik. "How do *you* know he was in the tree when I got here?"

"I don't know, man!" the guy on the floor said at the same time. "It was just a job! We got it off the freelancer board. We were supposed to watch this place, and if anyone came looking for stuff, we were supposed to take whatever they found and bring it to a drop box downtown."

Nik tilted his head. "Just take? Not shoot?"

"That was Andy's idea," the man insisted, flicking his eyes frantically toward the kitchen window where the first guy had been waiting. "He was the one who said we should shoot first 'cause it was a mage. You have to get the drop on mages before they see you or they'll fry you like a catfish." He glanced at me. "No offense, miss. We didn't mean nothing by it. It was just a job."

He gave me a little shrug as if that excused everything, but I take getting shot *very* personally. I was about to tell Sibyl to call the cops when Nik lifted his boot off the guy's chest.

"Get out."

The man on the floor blinked. "Wait, for real?"

"Are you serious?" I said at the same time. "He tried to murder us!"

"He tried," Nik agreed, hitching the bottom hem of his jacket up to slide his pistol into the chest holster hidden beneath it. "But he failed."

"So what?" I cried. "Even in the DFZ, attempted murder is still illegal. We should call the police!"

Nik arched a dark eyebrow at me. "The average DFZ PD response time for a non-life-threatening event in the Underground is two hours. Do you really want to stand around watching him for that long?"

Not particularly. Still. "You can't just let him go!"

"Why not?" Nik asked, tilting his head as though he truly did not understand the question. "You heard what he said. It was just a job. It's not like he's a stalker who's going to hunt you down, right?" He glanced at the man, who frantically shook his head no. "There you go," Nik said, turning back to me.

"But we don't know who he's working for yet," I pointed out.

"Neither does he," Nik said.

"And you believe him?"

Nik gave me that infuriating shrug of his, and I reached up to rub my throbbing temples. "Look," I said at last. "Even if he doesn't know whom he's working for, he's still a dangerous criminal. You can't just let him run free. What if he tries to murder someone else?"

"That's their problem," Nik said. "There's always someone willing to shoot someone else for money. If he doesn't take the job, someone else will. But if you get him booked for attempted murder, we'll be dragged into court every few weeks for the next year. That's a punishment for *us*, not him, and I'd rather not pay my time for his crime."

That made a strange sort of sense, but…

"Look," Nik said, his voice growing soft, as if he were trying to cajole me. "If you want to see him punished, just think about how much it'll cost him to get his leg fixed. I can call an ambulance right now if you want."

"Please don't," the man begged, his dirty face going ashen. "I can't afford that shit. Just let me out of here and you'll never see me again. I swear."

He started crawling toward the door before he'd even finished, dragging his shot leg behind him. It must have hurt like hell, because he groaned pathetically every time he moved, leaving a trail of bright-red blood on the floor behind him. Too much blood. He was going to bleed out before he got down the stairs at this rate. From the look on his face, Nik was fine with that. I, however, was not, and after thirty seconds of this macabre fiasco, I broke.

"Stop," I said. "Just stop."

The man looked back at me in confusion. The feeling was mutual, because I couldn't believe I was doing this either, but that didn't stop me from digging into my bag for my emergency first aid kit.

"Hold still," I muttered, grabbing a skin-mimicking bandage from my stash and shoving his loose pants up to place it over the hole in my would-be-murderer's calf. When I had the bandage where I wanted it, I shoved a bit of magic into the machine-printed spellwork woven into the adhesive. When the light faded, the bandage was bound to his leg as if it had grown there, and the man's face lit up with a euphoric smile as the magic-activated painkillers flooded into his bloodstream.

"Wow, baby," he slurred, head listing to the side as he grinned at me. "You got the *good* stuff."

"Shut up," I growled, furious with myself for wasting an expensive healing strip on the idiot who'd shot at me because I was too soft to sit through a little moaning. "That strip will hold for six hours. Get out of here, and if I ever see you again, I'm recouping my costs out of your face."

The man nodded frantically and pushed himself up, grabbing his bloody goggles off the floor as he went. "Thank you very much, ma'am," he said as he hobbled toward the door. "You'll never see me again, I promise."

I didn't even want to hear it. I just shoved my first aid kit back inside my bag. I also checked the notes, breathing a sigh of relief when I saw that both sets had made it through this fiasco undamaged. Forget being shot; I would have died of sheer frustration if the only thing I had to show for this mess had gotten destroyed. I was moving the papers to the slightly safer interior zipper pocket of my shoulder bag when Nik said, "What's that?"

I jumped. His voice was so close he was practically speaking into my ear. By the time I whirled around, he was even closer, hooking a finger over the edge of my bag to peer inside. "Did you find something?"

"What's it to you?" I snapped, yanking my bag away.

I felt bad about the words the moment they were out of my mouth. If Nik hadn't shown up when he did, I'd be dead right now. Even if he was invading my personal space, yelling at the man who'd saved my life was a pretty sorry way to behave. That said, now that I was no longer in imminent danger, it was finally starting to break through to me just how little sense this situation made.

"Wait," I said, stepping back. "What are you doing here?"

Nik gave me an innocent look. "I was following you."

A chill shot up my spine. "*Why?*"

"Because you bid two thousand dollars on a unit that wasn't worth twenty," he explained. "You clearly saw something here that the rest of us didn't. I wanted to know what it was."

"So that's why you stalked me?" I asked, incredulous. "Because you were curious?"

"That and I wanted to be in position in case whatever it was turned out to be more than you could handle," he said, a sly smile creeping across his face. "Which it *did.*"

As he spoke, the chill in my spine grew into a full-body freeze. "You want a share, don't you?"

"Damn straight I want a share," Nik said, looking down at me as if I was a goose who'd just laid a golden egg. "Considering I saved your life, I think half is fair."

"*Half?*" I cried. "That's robbery! You don't even know what it is."

"I know it's good enough to make you wager two thousand bucks at a time when you're desperate for cash," he said with a shrug. "You think I haven't noticed how hard you've been bidding these last few months? Something's got you up against the wall, and given how much I've seen you turn units around for, I bet you're up against it for a *lot.*"

My jaw tightened in fury. "If you knew that, why'd you bid me up?"

"Because I'm in this for the money just like you are," he said, looking me straight in the eyes. "I didn't know what you saw in this place, but I knew you wouldn't have gone after it so hard if you didn't think you were going to make your money back in spades. Your instinct for these things has always been top notch. If you thought there was money here, that was good enough for me."

That was the closest thing to a compliment I'd ever heard come out of Nik's mouth. If it hadn't cost me so much, I would have been flattered. Right now, though, his blind faith in my professional skill was highly inconvenient. "How do you know I'm not here for personal reasons?"

"Because I'm not an idiot," Nik said, looking around at the trashed house. "No one breaks up a place this thoroughly *and* hires thugs to watch it unless there's serious money on the line. You clearly think so too, or you wouldn't have let me bid you up so high. Now I know, and I want in." He turned back to me, crossing his arms over his chest. "Sixty-forty split, in my favor."

I gaped at him. "You just said fifty-fifty!"

"That was before you tried to wiggle out of it," he said, reaching down to pat his black-gloved hand against the gun I now knew he carried under his jacket. "This is clearly a much more dangerous job than you're used to, and there's the matter of the guy in the window who got away. The idiot you saved might be too grateful to talk, but the runner *definitely* will. That means it's just a matter of time before whoever paid for this knows you found something. If you want to keep it, you're going to need me, and sixty-forty is a lot better than seventy-thirty, which will be my next offer if you keep trying to freeze me out."

I glared murder at him. "This is extortion."

Nik shrugged. "That's not illegal in the DFZ."

"He's right," Sibyl whispered in my ear.

"Shut up," I snapped. Nik gave me a funny look, and I sighed. "Not you."

"If you're serious about continuing this job, you should take him up on his offer," Sibyl went on. "We could use the help."

I held up my finger and stepped away, cupping my hand around the microphone at the base of my goggles so Nik wouldn't hear me. "I thought you didn't even want to do this!"

"I don't," Sibyl said. "But you're not listening to me, so I figured the best thing I can do for you now is try to minimize the pain. It's obvious Mr. Kos is no stranger to violence, but I just replayed that fight to take measurements, and dude is *fast*. I don't know what he's packing to get that kind of speed, but we couldn't hire a bodyguard with moves like that for sixty percent of two hundred grand. And that's assuming we recover anything of value. The way he's worded things, you won't have to pay him at all if you fail. Sixty percent of nothing is nothing, which is the only number that fits our budget right now. Having someone else along to split costs and stop bullets will make this idiocy a lot less scary and expensive. Obviously, the best choice would be to run away as fast as possible, but since you're not going to do that, teaming up with Kos is the least terrible of the remaining options."

"You're really selling it," I muttered, glancing over my shoulder at Nik, who was staring at me like I'd gone crazy.

I couldn't say that he was wrong. If this had happened to me a year ago, I'd have already been running for the hills just like Sibyl wanted me to. I *definitely* wouldn't have been planning how to get into even more trouble, but Nik had made a lot of good points about the cost of watching this place. You didn't pay people to keep an eye on a robbed house if you didn't think there was something still inside. Clearly, whoever had smashed up the dearly departed Dr. Lyle's home thought his work was more than just chicken-scratch theories. Maybe a *lot* more. I didn't know the going rate for cheap thugs, but I had the feeling that anyone who went this far wasn't interested in cashing in on a pile of mail-order reagents.

The fact that Nik had noticed all of this earned my respect even more than his quick hand with a gun, but what really made up my mind about the situation was the other thing he'd gotten right. I *was* up against a wall. Not for as much as he'd insinuated, but ten thousand dollars might as well be a million when you need it and don't have it, and I needed it bad. If Nik wanted to help me get it, who was I to say no?

"All right," I said, turning back around. "We've got a deal."

"Great," he said. "I want to know everything, but not here. Whoever put eyes on this place is probably already on their way over, which means we need to be somewhere else. Do you have a car?"

When I nodded, he started hustling me toward the front door. "Then let's go."

With a final look at the trashed, bloody living room, I tightened my grip on my bag where I'd hidden the notes and marched out, Nik following on my heels like a deadly, unwanted shadow.

CHAPTER 4

"I'm never going to actually finish a Cleaning job, am I?" I muttered as I walked down the stairs.

"Hey, the contract just says you have to clean the unit. It doesn't specify when," Sibyl said helpfully. "So long as you have Dr. Lyle's place ready for a new tenant before the end of the month, you won't have to pay rent on it. You can just come back and finish cleaning it out next week when things calm down."

Or hire someone to do it for me when I hit it big, I thought to myself. Now that we were away from the blood and the bullet holes, it was starting to hit me just how much money we might be trailing. Forget making my payments. If this went big, I might be able to pay off my entire loan balance, which meant I'd be free. *Actually* free, for the first time in my life. I was getting all giddy at the thought when I spotted my truck.

"Oh, come *on!*"

The tires were slashed. All four of them. Someone had knifed huge gouges in the rubber right down to the wheel well, which meant there'd be no patching them. And since I'd waived the insurance option, there'd be no free repair service either.

"Guess they didn't want you to be able to get away if you ran," Nik said, poking his finger through the sliced rubber.

If that was true, then I was seriously regretting letting that bleeding guy go. "This day cannot get any worse," I moaned, putting my face in my hands.

"No fixing it now," Nik said. "You want to call for a tow?"

I couldn't afford a tow any more than I could afford to pay the fee the rental company was going to charge me for four new tires. My face must have showed it, too, because Nik rubbed the back of his neck awkwardly.

"This is a reasonably safe neighborhood," he said, looking up and down the street, which was filled with happy drunken college students moving between house parties. "It probably won't get stripped if you leave it until later."

That was not as reassuring as he probably meant it to be. It also didn't help. "But how am I going to get around?" I asked. "That's my only car."

Nik scowled. Then, wincing as though the words caused him physical pain, he said, "We can take mine."

My head shot up in surprise, which was silly. Of course Nik had a car. How else could he have followed me here? I couldn't remember seeing it before, though, which suddenly struck me as crazy. We'd been parking in the same lot for a year and a half. I knew every other career Cleaner's car, so why didn't I know Nik's? I was about to ask if he used a rental service too when he walked two spaces down the street and stopped in front of a sleek black sports car I'd assumed belonged to one of the Magic Heights trust fund kids.

"Wait," I said as he opened the door. "That's *your* car?"

"Yes," he said, pulling off his Cleaner boots to reveal a second pair of tight-laced combat boots underneath. "And I don't like dirt in it, so take off your shoes before you get in."

I did as he asked, though I didn't have a second set of shoes under my boots, so I had to get in wearing only my socks. "If you had a ride like this, why did you want to take my truck?"

"Because then they'd shoot at your car, not mine," he said, plucking my filthy—and now slightly bloody—boots out of my hands and bundling them in a plastic bag before setting them down on the floor of his pristine back seat.

I didn't appreciate Nik's willingness to use my car as a sacrifice, but it was hard not to see his logic when I was sinking into buttery leather upholstery. I didn't know as much about cars as I did about art prints, but I knew expensive when I felt it, and Nik's car was *nice*. It was a manual, too, as in he drove it himself. I wasn't aware people even knew how to do that anymore, but Nik grabbed the wheel like it was second nature and started the quiet engine.

"You must have Cleaned a lot more than I realized to afford something like this," I said as he pulled us into the street. "Or have I been vastly underestimating Eviction payouts?"

"A bit of both," he said as we merged into traffic. "But it's mostly that I don't waste money on things that don't matter."

I smirked. "A flashy sports car counts as a necessity?"

"Yes," he said, sounding slightly irritated. "Because it's *not* flashy. It's black, and it's quiet. It *is* a sports car, but that's only because I needed the bigger engine. This car's fast enough to catch anything I need to catch and outrun anything that's trying to catch me. The manual steering and transmission mean it does exactly what I tell it when I tell it with no computer to be compromised. It's a quality tool that helps me do my job. Those are worth investing in."

He glanced over to see if I was appreciating his practicality, but I'd gone stiff in my bucket seat. "Wait," I squeaked. "There's no computer?" I pointed at the stick shift in the center console. "That's a *real* gear shift? As in not just for show?" When he nodded, I made a choking sound. "We're going to *die*."

"You know, people drove their own cars for over a hundred years, and the species somehow survived," Nik said dryly.

"Not all of them!" I cried. "Car accidents used to be the number-one cause of death before self-driving AIs took over. Next thing you're going to tell me is it runs on gasoline."

Nik reached down to shift gears without a word, and my stomach dropped. "You're *kidding*."

"You can't run an electric car without a computer," he said with a shrug.

I stared at the dash in horrified wonder. "I can't believe we're actually driving around in a metal box powered by explosions. Where do you even *get* gasoline anymore?"

"If it bothers you so much, you're free to walk," Nik growled, gripping the wheel.

"No, no, no," I said quickly, putting up my hands. "It's a very nice antique. I was just surprised, that's all."

"It's not an antique," he said sharply. "It's a highly tuned, custom machine!"

"Of course it is," I said, though I couldn't stop my smirk. "So does it have a name?"

His silence was answer enough, and I smiled wider, piling my poncho's folds into my lap so I wouldn't get dust on his darling, whatever her name was. "Where are we going?"

"You tell me," Nik said, keeping his eyes on the road. "You're the one who spent two thousand bucks on a house full of diced furniture."

Good point. "Okay," I said, pointing at a fast food joint across the street. "Pull over there."

"Why?" Nik asked.

"Because I don't want you distracted while you're holding my life in your hands," I said. "It would be just my luck today if you got all excited about money and crashed us into a truck."

Nik looked terminally insulted. "I would never do that to my car," he said, but he did as I asked, turning us into the crowded drive-thru line. I was half-hoping he'd stay there—I hadn't had dinner yet, and this place looked cheap enough to be in my remaining budget—but he pulled through the traffic and parked in an empty spot at the back by the dumpsters.

"There," he said, cutting off the engine and turning around in his seat so that he was facing me. "Now tell me how we're making our money."

With a final, hesitant breath, I told him. It was a little surreal talking out loud about the subbasement and finding Dr. Lyle's body. Even though I was just reporting what I'd seen, it felt as if I was telling a story that had happened to someone else. It also sounded a lot crazier than it had in my head. The more I tried to explain the notes and what I thought they were, the more I realized how desperate and cockamamie this must seem from the outside. To his credit, though, Nik didn't interrupt. He didn't even roll his eyes. He just listened quietly until I reached current events, tapping his gloved fingers quietly against his knees.

"So you think these reagents haven't been used?" he asked when I finally stopped talking.

"Actually, I'm hoping they have," I said, pulling out Dr. Lyle's ritual notes. "Two hundred grand in magical materials would be a fantastic score for us, but it's nothing by criminal standards. Like you said, it takes serious money to hire thugs to bust up a house and then sit around watching it for thirty days. If someone cared enough to foot the bill for all of that, then I bet this ritual is worth a lot more than the sum of its parts."

Nik scratched his chin thoughtfully. "Your expert said the ritual was for a cockatrice egg, right? How much are those worth?"

"Technically nothing," Sibyl answered, though her voice was only in my ear. "Due to their complex breeding practice, they're highly endangered. Not that the protected species list means anything in the DFZ, but they were also added to the Peacemaker's Edict last year, which makes things complicated."

It did indeed. I had no idea why the Dragon of Detroit cared about cockatrices, but if they were protected under his Edict, that made selling their eggs problematic. The Peacemaker couldn't actually make laws since he only controlled the dragon population of the city, but he had a lot of monsters working for him and the goodwill of the DFZ herself. If he said "don't do that," it was very much in your best interest to listen. That said, selling cockatrice eggs wasn't *actually* illegal, and if there was anything I'd learned living in the DFZ, it was that anything that could be sold would be.

"If they're troublesome to sell, that just means you can charge more," I told Sibyl. "Someone has to be buying. Why would you use all of those expensive reagents to make something that had no market value?"

"Because it's the only way you can get one?" my AI guessed. "The last recorded sale I see for a cockatrice egg was over a year ago for fifty thousand dollars. Obviously, I don't have access to private transactions, so it's possible there's a vast underground cockatrice breeding industry I'm unaware of, but it looks like they're just super rare."

I frowned. Considering what had gone into making them, fifty thousand sounded low to me. If they really were as rare as my AI suggested, though, it was possible that the price had gone up. We also didn't know how many eggs the ritual created. Fifty grand might not be enough to justify paying thugs to watch a house for a month, but multiply that by a dozen and you had a whole different ballgame.

"Sounds legit to me," Nik said after I'd explained all of this. "So how do we find these eggs?"

"That's the tricky part," I said, pulling out the second stack of papers I'd found in the pantry and shuffling the yellow legal-pad sheets until I found the one containing the final to-do list Dr. Lyle had made before he'd passed away. "See here?" I said, pointing at the last two crossed-out items, the ones that said *Move final reagents to ritual location* and *Parse coords to VCI.* "I think 'coords' is short for coordinates. I don't know about VCI, but if we can figure out how the coordinates are parsed to it, I bet we can use them to find the ritual location."

"VCI, huh?" Nik's scowl deepened. "This dead mage, did he have any body augs? Fake eyes, integrated computer systems, anything like that?"

I nodded rapidly. "He had a cybernetic hand. I thought it was weird because cybernetics mess with magic, but I definitely saw it." It was the only part of him that hadn't rotted. "Why do you ask?"

"Because VCI stands for Vivere Code Index," he said, cranking the engine. "It's the base computer language that controls all cyberwear, at least the nonproprietary stuff."

My eyes went wide. "You think he hid the location in his *hand*?"

"Safest place there is," Nik said, turning around in his seat to back us out. "Where's the body now?"

"The morgue, I suppose," I said, biting my lip. "But it's already been committed to the Empty Wind."

"Then we'll just take it back."

I stared at him in horror. "But that's stealing from the dead!"

"Who said anything about stealing?" he asked as we rejoined the flow of traffic. "We're just going to borrow it for a while. It's not like he's using it anymore."

"But—"

"Did you miss the part where this is our ticket?" Nik snapped. "VCI is a machine language. It doesn't even support wireless access because why would you want to risk someone being able to hack your limbs? If those notes are right and our mage hid the location in his VCI code, then the only way to access it is to get that hand."

It all made sense when he said it that way, but this whole thing still made me extremely uncomfortable.

"Look," Nik went on. "You said Peter was the one who picked up the body, right? Just tell him you need to see it again. He'll let you do it."

I gaped at him. "He's a priest of the Empty Wind! Why would he let me see a body he's already committed to his god?"

"Because you're a pretty girl who doesn't treat him like garbage," Nik replied without missing a beat. "He'd probably let you waltz out with a whole bag full of corpses if you asked nicely enough."

Now he was just being insulting. "Peter is a public servant," I said angrily. "He's also a decent guy who believes wholeheartedly in what he's doing. He would never be so irresponsible! He's not like—"

Nik flicked his eyes in my direction. "Not like who? Me?"

That had been what I was about to say, but it no longer seemed fair. "Not like us," I finished instead. "We're talking about stealing a dead guy's hand so we can sell off his last great work. Work that technically belongs to his next of kin, I might add."

"If he's claimed by the Forgotten Dead, then he has no next of kin," Nik said. "At least none who care."

"Then we're stealing from a spirit, which is even *worse*."

"Do you want the money or not?" Nik demanded as we pulled up to a stoplight.

I sighed. Want was the wrong word. I *needed* that money, and Nik knew it.

"The cost of survival is doing things you don't like," he said coldly. "Suck it up or give up, but don't sit on the fence and complain. It does nothing but waste time. Now are you going to bail, or are we going to the morgue?"

I should have told him no. The me of five months ago would have, but having your back against a wall does funny things to your better judgment, and in the end, all I could do was nod. "Peter's still not going to let me see the body, though."

A smile ghosted over Nik's face. "I think you'll be surprised," he said as the light turned green. "And if he does turn you away, we can always just steal it. I've broken into the morgue before. It's not exactly well defended."

"Why did you break into the—" I stopped myself with a sharp shake of my head. "Never mind, I don't want to know. But if we're going to anger a death god, at least take me home first so I can recharge my wards." Because if I was going to steal from the Empty Wind, I needed every edge I could get.

"Why can't you just recharge them here?" Nik asked. "You're a mage, right?"

"Yeah, but these aren't my wards," I said, pointing at my spellworked poncho. "This is corporate-level protection. I can't refill that freehand. I need to use the circle they came with from the dealer."

Nik frowned. "I thought mages did all their own spellwork."

"*Some* do," I huffed. "But just because you're born magical doesn't mean you have to make a career out of it. I wanted to study art, not spend eight years of my life earning a doctorate in Socratic Thaumaturgy, which is what I'd need to make something this complicated on my own. There's no point, anyway. Why kill myself reinventing the wheel when I can buy wards written by a whole lab full of professionals and backed with years of testing?"

"No need to get defensive," Nik said. "I was just asking."

I was *not* being defensive. I was just sick of people assuming that being a mage meant I'd mastered every aspect of the art. Being born with the ability to move magic didn't mean you were good at it any more than being tall meant you were good at basketball, and it wasn't as though I hadn't tried. My whole childhood had been nothing but spells blowing up in my face while various highly paid professionals shook their heads in dismay. Frankly, I found the make-it-up-as-you-go, slapdash magery I'd picked up since I started Cleaning a lot more useful than the "correct" forms I'd been taught back home. So long as I could crack safes and knock open doors, I saw no problem with my way of using magic.

"Until you slip up and burn yourself out," Sibyl whispered.

I yanked my goggles off my head. Despite having access to my surface-level brain waves through the mana contacts that powered my AR, Sibyl wasn't supposed to *actually* be able to read my thoughts. At times like this, though, I wasn't entirely sure that was true. I was fiddling with her sensitivity settings to make myself feel better when I caught Nik looking at me.

"You have an AI, don't you?"

"Of course," I said, moving my eyes around to remind myself what the world looked like without an augmented-reality overlay. "Doesn't everyone?"

"I don't," Nik said proudly. "AIs are expensive and invasive. They don't do anything except talk when you're trying to listen and look up things you could have looked up yourself."

"Wow, curmudgeon much?" I said. "AIs are great. I use mine for everything."

That was not an exaggeration. Sibyl took care of every aspect of my life. She kept my calendar, upgraded my security, managed my contacts, and paid my bills on time. She even kept track of all the local grocery stores' final sale notifications, which was the only reason I still had food in my apartment. She could be a little much sometimes, but if I didn't have her, I was pretty sure I'd be curled up naked and starving in a ball on my bathroom floor by the end of the week. She was my keeper. Literally, sometimes.

"She's a liability," Nik said when I explained this to him. "Any convenience AIs offer is outweighed by the fact that they can be hacked. Why would I entrust my bank account and real-time location data to something someone else can access?"

"Because life sucks without them," I said, exasperated. "Why are you such a Luddite?"

"A what?"

"Someone who hates technology," I explained, and then I smirked. "See, if you'd had an AI, it could have looked that up for you."

"I have no problem admitting when I don't know something," Nik said flatly. "And I don't hate technology. It's the loss of control that I resent. I don't think it's weird to not want a car that can drive itself off a bridge or a voice in my head that someone else could talk through."

It sounded almost reasonable when he put it that way, but seriously, how did he live without AI? How was it even possible to drive in the DFZ without a computer to check the ever-changing roads and redirect you? I couldn't imagine it. Fortunately, Nik seemed to be navigating the cloud of self-driving cars surrounding us just fine, and so long as he wasn't actively getting me killed, I supposed his paranoia was none of my business. The spirits knew I had enough paranoid hang-ups of my own, so who was I to judge?

"It's your life, I guess," I said, leaning back in my seat. "So long as you can get me to my house without driving us off a bridge, I have no complaints."

"I think I can manage that much," Nik said, though his voice was so dry I couldn't tell if he was joking or not. "We'll swing by your place, get you what you need, and then head for the morgue. Now, where do you live?"

Speaking of paranoid hang-ups, I had a slight panic attack when I realized I was going to have to tell this man where I slept. I almost told him to forget it and head to the morgue, but I felt naked without my wards, and it wasn't like I could get myself in more trouble. I was in this mess up to my chin already, so I sucked it up and gave Nik my address, which he punched into a cheap plastic phone that looked like one of the ones they sold out of vending machines to kids whose real phones had been confiscated. The chintzy little thing barely even had a touch screen, but it wasn't so terrible that it lacked a map. The lag was a bit annoying, but we managed, snaking through the Underground's neon-lit streets to the sound of the cheap GPS's emotionless voice telling us where to turn.

***

My current apartment was a one-bedroom walk-up on the top floor of an old converted motel.

It was a pretty nice building by Underground standards. It was a little old—not Old Detroit old, but still more than forty years—but it was solid brick, which was a lot prettier and better insulated than the cheap cement block Dr. Lyle's subbasement had been at the bottom of. The only downside was that since it had been a motel, it was still located right next to the busiest Skyway ramp for this area, which meant I basically had a highway going right past my window. I kept hoping the DFZ would move it, but in the year I'd lived here, she never had. Still, I couldn't complain too much. Loud as it was, the road noise kept the rent affordable on what would otherwise have been a very expensive apartment in one of the safest parts of town.

The former city of Hamtramck was where all the big private security firms had their offices. The whole place was full of rent-a-cops, which did wonders for keeping the crime rate down. That was a big deal for me given how much nice stuff I'd picked up in my early days of Cleaning. Of course, I'd had to sell most of it recently to make ends meet, but I still appreciated having a parking lot full of security cars, even if it did mean I had to sleep with earplugs and a pillow over my head.

I hopped out the moment we pulled into the loading area, grabbing my boots out of the back and shoving my feet into them so I wouldn't have to walk up in my socks. Feet protected, I slung my bag over my shoulder and leaned down to look at Nik through the open door. "Wait here. I'll be right back."

"Aren't I coming up with you?" he asked, giving me—and the bag on my shoulder that contained all of our leads—a suspicious look.

"No."

His suspicious scowl deepened. "Why not?"

Because I didn't want him to know which of the fifty units was mine. "Because my place is a mess."

Nik set his jaw stubbornly, and I rolled my eyes. "Please, I'm not going to bolt. First, I don't have a car right now, and second, even if I did try to run, you know where I'm going."

"If you're not going to run, why are you taking everything with you?"

I gave him a stubborn look of my own. "To make sure *you* don't run."

A normal person would have been offended by my blatant lack of trust, but Nick was a Cleaner like me. "Reasonable enough," he said, leaning back in his seat. "Ten minutes. Don't be late."

"What's the rush?" I asked. "We're going to visit a body in the morgue. It's not like he's going to run away." I checked my phone. "It's also ten o'clock at night. Peter probably won't even be there."

"He'll be there," Nik said with a certainty I found highly suspicious. "Ten minutes. Go."

Too tired to argue, I just shook my head and shut the door, starting up the worn stairs toward the building's second floor.

Since this was a converted motel, all of the hallways were open to the air. My apartment was on the western corner of the third floor, right under the Skyways where the on-ramp curved around. I knew Nik couldn't see my door from where I'd told him to park, but I still took the long way around, just in case. When I unlocked my door, I was doubly glad I hadn't invited Nik up. I'd been lying when I'd said my place was a wreck, but that didn't mean it didn't still look awful.

It hadn't always been this way. Before my luck had gone suddenly and indomitably downhill, my place had looked great. I'd been at the top of my Cleaning game, and my apartment had been a treasure trove of all the weird and wonderful stuff I'd found along the way. There'd been nothing truly spectacular—even back then, I'd needed the money too badly not to sell the *really* valuable stuff—but I'd still managed to acquire a very respectable collection. My walls had been covered in original paintings from up-and-coming DFZ artists, and my front window had featured an entire two-paned stained-glass panel I'd salvaged from one of the Old Detroit cathedrals. I'd had fossils, some nice fired glass vases, and a taxidermy tank badger the size of a Labrador beside my TV.

Anything and everything I'd found interesting I'd kept, turning what would otherwise have been a ho-hum one-bedroom efficiency into my very own gallery of curiosities. I'd been in the middle of installing track lighting to really take the place to the next level when I'd slammed into the wall.

Now, five miserable, bottom-of-the-barrel-scraping months later, my shelves were nearly bare. One by one, all my treasures had gone to auction so I could make my debt payments. I still had a few things—my absolute favorite and most irreplaceable pieces, plus all the interesting but not-actually-valuable stuff that wouldn't sell anyway—but the little that remained only served to make the gaps look bigger. My furniture was too cheap to resell, so my place wasn't *completely* empty, but I wasn't sure that was a good thing. A mattress on the floor was sad in its own way, but at least it had no pretensions. When I stepped through my door now, all I could see was how much I'd lost, and that almost hurt more than having nothing at all.

"Home sweet home," Sibyl said, her voice tinny and distant from my goggles as I dropped them, and my bag, on the coffee table. "Are you going to put me back on now?"

"Not before I brush my hair," I said, closing the cheap lace curtains over my front picture window. What I *really* wanted was a shower, but there was no way I could squeeze one of those in and recharge my wards in the ten minutes Nik had given me.

"Aw, come on," Sibyl said, her voice ringing loud and clear as she took over the speaker function on the cell phone in my pocket. "You're not mad because I told you to pair up with Mr. Kos, are you? I was just being realistic."

"I'm not mad," I said, walking into my tiny bathroom to wash my face. "It's just frustrating when you act like you know everything."

"That's what the 'I' in 'AI' is for," Sibyl said cheerfully. "It's my job to think of everything so you don't have to. But if it's hurting your self-esteem, I can tone it down. I'm here for your mental well-being, never forget."

"How could I?" I asked, patting my face dry before reaching for my brush to attempt an emergency rescue on my poor hair. "You remind me constantly."

"Just making sure you remember how useful I—" Sibyl cut off with a beep as my phone buzzed against my thigh. "Hey, you've got an incoming call from Heidi Varner! Should I put her through?"

I had to think about that one. On the one hand, I'd just told Heidi I'd stop ignoring her calls. On the other, I'd already decided to cut off contact. That said, it had only been a few hours since I'd seen her, which meant ignoring her now felt extra rude. There was also the chance she might have more to tell me now that I knew Dr. Lyle's name. They'd been at different schools, but he was still a professor who specialized in Alchemical Thaumaturgy. Even in a city as big as the DFZ, that *had* to be a small pond. Definitely worth the risk, especially since it meant I wouldn't have to be the world's worst friend again quite so soon.

"Okay, I'll take it," I said, smiling at my pale, tired reflection in the mirror as I began teasing out the complicated system of braids and bobby pins that kept the majority of my long black hair more or less safely bundled at the back of my head. "Put her on speaker."

The phone clicked as Sibyl patched the call through. "Hey, Heidi," I said when I heard the connection pick up. "Forget something?"

There was a long pause, and then a woman who was *definitely* not Heidi began speaking in Korean.

"Please hold for a call from Lady Yong-ae."

My stomach dropped so fast I was almost sick. "Sibyl!" I cried. "Cut the—"

"Opal."

I closed my eyes. Even on a staticky, hijacked connection, no one could say my name as sweetly, or as terrifyingly, as my mother could.

"Why are you calling from Heidi's number?" I demanded in English.

"Because you never answer when I call you from my own," she replied in Korean, which was nothing but a power move. She spoke English—and French and Japanese and German and Chinese—better than I did. Korean was for family matters, which meant this was not a happy call. Not that I'd ever gotten one of those.

"I hear you're going to miss your debt payment," my mother continued. "That's very irresponsible of you."

"Where did you hear that?" I demanded, sticking to English because I could do that now that I was on the other side of the world.

"Mother's intuition."

"That's not a real thing."

"But I'm still right," she said confidently. "Aren't I?"

My answer was a long sigh as I slumped against the sink. "I'm not late yet," I said stubbornly. "It's only Monday. The money's not due until Friday."

"It's already Tuesday here," she reminded me. "Your father—"

"I'll make the payment," I said through clenched teeth. "Tell *Father* he can mind his own business."

"But you are his business," she reminded me. "You made yourself his business when you made this about money."

My father had been up in my business *way* before actual money had gotten involved, but I didn't bother to point that out. As always, my mother had an uncanny knack for turning complicated situations into simple faults, usually mine. Still, it was hard to argue that she was wrong considering my father was the one I owed all this money to.

"It doesn't have to be this way, you know," she said, her voice so sweet that I almost fell for it even though I knew better. "Your father doesn't care about the money. Such amounts are trivial to one as great as he. He just wants you to come back home where you belong. It's obvious your little experiment in independence is a failure. You're living in the Underground, working as a *maid*—"

"Cleaner, Mom," I said. "I'm a *Cleaner*. It's an entirely different job."

"Whatever," she said dismissively. "It's still menial, and you're still broke."

"How do you know I'm broke?" I challenged. "Cleaning's a lucrative business. Maybe I'm rich and just too busy to worry about little family debts."

She laughed at that, a beautiful, musical sound. "*Please*, darling, don't play these games with me. You've been down to the wire on every payment since March. It's painfully obvious that you're drowning, so stop being stubborn and come home. You're so young, and your magic is so dreadful. The DFZ is no place for lazy, sloppy children."

"I'm twenty-six, Mom," I said, reaching up to rub my suddenly aching head. "Get a better argument."

"How can I see you as anything but a child when you insist on acting like one?" she snapped, the sweetness vanishing from her voice to reveal the steel that was always waiting just underneath. "Your father has been exceedingly generous letting you roam for as long as he has, but enough is enough. Your failure is obvious to everyone. A better daughter, one worthy of being called Yong-ae, would have realized this and come home ages ago, but alas! I am cursed with an ungrateful, defiant sow of a child who is incapable of appreciating the great privilege she was bred into. Can you even comprehend the suffering your selfishness has caused?"

"I'm sure you'll survive," I grumbled, rolling my eyes. "I'm hanging up now. Tell Dad I'll have his money on time."

"You can tell him yourself," she said. "He's already there."

I froze. "He's here? In the DFZ?"

"Not for *you*," she said. "He has business in the city this week, but that just makes it more convenient for him to pick you up when you inevitably miss your deadline."

"Well, I hope he didn't change any plans," I growled. "Because I'm *not* going to miss the deadline."

"Don't make promises you can't keep," she warned. "Never forget, Opal, this is a bed of *your* making. You were the one who insisted on this debt. Your father has been very lenient thus far. *Too* lenient, I think, but even his patience is not infinite. You know what he is capable of. If you continue to defy him, you'll have no one to blame but yourself."

She was right. I knew *exactly* what my father was capable of. It was why I'd risked everything to go to school overseas. Why I worked an untraceable job and cut myself off from all of my legitimate friends like Heidi, who'd only seen me four hours ago and yet had somehow already managed to leak my new number to my mother. Now I'd have to change it again.

I'd already warned her I was hanging up, so I didn't feel the least bit bad when I cut off the call without a word. I brushed my hair with furious strokes until it hung straight, black, and shiny again, and then I pulled it back into a ponytail to keep it out of my face and because my mother hated ponytails. I did my poncho next, pulling the plastic over my head and rinsing it off in the shower. When all the dirt was on the floor of my tub instead of the spellworked plastic, I shook off the excess water and walked back into my living room to start recharging the wards.

The preprinted magic circle that had come with my poncho was in the corner of my living room where I'd left it yesterday, draped over the top of my empty mini fridge. I knocked the stiff plastic ring onto the floor with my foot and dumped my heavy plastic warded coat into the middle, sucking magic into my hands as I went. When I had enough—or maybe too much—I shoved the power into the circle, filling it until the tiny lines of laser-printed spellwork flared and the magic pushed back at me. Satisfied I'd dumped enough in to replace what I'd used, I left my wards cooking and went into my bedroom to change.

Cleaning is a dirty job. Even with my poncho to keep the worst off, my jeans and T-shirt were sweaty, dusty, and still smelled vaguely of dead body. Disgusted, I stripped naked and shoved everything I'd been wearing into my work clothes hamper, the one with the sealed lid. Since I was still working, changing into another pair of jeans would have been best, but it was beastly hot, so I opted for shorts and a tank top, which, though far less protective, were *much* cooler. I was still lacing up my running shoes, because like hell was I putting my bare legs into my filthy work boots, when someone knocked on my door.

"Dammit, Nik," I muttered, checking the clock on my nightstand. Sure enough, it had been exactly ten minutes. I would have wondered how he'd known which apartment was mine, but after everything else he'd pulled tonight, I was starting to think Nik could follow my scent like a bloodhound. Cursing my stupid mother for wasting my time and stupid punctual jerks for rushing me, I yanked my shoelaces tight and stomped to my front door.

"Seriously," I said as I yanked it open. "You couldn't give me one extra minute before…"

I trailed off, eyes going wide. The man standing in front of my apartment was *not* Nik. He looked very legitimate at first glance: tall and handsome with a tailored suit, slicked-back brown hair, tan skin, and expensive leather shoes. But his blindingly white smile was too aggressive to mean anything good.

"Miss Yong-ae?" he said politely.

My answer was to shut the door in his face. It might have been too much—I got a lot of door-to-door salesmen, and annoying as they could be, they weren't usually bad people—but this was too close on the heels of being shot at and my mother's phone call to take risks. Also, door-to-door salesmen didn't ask for me by name. I almost managed to get my door slammed and locked before the man wedged his foot in.

"I just need a moment of your time," he said quickly. "I want to make you an offer. My name is—"

He stopped suddenly, voice cutting off like a switch. It happened so fast my first thought was that he'd finally realized how much getting your foot slammed in a door hurt. A second later, though, I realized his silence had nothing to do with me or the door I was shoving against his wing-tipped shoe. He'd shut up because there was a gun sticking past the side of my door frame, its muzzle pointing directly at the side of his head.

CHAPTER 5

"**W**hy, Mr. Kos," the stranger said, raising his hands over his head. "Fancy meeting you here."

I couldn't see who was holding the gun from where I was standing, but sure enough, when I opened my door wider, Nik was standing in the old motel's open hallway with his sleek gun pointed at the tanned man's temple.

"What are you doing here?" he asked in a deadly voice.

"Same thing you are, I imagine," the man at my door replied. With remarkable calm, I thought, given the situation. "Pursuing a business opportunity." The stranger's sly brown eyes flicked back to me, and the brilliant white smile returned to his face. "You're Miss Opal Yong-ae, correct? The Cleaner?"

I glanced nervously at Nik, but he was keeping his eyes—and his gun—pinned on the newcomer. He looked more pissed off than worried, though, and I took that as a cue to play it cool. "Who's asking?" I said, opening my door all the way to show that I wasn't afraid.

The tanned man smiled wider, which didn't seem physically possible. "My name is Kauffman," he said, nodding down at his chest. "There's a business card in my front jacket pocket."

Which he couldn't get for me because he'd be shot if he moved.

Sighing at the ridiculousness of it all, I dug my fingers into his pocket to grab the card. I made sure to press my knuckles into his chest as I did, giving him a good feel of the magic I'd instinctively pulled into my hands. It was supposed to be a warning, a rattle of my own to match Nik's pulled gun. To my surprise, though, the man was already buzzing with power when I touched him. It was a neat, orderly pulse, much better shaped than my sloppy handful. Apparently, this Kauffman was a mage as well, and not a bad one. Better than me, actually, which made me much more grateful for Nik's gun as I stepped back into my apartment with the business card.

"Andrej Kauffman," I read, noting the expensive embossed printing and, more importantly, the tracking spell woven into the ecru card stock. "President, Creative Solutions LLC. Magical risk management and asset recovery."

That last one made me sweat a little, but I managed to keep the worry off my face, leaning casually on the door frame so that my body blocked Kauffman's view of the bag full of the papers we'd taken from Dr. Lyle's house, which was still sitting on the coffee table not three feet behind me.

"If you're here to recover something, I'm afraid you're out of luck," I said innocently, reaching out to tuck the bugged business card back into Kauffman's pocket. "I haven't found anything worth sending someone after in weeks. Just ask Nik. He knows how bad my luck's been, and you two seem to know each other."

"We're not friends," Nik said sharply, sliding his gun a bit closer to Kauffman's skull. "He's a fixer. He helps corporations find criminals to do their dirty work."

"I prefer the term 'consultant,'" Kauffman said crisply, giving Nik a cutting look before turning his dazzling smile back on me. "I understand you recently purchased the Cleaning rights to a town home in Magic Heights, yes?"

I could have said no. Cleaning auctions weren't public record, but it was easy enough information to get. All he'd have to do was talk to any other Cleaner, and they'd tell him all about my crazy bid. Kauffman also struck me as the sort of person who didn't ask a question unless he already knew the answer, so I nodded, and his smile grew even brighter.

"Excellent," he said, clapping his still-raised hands together above his head. "I'd like to buy it from you. My employer has authorized me to offer you a hundred thousand dollars for full rights to the house and everything therein. If you could just tell your attack dog to lower his weapon so I can use my phone, I'll be happy to transfer the full amount to your account immediately."

Nik looked more pissed at the dog comment than I'd ever seen him, but I was too shocked to pay his reaction proper attention. A hundred thousand dollars was a *lot* of money, and "immediately" was definitely my kind of timeline. If I took his offer, I could pay my debt *tonight*. But eager as I was to get out of my current squeeze, I wasn't a total idiot. If Kauffman really was a fixer like Nik said, then he was undoubtedly the one who'd hired the guys who'd attacked me. He was also *vastly* overpaying, which told me the information I'd found in Dr. Lyle's home was worth a lot more than a hundred grand.

"Opal," Nik whispered, but I held up my hand.

"You're offering for the Cleaning contract, right?" I said, choosing my words carefully. "Meaning you'd clean the house up and hand it back to the city ready for a new tenant in exchange for ownership of everything that's inside it right now."

Kauffman's eyes sharpened above his smile. "Considering you've already been there, that wouldn't be a very good deal for me, would it?" He shook his head. "We're not making a new deal, Miss Yong-ae. I'm offering a hundred thousand dollars for *your* contract, meaning I would own everything on the property from the moment you won it at auction, including any objects or papers you might have already salvaged. But I'm sure that won't be a problem," he added quickly. "After all, you already said you've found nothing of value for weeks, so selling all that nothing to me for a very nice profit should be a no-brainer, right?"

He finished with a cheerful grin, but I was already shaking my head. Nik was as well.

"No deal," he said.

Kauffman shot him a sideways look. "I don't see how your opinion enters into this, Mr. Kos."

"It enters because sixty percent of that contract is mine," Nik growled, keeping his gun up as he stepped around Kauffman to join me in the doorway. "Opal and I already made a deal, and if you're throwing around that much money, all you're doing is telling us that what was in that property is worth a lot more." He looked at me. "Right?"

"Damn right," I said, crossing my glowing hands over my chest.

Kauffman shrugged and lowered his hands even though Nik's gun was still pointed at his head. "That is your prerogative. But before you close the door, you should know that the previous tenant, Dr. Theodore Lyle, is a dangerous and deranged man."

I blinked in confusion at his use of the present tense, and then it hit me. Kauffman was only trying to buy my Cleaning contract on Dr. Lyle's townhouse. That meant he must not know about the basement I'd won this morning, or that Dr. Lyle was dead.

"A dangerous man, huh?" I said, keeping my face neutral. "What's so bad about him?"

"He's a thief, for one," Kauffman said. "He was a magical contractor for our mutual employer, but he absconded six weeks ago with some expensive and very dangerous property. I'm merely trying to get it back."

"If he's a thief, why didn't your 'client' call the authorities?" Nik asked.

"He's a man who greatly values his privacy," Kauffman replied innocently.

"Right," Nik said, giving me a pointed look.

As if I needed the hint. This was obviously a case of criminals all the way down. But while I had no idea why Kauffman's "client" cared so much about a ritual that made cockatrice eggs, I now knew for certain that that spell was worth a *lot* more than a hundred thousand. No one made money paying fair market price on a buyout. For Kauffman to show up this fast with a six-figure starting number, the actual value had to be multiple times that. Maybe even more than a million.

My stomach began to flutter. Forget making my payment. Forty percent of a million would clear all the money I owed to my father and then some. I just had to get my hands on it, and that meant getting rid of Kauffman.

"Thank you so much for coming all the way out here, Mr. Kauffman," I said sweetly, trying not to cringe at how much I sounded like my mother. "But I'm afraid we can't do business. I have a previous arrangement with Mr. Kos, and I could never go back on a contract with a fellow Cleaner."

"You really should reconsider," Kauffman said, the smile slipping from his face. "This is a one-time offer. I'd hate for you to miss it."

"Sorry, but the answer is no," I said firmly, clenching my fists around the magic I'd packed so tight it was starting to burn my skin. "Good *night*, Mr. Kauffman."

Kauffman's perfect square jaw tightened as he realized I was serious. Nik tensed as well, his body still and hard as an iron post beside mine. To my enormous surprise, though, no violence broke out. Kauffman simply backed away.

"A no is a no," he said, charming smile right back in place as though it had never left. "I'm sorry we couldn't come to an agreement, Miss Yong-ae." He nodded to Nik. "Mr. Kos."

Nik didn't answer. Neither did I. We just stood side by side in the doorway, watching Kauffman like hawks as he strolled away down the open hallway, whistling to himself in the hot, dark night.

When he'd vanished down the stairs, Nik slammed my door. "You need to pack."

"What?"

"Kauffman's a professional," he said, holstering his gun. "He only asks nicely once. The next time it's going to be men through your window."

I gaped at him. "Are you serious?"

"What part of this strikes you as a joke?" he demanded. "You've already been shot at once today by men Kauffman probably hired. You think he'll hesitate to do it again?"

Not when he put it that way. "Should we call the cops?" I asked, grabbing my bag off the table and digging for my goggles, because if this was getting serious, I needed Sibyl's eyes. "Even in the DFZ, it's illegal to bust in through people's windows, right?"

"It is," Nik said. "But DFZ police are all private security contractors. They practically have an 800 number for bribes, and given the numbers Kauffman's thrown around tonight, he's probably already paid."

I cursed under my breath. Sometimes I hated this city. "So what do we do?"

"We run," Nik said, nodding at my poncho, which was still lying in the center of its charging circle. "Is it done yet?"

I walked over and stuck my hand in the circle to check. "Almost," I said, swirling my fingers through what was left of the nearly absorbed magic. "So what should I bring? Are we talking overnight or days or what?"

Nik shrugged. "Kauffman knows where you live now, so I'd say bring whatever you don't want smashed."

I froze, eyes going wide as I remembered the rubble they'd made of Dr. Lyle's house…and then imagined the same thing happening to mine. "Oh no," I said, dangerously close to tears as I turned to my nearly empty shelves, the last treasures I had left. "No, no, no."

My reaction seemed to freak Nik out even more than the prospect of gunmen crashing through the window. "What's wrong?" he asked, voice slightly panicked. "Why are you crying?"

I was *not* crying, though I did have to sniff a few times before I could answer. "I don't want him to break my stuff. I know it's stupid and it's not worth much, but…" I shook my head, pushing my goggles up so I could wipe my eyes. "It's mine."

That was all I could say. Before I'd come to the DFZ, nothing had been mine. Everything had belonged to my father, including me. I couldn't say that to Nik, though. I could already see him assessing my apartment as a Cleaner would. I'd done the same myself countless times, and I knew what he was going to say. The stuff in my apartment wasn't worth a thousand bucks altogether. It was useless, pointless, sentimental junk, and I was an idiot for caring about it when so much more was on the line. I was telling myself to get a grip when Nik turned back to me.

"We'll move it."

I stared at him, uncomprehending. "What?"

"We'll move your apartment," he said, his face breaking into a rare smile. "We're Cleaners, right? We do this all the time. I've only got my car, so we can't get the furniture, but we can do the rest. Just tell me what you want to save, and I'll help you get it out."

He said all of this quickly and confidently, but I still couldn't believe it. *I* thought this was stupid, and I was the one who was upset about it. Nik had to think I was the biggest idiot on the planet for going to pieces over a bunch of quarter-full shelves. It would be in everyone's better interest for him to tell me to suck it up, but he was already grabbing the big empty box that my bulk order of Cup Noodles had arrived in.

"It's the stuff on the shelves, right?"

I nodded, unable to speak. He nodded back and started carefully but quickly packing my things into the box with a Cleaner's efficiency. I stood there watching him for a good minute and a half before it hit me that if I wasn't being an idiot before, I was *definitely* being one now.

"I'll do my room," I said in a rush, grabbing a black trash bag from the box I kept in my closet before sprinting for my bedroom door. "Prioritize the ceramics. If it doesn't fit in that box, just leave it."

"I can get it all," Nik said confidently. "I do this all the time."

I could have hugged him right then. If I hadn't wasted so much time already, I would have fallen at his feet and thanked him from the bottom of my heart. It was such a small kindness, just a few extra minutes, but while plenty of people had been kind to me in my life, no one had done it for as little as Nik had just now. *I* wouldn't have done it. I was already furious with myself over how selfish I was being. It was just junk, the unsellable dregs of a collection that had only taken me a year to put together. The only reason it mattered was because of my weird attachment issues. If Kauffman already had guys lined up in case we rejected his offer, I might have just gotten us killed over trinkets. Nik *had* to know that, and yet here he was, working to save my stuff without complaint or condemnation.

I had no words for it. "Thank you" felt too shallow and cheap to attach to the big, formless emotions boiling inside me, so I said nothing at all. I just kept working, throwing whatever clothes and toiletries would fit into my trash bag as fast as I could.

***

We had the whole place done in ten minutes.

"What did I tell you?" Nik said as he put the box containing the final bits of my collection and my trash bag full of clothes and toiletries into the trunk of his car. "Cleaner efficiency."

"Thank you," I said, repeating the words even though I knew they weren't enough because really, what else could I say? "Thank you so much."

Nik shrugged and took the preprinted magic circle I used to recharge my poncho from my hands. We'd finished before it had, but we'd already wasted too much time, so I'd declared my wards good enough and grabbed the whole thing, pulling the protective poncho over my head while Nik crammed the soft-ribbed spellwork-covered circle into his trunk and shut the lid. "Is that all?"

"It's everything I care about." My apartment wasn't empty, but I could buy more cheap furniture and packs of instant noodles. The stuff I couldn't replace—my salvaged block of limestone fronting engraved with nineteenth-century Masonic imagery, my ammonite fossil where you could see the full Golden Ratio spiral, my brass letter opener shaped like a crane that *might* have been a limited-edition Crane Paper Company retirement gift from the 1920s—was all safely stowed in Nick's trunk, and I couldn't thank him enough.

"Thank you," I said again. "Really, thank you."

"It's fine," he said, looking as awkward as I felt. "You're welcome. Now let's *go*. I don't want to push our luck any further than we already have."

I nodded and dove into the car, remembering to take my shoes off at the last minute even though I was wearing my reasonably clean sneakers rather than my Cleaning boots. I was still fastening my seat belt when Nik hit the gas, shooting us out of the quiet parking lot like a bullet. He turned the moment he hit the street, almost fishtailing the car as he swung around and gunned it up the ramp toward the Skyways.

"Wait," I said as he pushed us faster. "Why are we going up? I thought the morgue was in the Underground." And while you could get there through the Skyways, the tolls were ridiculous.

"We're not going to the morgue," Nik said, eyes pinned on his rear-view mirror as he wove us through the late-night traffic. "If Kauffman didn't smash a team through your window the moment he got to the parking lot, it's probably because he decided it would be easier to follow us to the prize instead, which means I'm not going anywhere important until I'm certain I've lost any tails. When I know we're not being followed, we'll pull over, check the car for bugs, and then drive some more. *Then* we can head to where we're actually going."

I smiled at him, impressed. "Good thinking."

Nik shrugged, a move I now recognized as his default for when he didn't know what to say. Fortunately, I did. "We should cover our magical trail, too," I said, pulling off my poncho so I could turn it inside out. "Kauffman's a good mage. I caught his bugged business card, but if he got something off me—like a hair from my apartment—he could use it to cast a finding spell that will track us anywhere. The only way to stop him is to cut the connection ahead of time."

Nik nodded. "Sounds good. How do we do that?"

"With this." I held up the inside of my poncho. "I didn't buy this thing for Cleaning. It's actually a security garment meant for protecting high-value targets: CEOs, foreign dignitaries, that sort of thing. My mom bought it for me when I first moved to the DFZ."

"Then she must love you a lot," Nik said. "I've seen those in catalogs. They're stupid expensive."

I'd never doubted that my mother loved me. It was her judgment I didn't trust. But unlike the designer clothes she still sent me every season (always one size too small, for "encouragement"), the poncho was actually useful, which was why it had survived long after I'd sold everything else. "It's worth the money," I said, pointing at the far-more-delicate ward lines that covered the poncho's interior. "The outside focuses on external threats—bullets, dirt, blunt trauma, and so on—but the interior's all about magical protection, including a burn command for separating material links."

I just had to remember how to use it.

"Sibyl," I said, pulling my goggles back down over my face.

My AI's icon fluttered. "Oh, are you speaking to me again?"

"I wasn't ever *not* speaking to you."

"That's not what it felt like to me."

I rolled my eyes at her grumpy tone. "I thought AIs weren't supposed to hold grudges."

"I wasn't holding a grudge," she said defensively. "I was giving you your space. You always get snippy after you talk to your mother."

I couldn't deny that one, so I just moved on. "I need you to look up the manual for my poncho. I can't remember the activation sequence for the material links disposal system."

"Here you go," she said, bringing up the diagram. "I highlighted the hand gestures since I know you have trouble with those."

I smiled at her thoughtfulness. This was why computer assistants were awesome. They knew you better than you knew yourself. "Thank you," I said, wiggling into the inside-out poncho. The rough plastic exterior felt awful against my bare shoulders, like a combination tarp and trash bag, but at least I didn't have to bear it for long. Even without a full charge, I could feel the magic through the spellwork as I followed the diagrammed instructions my AI had projected in the air in front of me.

"Clear!"

A pulse of magic filled the car, making Nik jump. "A little warning next time!" he snapped, gripping the wheel. "I almost rear-ended someone."

"Sorry." I coughed, waving the smoke away from my flushed face. "Didn't realize it was going to do that."

I'd never used this particular feature of my poncho before. I honestly had no idea how the material link disposal spell functioned since the whole point of owning a high-end piece of magical equipment was so I didn't have to learn how to do all this stuff myself, but my entire body felt sunburned, which I assumed meant it had worked. According to the manual, the burn-off wouldn't save me from a really strong link like blood, but all the minor connections such as hair, skin, recently worn clothing, treasured objects, and so forth should have been neutralized.

"I'll do you next when we pull over to check for bugs," I told Nik, pulling the poncho off my head again.

"No thank you," Nik said, cringing. "Kauffman doesn't know where I live, and I didn't get close enough for him to grab anything, so I'll pass."

"You should still do it," I said. "Better safe than sorry."

"Better anything than what just happened to you," he said with a shudder, shaking his head. "If it felt that awful from the outside, I don't ever want to be inside."

I hadn't thought it was that bad, but then, I'm a horrible mage. I'd backlashed myself with magic so many times I didn't even feel it anymore. Now that I thought about it, I remembered that this kind of internal magic was always way scarier for non-mages who weren't used to having their souls moved around on the regular. No wonder Nik didn't want to do it.

"Your choice," I said, draping the poncho over my lap since we weren't being shot at right now and I wanted to savor life outside a plastic bag for a while. "How long are we going to drive?"

"Until I'm convinced there's no one following us."

"Do you need me to navigate?"

He shook his head. "Don't need to know where you're going if your only destination is *away*."

I shrugged and leaned back in his seat, determined to rest if he didn't want assistance. Now that I'd stopped moving, it was starting to hit me how tired I was. Tired and *hungry*. According to the clock at the corner of my augmented-reality vision, it was after eleven. I'd gotten up at five to get a good spot at the morning Cleaning auction, and I'd been going nonstop ever since, which meant I'd missed lunch *and* dinner. My stomach clenched at the reminder, but I couldn't do anything about it. I'd left my supply of Cup Noodles back at my apartment, and I was flat broke. Even vending machine sandwiches were out of my budget right now if I wanted to have any money left for tomorrow, so I told my stomach to STFU and leaned my head against the window of Nik's car, looking up at the night sky as we came out on the Skyways to see if I could spot the moon. Living Underground, I almost never got to see it. But my bad luck must still have been going strong, because the night was overcast, leaving me staring at yet another ceiling as the low clouds rolled between the brightly lit columns of the superscrapers.

***

After an hour of driving in circles and a very thorough check for bugs at what had to be the last petroleum pump in the DFZ, Nik finally deemed us free of tails, which meant we could move on to our *actual* destination: the city morgue. Today's events notwithstanding, I didn't normally encounter dead bodies, so I'd never actually been there before. I wasn't sure what I was expecting, but the giant industrial warehouse Nik pulled us up beside definitely wasn't it.

"Are you sure this is the right place?" I asked, squinting out the window at the brightly lit white walls. "It looks like an auto plant."

"It has to be big," Nik said as he cut the engine. "There's ten million people between the Underground and the Skyways. Even when you account for all the ones who die in hospitals and get processed there, that's still a lot of dead bodies."

I'd never really thought about it. I supposed it was comforting to know that even in the capitalistic dystopia of the DFZ, bodies weren't left to rot in the street. The industrial scale of the facility still gave me the creeps, though, especially once I noticed the giant smokestacks rising up through a special hole in the Skyways above.

"So what's the plan?" I asked, tearing my eyes away from what had to be the biggest crematorium in North America.

"Same as before: get to the body," Nik replied, leaning down so he could peer at the morgue's towering wall through my window. "There are thousands of corpses in there. We'll never find our mage in that haystack, so you're going to go into the office and ask Peter where he put him. Once we get the slab number, we can sneak into the main building and get the hand."

By which he meant *steal*.

"Are you sure we have to do this?" I asked nervously. "There has to be some other way of accessing the information in that hand that doesn't involve taking from the Forgotten Dead."

"I already told you there isn't," Nik said sharply. "You're the one who said the location info was hard-coded into the VCI. If you're right, then there's no way to hack into that without literally sticking a wire into the inputs, so unless you want to bring a hacker into the morgue, we need that cyberwear."

I winced, fingers twisting in my lap, and Nik sighed. "Look," he said, dragging a gloved hand through his short-cropped dark hair. "I'll do the actual snitch if you don't want to, but you're the only one who can get the info out of Peter. If I show up out of nowhere and start asking for slab numbers, he'll know something's up, but you're the one who found the body. You've got all kinds of reasons why you'd need to see it again. Just pick one and get in there. Most death priests are night owls, but it's getting close to one a.m. If we don't do this quick, Peter will go home, and we'll be stuck until tomorrow."

I sank deeper into my seat with every word. He was right, of course. I'd already made up my mind that I had to do this for the money, but now that I was actually here, it felt utterly wrong. I also had no idea how I was actually going to convince Peter to lead me to the body. Nik said I had all kinds of reasons, but all the ones that came to my head sounded like transparent ploys. I was going through Dr. Lyle's notes again to see if there was anything that could give me a legitimate reason for needing to see his body again when I found his expired ID.

And got my idea.

"I'll be back," I said, putting my shoes on before sliding out of the car. "Wait here."

Nik nodded and settled into the driver's seat, watching me like a falcon as I walked down the street and up the stairs to what I hoped was the morgue's front office.

***

The inside of the DFZ's clearing house for dead bodies turned out to be a lot more mundane than you'd expect. With its beige walls, fluorescent lights, and cheap blue carpeting, it actually looked more like a traditional government building than anything else I'd seen in this crazy city. The front steps led me up to a pair of double doors that opened into a receiving area, where a bored security guard asked me what I wanted. This was the point at which I suddenly realized I didn't actually know Peter's last name. Fortunately, despite his prominence in the DFZ, the Empty Wind didn't actually have a lot of full-time priests. The guard knew exactly who I was talking about, and a few minutes later, I was walking down the fluorescent-lit hall with a temporary visitor's stamp on my hand, counting the endless identical doors until I reached the one the guard had told me to knock on.

"Opal!" Peter said, his face surprised when he opened his door and saw me standing outside like a guilty kid. "What are you doing here?"

"I had a question for you," I said, trying not to fidget. "Can I come in?"

Peter stepped back at once, holding the door for me. His office was surprisingly large and even more surprisingly normal. I'd been half expecting altars of bones, but his large desk was covered in a perfectly ordinary mix of publicly projected AR and good old-fashioned paper. He had several lamps to soften the harsh overhead light and a few potted plants to make the place feel a bit less like a windowless box. There was even a cat tower in the corner, where Peter's orange tomcat was lounging on his back, watching me with curious yellow eyes as I sheepishly scuttled inside.

"Sorry to bother you," I said as Peter shut the door behind me.

"No bother at all," he replied, pointing at one of the two padded chairs in front of his desk. "I'm happy to have the company. I don't exactly get a lot of visitors."

I could see how someone whose clients were alone by default wouldn't have a lot of foot traffic.

"There," Peter said, sitting down in his own comfortably worn office chair. "Now, what can I do for you?"

He finished with a warm smile, which made me feel absolutely awful. Unlike mine, Peter's job was a noble calling, and here I was trying to take advantage of it. But while there was no sugarcoating the fact that I'd come here as a thief, I did have something legitimate to share with him, and I clung to that shred of decency with all I had.

"Actually, I have something for you," I said, holding out Dr. Lyle's ID.

He took it curiously. "Who's this?"

"The man you removed from the apartment this morning," I replied. "He was Dr. Theodore Lyle, a professor of Thaumaturgy, or at least a former one."

An exultant grin spread over Peter's face. "Where did you find this?"

"In the unit," I said, which wasn't technically a lie. I *had* found it while Cleaning, just not in the place I was implying.

"Thank you so much for bringing this to me," he said, putting the ID on his desk so he could take a picture of it with his phone. "It will help enormously."

"Glad to hear it," I said, trying not to sound too excited as I moved on to my real object. "So now that we know who he is, he's no longer one of the Forgotten Dead, right?"

Peter shook his head. "That's for the Empty Wind to decide. I just do the grunt work."

"But we know who he is now," I argued. "How can he be forgotten if he's known?"

"Knowing isn't the same as remembering," Peter explained, taking one more picture of the back of the ID before sliding the card into a manila folder marked "pending." "We know who he was, but we don't *know* know him. Not like family or a friend would. But this is still fantastic! Even a little remembrance can help keep a soul together on the other side. The world of spirits is not a kind or gentle place. It's the source of all magic in the world, and the torrents of power there will shred a human soul in seconds if it's not properly protected by the memories of those who knew them. It's not as good as the love of a relative, but just the two of us knowing Dr. Lyle's name can still be a shield for him in the swirling void. It'll also make Collections' job a lot easier when they search for his next of kin." He beamed at me. "You did a very good thing bringing this to me, Opal. The dead and I thank you."

His heartfelt gratitude made me feel ten times worse than if he'd yelled at me, as did the fact that none of this was going according to plan.

I'd hoped that Peter would see the ID and proclaim that Dr. Lyle was no longer forgotten, which meant taking his hand would be just the normal sort of illegal and not stealing from a death god. Clearly, this wasn't going to be as simple as I'd hoped, but I wasn't giving up yet.

"So what happens to him now?" I asked, finally sitting down in the chair he'd offered when I'd walked in. "Are you holding his body in case any relatives come looking?"

"Normally we would," Peter said. "But his body was so decayed, I decided cremation would be kinder. He's in the queue for the ovens right now."

My heart skipped a beat. "But you haven't burned him yet, right?"

"I'm not sure," Peter said, giving me a curious look. "Why do you ask?"

"I was just wondering," I said, keeping my voice desperately casual. "What about organ donations?"

Peter chuckled. "Opal, he was dead for thirty days before you found him. I don't think they'll be getting any viable organs out of that."

"What about cybernetics?" I pressed. "He had a cybernetic hand, didn't he? Surely you don't burn that."

"Normally, no, but he came in with the Empty Wind. When that happens, we burn everything the living would have considered their body to make sure that nothing they might need is left behind." Peter's eyes narrowed suspiciously. "Why the sudden curiosity? Is there something of his you want?"

This was where I could have played the ruthless, greedy Cleaner and claimed I wanted the cybernetics for resale, but that was so shameless that I couldn't even get the words out of my mouth. "I don't want anything," I lied, pulling the notes I'd taken out of my bag. "It's just that I was going through his spell notes, and I found some stuff that looked like it was meant specifically to get around the casting limitations caused by having a fake hand. I've never seen anything like it, so I wanted to examine his fingers to see if they matched the description of the altered motions in the spell."

That was the biggest BS I'd ever spewed in my life. I didn't even know if spells *could* be modified to account for cybernetics, but it sounded plausible, and it gave me an innocent reason to look at Dr. Lyle's body. I was congratulating myself on my fast thinking when Peter suddenly rose from his desk. "Why didn't you just say so?" he asked, giving me a smile. "I can take you down myself right now. If Dr. Lyle hasn't gone into the oven yet, you're free to look him over all you want."

I smiled back, panicking inside. If Peter was with me, there was no way Nik or I could steal the hand. But while I was scrambling to think of how I was going to salvage the situation, Sibyl's voice whispered confidently in my ear.

"I've got this."

Peter's phone rang the moment she finished. Flashing me an apologetic smile, he picked it up, sitting back down at his desk so he could access his computer. "Office of the Forgotten Dead, Peter speaking."

What followed was a conversation too low for me to hear. It must have been very serious business, though, because Peter's normally cheerful face grew dire. "Of course," he said, scribbling an address down on the yellow sticky pad beside him. "I'll head over right now."

What did you do? I typed to Sibyl on my AR keyboard.

"Called in an emergency," my AI replied smugly. "Now he'll be out of your hair."

The horror I felt at that must have been loud and clear on the surface brain waves she had access to, because Sibyl's voice grew instantly calm and cajoling. Before she could explain herself, though, Peter hung up and turned to me.

"I have to go," he said, his voice deadly serious. "If I give you the slab number, will you be all right checking the body by yourself?"

"I'll be fine," I said, happy to let him assume my shaking voice was nerves over being alone in a morgue and not crippling guilt. "What's the number?"

He wrote it down on another sticky note and handed it to me. "I'm so sorry to leave you in the lurch. I'd tell you to come back later so I could guide you myself, but I don't know how long this will take, and there's no stopping the cremation queue. I'd hate for any part of Dr. Lyle's legacy to be lost because you were waiting for me. Just tell the front guard I said it was okay, and he'll let you in. Again, I'm really sorry about this."

Not half as sorry as I felt. "Thank you, Peter," I said, taking the sticky note. "I owe you big time."

"Not as much as we owe you," he assured me, grabbing his bag and holding out his arm so that his cat could climb onto his shoulder. "You're the one investigating his spells. The things we create in this life are so much more important than our names. By pouring your energy and interest into something Dr. Lyle made, you honor his memory and keep his flame alive. I couldn't ask for a greater service to the Forgotten Dead."

I couldn't even fake a smile after that. I followed him out of his office feeling like an absolute villain. Fortunately, Peter was too busy to notice. He was already jogging away down the hall, calling for the service mechanic to get his truck pulled around.

"*Sibyl!*" I hissed when he was gone.

"Why are you mad at me?" my AI cried. "I exist to help you! And it's not as if I put the priest in danger. I just sent him on a wild goose chase. By the time he gets back, you'll have the hand and the corpse will be in the cooker. No one will even know it happened."

That did sound like a pretty clean getaway, but even though everything was now going as well as I could have wished, it felt like the world was collapsing on my head. "I'm going to get cursed forever," I groaned, pulling out my phone to message Nik to meet me at the front. "The Empty Wind's going to damn my soul, and Peter's going to *hate* me."

"Peter will never know," Sibyl said confidently. "And the Empty Wind probably isn't even paying attention. He only cares about the Forgotten Dead. You're alive and remembered. You'll be fine."

As an AI, Sibyl was the least qualified entity to give her opinion on Mortal Spirits, but there was no point in arguing. I was already deep in the hole; might as well get what I'd paid for. So with that, I sucked it up and marched back to the front door to signal Nik.

CHAPTER 6

"Good job," Nik whispered as we walked into the morgue. "I'll admit, I was worried you wouldn't be able to pull it off, but this is fantastic. We don't even have a chaperon."

As Peter had promised, the guard had let us through as soon as I showed him the note. He didn't even ask about Nik, which struck me as sloppy, but I guess you didn't get many complaints when all of the people you'd been hired to guard were dead. Now we were walking together into the enormous, freezing warehouse that held the DFZ's corpses. Just as with the offices, it looked astonishingly normal: a big, open room filled with huge racks of metal shelving stacked all the way to the high-efficiency lamps built into the ceiling. If the plastic-wrapped objects we were walking past had been rectangular, I could almost have imagined we were in a normal warehouse for perishable items, but they weren't. They were body bags, very obviously so, and I was sorely wishing I'd never gotten involved.

"We are *so* cursed."

Nik harrumphed. "You're just being superstitious."

"It's not superstition!" I cried. "The mortal spirits are *real*. You live in a moving city! How can you doubt this?"

"I don't doubt it," he said, checking the numbers on each block as we went past. "I just don't think they care as much as you do. The Empty Wind is responsible for *all* the people who've ever died and been forgotten. What are the odds he's going to notice one cybernetic hand out of billions of souls? And even if he does, why would he care? It's just going to be cremated along with the rest of the body."

"It's the principle of the thing," I said stubbornly. "We're stealing from the dead."

"Stop calling it stealing," Nik chided, stopping in front of a tall stack of bodies beside the wall. "You bought both of his units. Technically, all of his material possessions are yours now, including his fake hand."

I didn't think the death god would see it that way. I had minored in religious folklore for my degree, and I knew from countless stories that trying to slip around divine edicts on technicalities usually got you into *more* trouble, not less. But it was too late now. Nik was already punching the number from the sticky note Peter had given me into the sorter. A few seconds later, a giant mechanical arm slid over along the rail set in the ceiling. When it was directly over our heads, it plucked the slab with the correct number on its bar code off the second-highest shelf and dipped down, pneumatic gears hissing as it lowered the body all the way to us on the ground.

"Right," Nik said quietly, pulling a heavy pair of Cleaning gloves very similar to mine over the thinner leather driving gloves he usually wore. "There's a camera directly behind us. *Don't look!*" he hissed when I started to turn. "Just stand there and block it. I'll get the hand."

I stood where he told me, heart pounding harder than ever. No matter what Nik said, I couldn't shake the feeling that this was wrong, probably because it *was.* I knew that, and here I was doing it anyway because apparently I'd rather anger a death god than miss a payment to my dad. But no matter how firmly I told myself I'd chosen the lesser of two evils, it sure didn't feel that way. Especially not when Nik reached out and unzipped the plastic, filling the morgue with the reek of decay I remembered from this morning.

"Ripe, isn't he?" Nik whispered, wrinkling his nose. "Which hand is it?"

"His left," I whispered back, wrapping my arms around my torso so I wouldn't shake. "Be gentle, please."

"Why?" Nik asked, shoving his gloved hand inside the white plastic sheeting to grab what was left of Dr. Lyle's left wrist. "He's dead. What's he going to do? File a complaint about—"

He cut off with a sound that made me jump. It was halfway between a choke and a gasp, but when I looked to see what was wrong, Nik wasn't moving. He was just standing there like he'd been frozen, his eyes so wide I could see the whites all the way around. I was still trying to figure out what had happened to him when a cold draft blew past me.

I jumped again, eyes going wide. A wind was rising. Since I'd left my protective poncho in the car like an idiot, I could feel it all the way up my bare legs and on the back of my neck. Even in the chill of the morgue, it was piercingly cold—as cold as the grave—and as it blew over me, it spoke.

What belongs to the forgotten remains to the forgotten.

Now it was my turn to choke. The words hadn't come from a voice. They weren't sound in my ears or even a pressure on my skin. It was my magic the voice spoke into, each word sending little puffs of icy breath through the secret space in the back of my mind I'd come to think of as my soul.

Leave, it whispered. *You both are guilty, but you showed remorse, so you shall be let off with a warning. This one, though...* There was a horrible creaking sound, and Nik gasped again. *This one will pay.*

The voice vanished then, leaving me gasping as I whirled to look at Nik. And started to panic. In the brief time I'd been caught by the voice, Nik's face had gone as white as the plastic body bag. He didn't look like he could move, but his eyes were darting frantically down. When I followed them, I saw why. Something invisible was pushing into the skin of his neck. I could only see it from the imprint the pressure made on his flesh, but it looked as though a giant transparent hand was wrapped around his throat. When I reached up to try to pry it off, the cold was so intense it burned my fingers, making me gasp in pain.

Leave the thief to his fate.

"No!" I said, scrambling into my bag for the notes I'd taken from Dr. Lyle's homes. "We're not thieves, and this man is *not* forgotten. His name is Dr. Theodore Lyle, and he died trying to hide his life's work from some very horrible people."

That was all supposition. I had no idea why he'd been hiding down in that hole. For all I knew, he really was a criminal who'd stolen from his boss just as Kauffman had claimed, but that wasn't what I believed. I'd never met Dr. Lyle, but I'd been through two of his homes now, and everything I'd seen told me that this was someone whose interests and values lined up with my own. He was also a collector, someone who appreciated history, and who'd died with work unfinished. I didn't know why he'd wanted cockatrice eggs so badly, if it was just for the money or if there was something else, but he'd cared enough to hide his notes in a hole at the bottom of the Underground rather than let Kauffman have them. I might not have known Theodore Lyle as a person, but I'd seen his work and how far he'd gone to protect it, and that was enough to let me jump to the conclusions I needed.

"We need this hand," I told the cold presence wrapped around Nik like a noose. "It's the only thing that can tell us where Dr. Lyle hid the project he died to protect. If we don't find it, his work will either fall to his enemies or be lost forever." I put my hand on Nik's shoulder, which was now as cold as the wind surrounding us. "Dr. Lyle might have died lost and forgotten, but he's remembered now. We know his work, and his enemies are after us because of that. But if you let us take his hand, we can beat them. We can find the ritual Dr. Lyle died working on and bring it back to the world. We can rekindle his memory, just as Peter said! That's what matters the most, right?"

Historically, lying to gods never went well for mortals. In my desperation, I'd decided to try anyway, but no one's surprise was greater than my own when I discovered that it wasn't necessary. I hadn't put it together until the Empty Wind had forced my hand, but as I spoke the words, I realized they were all true. Maybe not for altruistic reasons, but whether we made a profit or not wasn't really the point. What mattered to the Empty Wind was the fulfillment of the soul. He didn't care about me or Nik. He just wanted justice for the lost life I'd been digging through all day, so that was what I offered him, falling to my knees because that was what you did when you were begging a god.

"Please," I whispered, bowing my head. "I'm sorry we tried to take the hand without permission. I'm sorry I tricked your priest. I should have told him the truth from the start, because we're all on the same side, and that's Dr. Lyle's. That hand belongs to him, and I swear I will not sell it. When this is over, I'll give it back to you. I'll give it a proper burial or burn it or whatever you want, but until then, I need it to save his work. Ask Dr. Lyle if he's there with you. I'm sure he'll say yes. Just please don't kill Nik. I can't do this without him."

There was a long pause, which I hoped meant the god was considering my words. He must have found something in there to believe, because a few heartbeats later, Nik collapsed to the ground beside me, clutching his neck as he gasped for breath. I was slumping in relief when the cold tightened around my own throat.

The living forget, it whispered. *But I do not. I will hold you to your promise, Opal Yong-ae.*

I couldn't speak to answer. Every part of me was frozen as Nik had been, but unlike him, I was a mage. I wasn't strong enough to push the Spirit of the Forgotten Dead away—no mortal was—but I could let him in, dropping all my defenses to let the wind blow through my mind and see that I was sincere. There was no way to hide that I was also doing this for the money, but I hoped the rest would make up for that. The Empty Wind wasn't a god of morality, anyway. I'd never once heard of him judging the living. In all his stories, he only cared about justice for the dead, and there, at least, our objectives aligned.

I just hoped it was enough. But though it took a while for the icy wind to pass completely from my mind, in the end, he let me go, dropping me on the ground the same way he'd dropped Nik. Dr. Lyle's cybernetic hand hit the floor a moment later, the metal fist clanging against the smooth cement like a cymbal.

It is given, the god whispered over the noise. *Take it and go, but do not think I am not watching.*

I was coughing too hard to reply, so I nodded instead, but the supernatural cold had already vanished from my body, leaving only the normal chill of the morgue and the grip of Nik's gloved hands on my shoulders. "Opal?" he whispered, giving me a gentle shake. When I didn't reply, the shaking got less gentle. "*Opal!*"

I put my hand up before he shook my head off, coughing even harder as I struggled to clear my clenched lungs. When I could finally breathe again, I collapsed on my stomach on the cold floor. I was still wiping the stress tears from my eyes when Nik's hands returned.

"We need to go," he said, his voice tight. "I don't know if that thing is keeping the guard busy or what, but I don't want to push our luck. I've got the hand, and I've already put Dr. Lyle back, so let's get out of here."

I assumed "that thing" meant the Empty Wind, but I was pleased to hear him say the good doctor's name in such reverent tones. I was the one who'd done the begging, but it was Dr. Lyle who'd actually saved us. He was the one the Empty Wind cared about. All of that was too complicated to explain while my throat was killing me, though, so I just let Nik pull me out of the morgue and past the security guard, who didn't even look up from his phone.

"I'm chatting with him on a dating app," Sibyl explained when I wondered how that was possible.

The thank you was on the tip of my tongue when I realized she'd responded to a question I hadn't actually asked. "*Stop reading my mind,*" I hissed.

"You can turn it off in my settings," she informed me helpfully, bringing up her menu to show me where the option was. "But it's not recommended. If I can't access your surface thoughts, how can I get you what you need before you need it? The guard is a perfect example. I felt your brain waves go crazy, so I decided to run interference while I waited to see if you'd need medical assistance. Fortunately, you did *not* need assistance, and now, thanks to me, you're not about to be busted by the cops, either. All of this was made possible by my predictive brain wave technology, which, by the way, has been on for the last three years. Are you *sure* you want to turn it off?"

I wasn't prepared to make that decision yet, so I let the matter go. As she said, I'd had it on for years without a problem. It was probably only bothering me now because I kept doing things I didn't like, which said more about me than it did about Sibyl.

"Glad you can see reason," Sibyl said when I closed the options tab. "Just give me a moment to let Mr. Guard down easy and we can get to work on that hand. Speaking of which, I can already tell you the security on most VCI systems is too high for a social AI such as myself to crack. Does Mr. Kos have an expert in mind already, or should I look one up for us?"

Good question.

"I've got a place," Nik said when I asked him. "It'll be expensive, but it'll be done right."

My stomach sank at the word "expensive," but what could I say? I didn't know someone cheap to suggest as an alternative. I just hoped Nik's contact was willing to negotiate a payment plan.

I was still wobbly when we reached the car, so Nik got the door for me, which was unexpectedly thoughtful of him. I was still putting my seat belt on as he dropped into the driver's seat, but he didn't start the car. He just sat there with his hands on the wheel, staring down the orange-lit street with a distant, closed-off look on his face. I was starting to worry he'd gone catatonic again when he said, "Thank you."

"It was nothing," I assured him. "I just wish I'd had the idea to appeal to the Empty Wind from Dr. Lyle's side earlier. If I'd been faster on the ball, I wouldn't have had to lie to Peter." Which I would *absolutely* have to make amends for later. I was already planning where I would take the priest for an apology dinner the moment I had money again when Nik shook his head.

"Not that," he said. "I mean, it was a smart idea. Really smart, but that's not what I…" He trailed off, scrubbing his gloved hands over his face.

"What I'm trying to say is thank you," he finished at last. "You know, for saving my life."

Now I was embarrassed. "It wasn't a big deal," I said, brushing my hair awkwardly behind my ears.

"It was," he insisted, his always-moving gray eyes perfectly still when he turned to look at me. "I'm no mage, but I still heard the Empty Wind's voice speaking in my head. He was going to let you go. You could have run away and saved yourself, but you didn't. You stayed."

"Of course I stayed," I said with a huff. "What was I supposed to do? Let you die?"

The heavy silence that followed told me that was *exactly* what Nik had expected, and that made me furious. "Oh, come on!" I yelled at him. "What kind of monster do you think I am?"

"Not a monster," he said. "Just a person. It's only natural for people to look out for number one."

"Awful people, maybe," I huffed. "But not everyone. You saved my life earlier."

"Only because I wanted a share of your score."

If Nik had jumped in front of a bullet for a share of a wrecked unit before he even knew what was inside, I'd eat my goggles. "Yeah, right," I said, giving him a smirk. "Just admit it. You're a nice guy."

Nik jerked back like I'd stung him. "I am not nice!"

"Whatever you need to tell yourself."

"I'm *not*," he insisted. "I just..."

He trailed off with a frustrated huff, and I grinned in triumph. "Niiiiiiiice."

"Shut up," he growled, starting the car. "And for the record, we're even now. Let's just go get that hand cracked so we can get paid."

"Sounds good to me," I said, bringing up my map. "Where to?"

"Somewhere not on a map."

I gave him a *Really?* look through the glowing interface of my AR, but Nik was already driving down the street, eyes firmly on the road as we left the morgue behind.

***

Remember how I said there were places in the Underground where I didn't go? That's where we went.

It was out in the boonies by Eight Mile Road, only a few blocks away from the DFZ's northern border. Just across the line in Troy, Michigan, apartments were built right up to the border to house the millions of people who wanted to live within the security and laws of the United States while still enjoying the anything-goes freedoms of the DFZ. Naturally, then, the DFZ side of the border had metastasized into a maze of brothels, joy parlors, and drug dens. The whole place was a giant scam designed to separate naive suburbanites from their money. Everything was overpriced and of vastly lower quality compared to what you could get downtown, but behind the hard, candy-colored shell of cynical opportunism that coated the border was a real underworld that sold to the scammers, and that was where Nik took us.

"Are you *sure* we're in the right place?" I asked nervously as Nik turned down an alley behind a VR porn theater. "It seems kind of...dodgy."

"Then we'll fit right in," Nik said. "We're hiring someone to hack into a hand. Even for the DFZ, that's not exactly legitimate business."

Couldn't argue with that logic, but knowing I was part of the problem didn't make me any less jumpy as we turned into a gravel lot surrounded by razor wire. Nik passed a twenty to the old man sitting in a folding chair at the gate, which struck me as a lot. I didn't pay that much for parking on the Skyways, much less way out here. When I mentioned it to Nik, though, he shook his head.

"That's not for parking. It's for protection."

"Protection from what?" I asked, looking around at the lot, which, though surprisingly full, was definitely surrounded by a lot of nothing.

"Bad luck," Nik replied, pulling us into a space between two vans. "This area is owned by a gang. Which one changes depending on how the turf wars are going, but if you mind your own business and pay your fee, nothing will happen. Most of the time."

I cringed. "I'm surprised you're leaving your car here. Isn't it your baby?"

"It's a tool," he said as he cut the engine. "If it's not useful, what's the point? But nothing's going to happen to it. I paid my fee, and everyone here knows my car."

It was on the tip of my tongue to ask why before I came to my senses. Between his strange relationship with Kauffman and how blasé he'd been about getting shot at, it was becoming more and more obvious that Cleaning wasn't Nik's only job. Not that I was complaining—Nik's alternate skill set had been *very* useful so far—but it made me wonder what he'd done to make the exurb gangs respect his car.

Not that there was anyone around to do so at the moment. Other than the guy who'd taken Nik's money, the lot was empty. Of people, at least. There were plenty of surprisingly nice cars, but then, this *was* gangland. Gangers were famous for loving their cars. I'd actually been to one of their auto shows my first year in the city, back when I'd been super into all the "Oh, wow, look at all this stuff that's illegal everywhere else!" DFZ tourist crap. But while the cars were quite nice, they were the only show around. I didn't even see so much as a sketchy club in the surrounding buildings. Just cheap warehouse stores, fast food joints, coffin motels, and the back of the tacky vice strip that faced the border.

"So where are we going?" I asked, gripping the bag that held Dr. Lyle's hand with both of mine as Nik and I walked across the gravel lot. "You said you had an expert."

"I do," Nik said. "And we're here."

Unless Nik's guy was an expert at rigging slot machines, I didn't see what he'd be doing out here. I was opening my mouth to say as much when Nik opened a metal door in the back of the warehouse that formed the rear wall of the gravel lot and started to climb the cement stairwell inside.

I followed hesitantly, grumbling under my breath. I've been to some pretty sketchy places as a Cleaner, but this was pinging my bad-idea-o-meter big time. Bad things happened in small, enclosed stairwells at the edge of town. It didn't help that it smelled horrible, a mix of urine, old metal, and dead animal baking in the summer heat. Nik didn't even seem to notice the reek. He just kept going, taking the stairs two at a time up, up, up until we reached the door to the roof.

The moment he opened it, a blast of smoky, hot air and thumping music filled the stairwell. My first thought was a roof party, but I was thinking way too small, because when I stepped out after him, I found myself standing in the middle of an entire shopping district.

High above the cheap vice at the edge of the DFZ was a second, suspended world of metal walkways and corrugated steel buildings clinging like neon-lit wasp nests from the bottom of the giant commuter highway that connected the Michigan suburbs to the DFZ. But these weren't more tourist traps. Everything up here seemed to be targeted at the DFZ's working criminal community. I'd never seen so many high-end gun vendors and esoteric magical supply stores in one place. Going by the blinking AR signs, they seemed to be selling real quality products for pretty reasonable prices, which explained the crowd. The rooftop we'd come out on was packed with people carrying guns every bit as nice as Nik's, and it was just one island in a vast suspended network running down the underside of the highway for as far as I could see.

"Whoa," I said, stepping away from Nik to peer over the edge of the warehouse at the parking lot we'd just come from. "How did I miss this?" The music alone was loud enough to hear for blocks, let alone fifty feet down.

"It's warded," Nik said casually, pointing at the air, which I could now see was indeed shimmering with the biggest look-away ward I'd ever encountered.

I whistled in appreciation, glancing up the ramps at the packed nightclubs, bars, and noodle shops that were crammed in between the shops. This place beat the pants off my usual shopping destinations, which only made the fact that someone had spent so much magic and effort to hide it all the more surprising.

"I don't get it," I said to Nik as we walked up the nearest ramp. "I could see hiding a place like this somewhere normal, but this is the DFZ. Everything's legal here. Why would you want to keep such an awesome place secret from potential customers?"

"Because not *everything* is legal," he replied, pointing at a pawn shop that was pretty obviously a fence for stolen goods. "But the look-away isn't for the cops. The people up here run very specialized businesses. The last thing they want is a bunch of suburban tourists taking pictures and driving away real customers."

If that was what they wanted, then it seemed to me they shouldn't have set up shop above a tourist trap. That said, a lot of the suspended businesses had connections down to the roofs of the gaudy love palaces and theme-park-style opium dens below, which told me there was a symbiotic relationship going on here. They might not want the tourists, but the shysters who conned them were another breed of client entirely.

"Welcome to the DFZ," I said, shaking my head. "Criminals all the way down."

"It *is* called the 'City of Commerce,'" Sibyl whispered in my ear. "The place where anything is possible."

"And everything is sticky," I said with a grimace, pressing myself against the walkway's metal railing to get away from the drunk who was puking over the other side. "Don't think the ward's going to stop that."

"Um, no," Sibyl said, tilting one of my cameras down toward the ramp's floor, which, now that we were off the warehouse roof, was just an iron grid suspended fifty feet above the street. "Watch your step."

I winced and scooted closer to Nik, following so tightly that it was a challenge not to step on his heels. "Where are we going again?"

"Not much farther," he said, pushing his way through the heavily armed crowd that was waiting to get into a strip club. "Stay close."

If I stayed any closer, he'd be giving me a piggyback ride, but I didn't argue. Thanks to the narrow walkways, the place was dense. If we got separated, my chances of finding Nik again in the packed crowd were not good, especially since I didn't have his phone number. That was an oversight I'd need to fix pronto, but before I could ask, Nik turned sharply, yanking open the door of a large shop so covered in overlapping advertisements, I couldn't actually read any of them.

I scurried after him, eyes wide for my first look at…wherever it was we were. After all that buildup, I was hoping for some kind of smoky VR den like you saw in the movies, but the place actually looked more like a tattoo parlor than anything else. There was a waiting area with red-velvet couches and an attractive pink-haired receptionist fending off customers who ran the gamut from nervous to bored to high out of their minds. Being a hanging box like everything else up here, the walls were corrugated steel and the roof was the cement bottom of the highway, but you couldn't see any of that through the AR-projected posters of insanely attractive men and women flexing various artificial body parts, which was where I got my first clue as to what this place was. It was a mod parlor, a place that sold and installed cyberwear.

Ever since the Second Mana Crash had tripled the relative magic of the world, the enhancements industry had been booming. When forty percent of the human population was born magical, the other sixty was under intense pressure to compensate, and most did so in the form of better-than-human augmentations. Cybernetics could make you see better, run faster, jump higher, and punch harder. They could improve your memory, your balance, your reflexes. They could also leave you crippled and brain dead if done improperly, which was why most countries had laws prohibiting the more dangerous procedures. But this was the DFZ. You could get your phone wired straight into your frontal lobe if you were willing to pay for it. Installers didn't even have to have a medical license. Mod parlors like this were everywhere, offering superhuman improvements at a variety of price points depending on how picky you were about what went into your body.

I wasn't sure how nice this place was. The clientele in the waiting area looked like the usual mix of street thugs and blue-collar workers who liked a little something under the hood. But Nik walked right into the back with nothing more than a wave at the receptionist, so I could only assume they were good enough for what we needed them to do. I just hoped I could afford my half when the bill came.

Clutching my bag with the hand inside, I followed Nik inside, scurrying through the projected waterfall curtain that separated the waiting area from the installation rooms, of which there were a surprising number. The few mod parlors I'd seen had had two or three rooms at most, but this place had over a dozen, including what looked like a full-sized hospital-grade operating theater for putting in the really tricky stuff like artificial spinal columns. Clearly, this place was *way* more serious than your average strip-mall cyberwear vendor. I'd never even heard of some of the augments displayed for sale on the walls. I was still gawking like a tourist when Nik suddenly turned a corner and opened a door into one of the private rooms.

I followed tight on his heels, braced for some kind of crazy street-doc operating chamber, but the room wasn't bloody or scary. It was actually quite nice, a little cubicle the size of a dentist's office decorated with carpets and velvet-shaded floor lamps. There was an operating table, of course, and thick wall hangings to muffle the sound of drills, but otherwise the place looked more like a New Age massage parlor than an underground cyber clinic. If Nik had told me we were here to get our chakras aligned, I probably would have believed him if not for the woman organizing gleaming surgical steel tools on a rolling cart in the far corner.

While the rest of the room hadn't fit my expectations for this place, she surpassed them. With her white lab coat tossed on over black leather pants and high-heeled boots, the woman looked like she'd been sent over from central casting to play a back-alley doctor in a government film about the dangers of illicit cyberwear. Her dark hair was long on one side and shaved close on the other, but aside from the red light gleaming on her ear where an earring would have been, I didn't see any obvious modifications.

And then she turned around.

I must have jumped a foot. From the back, the woman had looked relatively normal, but her front told an entirely different story. She wasn't even wearing a shirt under her lab coat. It was all just silver—beautiful, gleaming silver engraved with leaves and birds. The enhancement ran from the top of her neck into her low-slung pants. Maybe it went back to flesh after that, but for all I knew, she was silver down to her toes. The only part of her that still looked human was her head, but even that was suspect when I looked closer. Her brown skin was too perfect, her dark eyes too sharp, and there was that red light in her ear, blinking like a warning as she flashed us an absolutely straight, absolutely white grin.

"Nikola!" she said in a voice that was as artificially perfect as the rest of her. "What are you doing back so soon? Don't tell me you've already broken the new..." She trailed off when she spotted me, and her eyes lit up with a delight so sharp it was terrifying. "You brought a *girl*!"

"She's not a girl," Nik snapped.

I whirled on him. "Of course I'm a girl! What did you think I was?"

"Not like that," he corrected, his ears turning ever so slightly red. "Not like she means, I meant. That is..." He gave up after that, throwing a hand out toward the machine woman instead. "Opal, this is Rena. Rena, Opal."

"So pleased to meet you, Opal," Rena purred, stalking across the carpet. "Are you getting something done today?"

"No," I said quickly, taking a step back.

That was when I knew that Rena's face was as artificial as the rest of her, because while her eyes were immediately disappointed, it took the rest of her expression a full second to catch up. "That's too bad," she said, looking at me. "It's *so* rare that I get to work on a virgin canvas."

It'd been a long time since I was a virgin anything, but I had the feeling saying as much would make this situation worse, not better, so I kept my mouth shut, digging into my bag instead. "The job's not for me," I said, pulling out Dr. Lyle's hand. "We need the information that's locked inside this."

Never taking her eyes off mine, Rena reached out and took the hand. Her silver fingers were the same temperature as the air when they brushed mine, which was a lot creepier than I expected. Usually, cyberwear keeps itself at normal body temperature so it won't feel false, but Rena's touch felt like an inanimate object. Like she wasn't there at all.

"Do you have the security key?" she asked, petting my fingers one last time with that dead touch before I jerked them away.

"No," Nik said. "No security question answers, either. Just the hand. There's a location hardcoded into its VCI. We need it out."

She wrinkled her nose. "That's a tall order," she said, turning the hand over to look at the connectors on the wrist. "And speaking of orders, the boss wants to see you, Nikki."

"Tell him to wait," Nik said, crossing his arms over his chest. "I'm doing this right now."

Rena snorted. "*You* can tell him to wait. My head might be replaceable, but that doesn't mean I like having it bitten off. It'll take me a few minutes to give you an estimate on the hand, anyway, and he's already seen you on the cameras, so you might as well go up. I'll keep an eye on your little Opal."

The way she said that made my skin crawl, but the boss thing must have been legitimate, because Nik sighed. "Fine," he growled, looking at me. "I'll be right back. Don't leave this room."

He didn't have to tell me that. As creepy as Rena was, I'd watched enough crime dramas to know that anywhere they called their boss "the boss" was not a place you wanted to go exploring by yourself. I'd already glued my back to the parlor's padded wall, pulling in just enough magic to activate my wards before pulling my arms inside my poncho to keep as much of my body inside the protective shield as possible. Sibyl was on high alert as well, running her full suite of security protocols and keeping my cameras moving so that I had a 360-degree view of the room.

Given how much machinery she was packing, I was certain Rena noticed me locking my doors, so to speak, but she was either too polite to comment or couldn't be bothered to care, because she went on as though nothing had changed. She just gave Nik a wink and turned around, carrying Dr. Lyle's hand to the back of the room, where she pushed the padded curtains aside to reveal a wall of equipment.

"So," she said, placing the hand inside a device that looked exactly like—but couldn't possibly be—a microwave. "Where did Nik pick *you* up?"

"I'm the one who picked him up, actually," I said, ignoring the blatant innuendo in her voice. "He wanted in on my job, I needed someone with a car, so we teamed up."

Rena's head snapped around to gape at me over her shoulder. "Wait, Nik let you ride in his car? For real?"

She sounded legitimately shocked, and I shifted uncomfortably. "It's just for tonight. My tires got slashed, so—"

"There is no 'just' when it comes to Nikola Kos," she said firmly. "He never lets anyone into his stuff. Not unless they're paying enough to buy him an upgrade." She pursed her lips. "So what's he charging you?"

"He's not charging me anything," I said. "As I already said, we're working together on a job."

"Must be some job," she said, turning back to punch a few buttons on the couldn't-be-a-microwave. "So you two aren't..."

"No," I said firmly, angry that my face was heating up.

Rena chuckled. "Pity. And here I thought he'd finally gotten himself a girlfriend."

I shook my head so hard it made me dizzy. "He's all yours."

"Oh, I'm not interested in Nikki," Rena said matter-of-factly. "I don't like men, and I don't take lovers who don't have at least as much cyber as I do."

That must have made her choices severely limited. I'd never even heard of someone with as much cyberwear as Rena who wasn't a military cyborg.

"Nik's just a client," she went on. "I do all his cyberwear."

My head shot up in confusion. "Nik has cyberwear?" Because I hadn't seen it. I mean, I knew he was fast, but all the cyberwear I'd encountered had been obvious: huge muscles, leg extenders, metal skin like Rena's, stuff you couldn't hide. But I'd been sitting next to Nik all night, and other than his quickness, which could have just been a combination of training and paranoia, I hadn't noticed a thing.

"Oh, honey," Rena said, giving me a wink. "He's got *features*. Not surprised you haven't seen them, though. Nikki likes to keep his cards hidden, but I'd bet he'd show you if you asked nicely."

"It's not like that."

"It could be if you wanted," she said with a smile. "He's already let you into his car, so he must like you. You should give it a try." Her eyes flicked pointedly to my warded poncho. "Aren't slumming rich girls like you always looking for the bad-boy experience?"

I didn't know what part of that statement to be more insulted by, the implication that the life I'd killed myself to build in this city was *slumming* or that I was only using Nik as a tourist attraction. Not that she could have known any of that, of course. I was just someone Nik had brought in, and I was wearing a magical security garment normally reserved for diplomats and the children of politicians. I should have given her the benefit of the doubt, but it had been a very long, very stressful day, and I wasn't in a mood to be charitable to someone who felt comfortable insulting me to my face.

"I don't know why you think I care," I said in a voice that was a perfect mimicry of my father's. "If you want to antagonize Nik, do it on your own time, but I'm on a deadline. Now how long will it take to get the information out of that hand?"

I braced for Rena to explode after I finished. Most people did when you talked to them as if they were beneath you, which was one of the reasons my father and I didn't get along. But while I would have—and had—blown up over being dressed down like that, Rena started to giggle.

"Oh, you are too precious!" she cried. "Look at you, trying to be scary. Like a hissing kitten!"

I rolled my eyes as she dissolved into laughter. Honestly, though, I wasn't pissed it hadn't worked. Even when I did manage it, I'd never liked being scary. I *was* getting really annoyed, though. So much so that I was considering just walking out when Rena finally got herself together.

"Sorry, sorry," she said, wiping her eyes, which were completely dry. "I'll stop teasing you, and the hand will take at least eight hours."

I blinked. "Seriously?"

"It takes time to crack a safe," she said, tapping on the door of the device where the hand was being scanned. "Cyberwear is made to be secure. Even the cheap stuff is nearly impossible to crack. If it wasn't, no one would use it. And before you ask, no, I can't do it faster. I have to fake a DNA sequence just to get the thing to turn on, and that's not counting dealing with whatever additional security might be inside. If you want your information, you'll just have to be patient."

I cursed under my breath. I didn't know enough about decrypting cyberwear to say if eight hours was reasonable or not, but it was a lot longer than I'd expected. If things had been normal, I would have welcomed the chance to go back to my apartment and crash, but if Kauffman had paid thugs to watch Dr. Lyle's empty house for a month, he'd definitely have someone camping my door. That meant home was out, but I didn't have money to go anywhere else.

"Aww, you look so sad," Rena said, reaching out to snag a lock of my hair before I could jerk away. "Don't worry, kitten. If Nikki isn't taking care of you, you can always stay with me. I don't have any more appointments tonight, and there's nothing I love better than easing newcomers into the joys of cyberwear." She tilted her head, looking my body over like an interior decorator deciding which pieces of furniture had to go first. "We could start with your eyes. I just got a pair in that would look gorgeous on you, and you could get rid of those bulky goggles."

"No, thank you. I like my eyes the way they are."

"Are you sure?" she purred, reaching up to stroke the skin at the top of my cheekbone. "I can give you a fantastic deal."

"Very sure," I said, backing over to the door. "I'm just going to wait outside for Nik."

She looked supremely disappointed, but she didn't try to stop me. I almost wished she had. Eight-hour wait notwithstanding, I *really* didn't want to abandon Dr. Lyle's hand in a strange place, and Nik had told me specifically not to leave the room. But I didn't like the vibe I was getting one bit, and while I was confident in my ability to defend myself with magic if it came to that, frying the person who was getting us our information was not how I wanted this job to end. So instead, I removed myself from the situation, slipping into the dark hallway to wait for Nik.

I didn't have to wait long. I'd only played two rounds of Monster Poker on my phone before I heard Nik coming down the hall. I hadn't even realized I could recognize his footsteps until that moment, but Nik had a very specific way of walking—full speed and straight ahead—that made him easy to pick out. I already had my game shut down and my phone back in my pocket when he came around the corner and froze.

"What are you doing?" he hissed frantically. "I told you to stay in the room!"

"You left me with a creepy lady!" I hissed back. "My choices were magic or hallway. Since she's the one decoding our hand, I chose hallway. You can thank me later."

Nik didn't look surprised. "Sorry about her," he said. "As you can tell from her body, Rena doesn't know when to stop. But she's reliable when it comes to work. Is she decoding the hand?"

"That or microwaving it," I said. "She said it'd take eight hours."

I expected him to balk at that, but Nik actually looked relieved. "It'll be safe with her for a while, then. We've got bigger problems."

I cringed. "Something happened with the boss, didn't it?"

"What?" Nik said, surprised. "No, no, Jonsey's solid. He'd never sell out a client. Bad for business. He just called me back to warn me that Kauffman's put a bounty on our heads."

"Wait, really?"

He nodded, and my eyes went wide.

"For how much?"

Nik cocked an eyebrow at me. "Does it matter?"

Not particularly, but I'd never had a bounty on my head. "I just want to know how much we're worth to him."

"Twenty-five grand each."

"Is that a lot?" Because it sounded like a lot.

"Enough to draw a crowd from the people who saw us come in," Nik said, pulling his gun. "Which is why we're going out the back."

He pushed past me down the hall, which I'd thought was a dead end. But when Nik reached out to touch the black-painted wall, it turned out to actually be a black-painted door leading out onto another suspended walkway. A much, *much* narrower one than the route we'd taken to get here.

"Stay close and keep your head down," Nik whispered, keeping his gun ready as he crept outside. "We follow this until it dead-ends. There's another stair we can use in the—"

He never got to finish. At that moment, the door he'd been easing open was ripped out of his hands. Standing behind Nik, I couldn't see our attacker's face, but I could see the machete in his hand, its gleaming blade already flying low toward Nik's stomach.

CHAPTER 7

After that, a lot of things happened at once.

I screamed. The man with the machete screamed. Someone outside screamed a demand to know what the hell was going on. The only one who didn't make a sound was Nik. He simply lowered his gun and shot his attacker in the foot.

The man dropped his machete with a roar of pain. He was reaching down to pick it back up when Nik kicked the weapon away and slammed the man's hand against the metal grate of the suspended walkway. Then, faster than I could follow with my eyes, Nik whipped a heavy plastic zip-tie out of his pocket and looped it through the bloody metal grating. He wrapped the other end around the man's wrist just as fast and yanked it tight, zip-tying his would-be attacker to the floor.

"There," he said, kicking the trapped, disarmed man to the side so we could get past. "Let's go."

I followed silently, eyes wide. I'd never seen anyone take down a knife-wielding maniac so efficiently. Of course, before tonight, I'd never seen anything like this situation outside of the movies. It was a lot messier in real life. As we stepped over him, I realized I could actually see the blindingly white bones of the guy's foot through the bullet wound. It was so mesmerizingly grotesque that I didn't notice him making a grab for me until his bloody hand snagged the edge of my poncho.

I kicked automatically, slamming my foot into the wound I'd just been staring at. Sadly, I was wearing my sneakers, not my metal-toed cleaning boots, so it wasn't as good as it could have been. Getting kicked on a gunshot clearly still hurt like crazy, though, because the man let me go with a wail, setting me free to run after Nik, who was already several feet ahead of me.

The narrow walkway we were running down must have been the crazy suspended version of a back alley, because all the stores we'd passed on our walk here also had hidden doors that let out on this side. I knew this because several of them were opening as people stuck their heads out to see what the commotion was about. Unfortunately, the doors were all the same width as the suspended railing, which meant each one was a block in our path.

"Move!" Nik yelled at me, slamming his shoulder into the door that had opened in front of him, which sent it slamming back into the face of the man who'd pushed it out. "Get down!"

I was opening my mouth to tell him to pick one when something slammed into my back. It was the same pressure I'd felt back in Dr. Lyle's kitchen, but it was still so new that I didn't recognize the feeling of my wards catching a bullet until the force sent me flying on to my face.

I was back on my feet a heartbeat later, covering my head as I ran to join Nik behind the door he'd ripped open again to use as a shield. "Are you all right?" he yelled at me. When I nodded, his face was relieved. Then it grew grim. "How many more of those can you take?"

"None," I said, pointing at the spellwork on my poncho, which was no longer glowing.

Nik cursed and pulled off his jacket. "Here," he said, dumping it over my head.

The weight almost sent me back to the ground. I'd already seen Nik's black leather bomber jacket bounce a bullet, so I knew it was armored. I just hadn't realized it was *this* armored. The thing felt like a dead body made of lead. It also struck me as something you definitely shouldn't take off in a gunfight.

"Don't you need this?" I asked, pushing the dead weight up just enough to look at Nik, who was now standing beside me wearing only his jeans and a short-sleeved black T-shirt.

"Not as much as you do," Nik said, pulling down his shirt at the neck to show me the metal underneath.

There was a *lot*. Rena hadn't been kidding when she'd said Nik was packing. The entire top of his torso was metal: a scratched-up, flesh-colored steel alloy that covered his chest down to at least the collarbone. I couldn't see if the metal plating extended to his back as well, but from the way he didn't even flinch at the bullets that were ricocheting off the edge of the steel door inches from his ribcage, my guess was that he had pretty full coverage. I just wished I was as protected.

"So what's the plan now?" I asked, clutching his jacket over my head.

"Same as before," Nik said, grabbing another zip-tie from his jeans pocket so he could tie the handle of the metal door to the walkway railing, locking it open and blocking the path behind us. "Get to the end, get down the stairs, get out alive."

"Good plan," I said. "But how—"

I cut off with a hiss. Directly in front of us, at the end of the walkway we were supposed to be fleeing down, a tall man with spellwork tattooed all over his bare arms was coming out of one of the doorways. The markings looked like Socratic Thaumaturgy, which meant I could have read what the spells did given enough time and a few searches, but I didn't think that was necessary. Whatever they did, I didn't want it, so I didn't wait for him to cast. I just grabbed all the magic I could and shoved it at him.

The wave of my magic hit the other mage dead in the face. I'd been in a hurry, so I wasn't sure how much I'd thrown, but what I lack in finesse I make up for in volume. He hadn't even finished lighting up the spellwork on his skin before I knocked him flat. I slammed him again to make sure he stayed down, taking the extra step this time to form the surprisingly dense magic floating through this place into a vaguely hammer-esque shape before I dropped it on his head.

"Good job," Nik said, lowering his gun as the other mage began to spasm on the walkway, bleeding profusely from his nose. "What did you do?"

I shrugged. "Punched him, I guess? It's not really a spell in the technical sense, but mages can only handle so much magic at once. Overload that limit and they drop like flies. Most of the time, anyway."

"Hell of a punch," he said appreciatively. "Does it work on non-mages?"

I'd never tried it on a non-magical person, so I wasn't sure. Before I could explain that, though, something crashed into the steel door we were using as cover, nearly ripping the handle off as the zip-tie strained to keep it attached to the railing.

There was no more talking after that. Nik and I sprinted forward in unison, jumping over the unconscious mage as we raced down the narrow—and now terrifyingly swaying—walkway. I heard a crash behind us as the door went down, and then a bullet whizzed past my ear.

"Idiots!" Nik yelled as I ducked. "The bounty's no good if we're dead!"

That was nice to know. Too bad nobody chasing us seemed to be paying attention to that little detail. But though the door was down and our cover with it, we'd made it to our destination.

The elevated back alley we'd been following dead-ended at a suspended building that was as big as all the others around it combined. Like everything else we'd run past, it had a back exit, but unlike all the other doors that had opened into our faces, this one was locked.

"Stand back," Nik said, pointing his gun at the lock.

I did as he said, covering my ears with my glowing hands as he pulled the trigger. But though the shot left a nice hole in the metal, the door didn't budge when Nik yanked on it.

"It's magnetic," Sibyl informed me in the very calm voice she always used during disasters. "Also, there are people closing in. I can't see how many since you've thrown a coat over my cameras, but the vibrations feel like at least four."

It was five, actually, coming up fast. They must have taken Nik's warning to heart, because they were no longer shooting at us, but they were big, and the first three were bulging with obvious cyberwear. Shoulders that huge simply did not occur in nature. But while there was no way I could have hammered all those guys the way I'd done the mage before they reached us, I didn't have to. We were standing on a rickety metal railing that was barely holding stable as it was, and that was all the edge I needed.

"Hold on to something!" I yelled at Nik, reaching up to grab the large, U-shaped metal walkway anchor where it had been hammered into the highway rumbling over our heads. "Here we go!"

It was more difficult without my hands to guide me, but it's amazing what you're capable of when your life is on the line. I'd barely finished warning Nik before I had the crowbar formed in my mind. I kept shoving magic into it until our pursuers were only a few feet away, cramming the shape so full of power that my nose started to bleed. It was *way* more magic than I had any business handling, but like I said, I've been backlashed a lot. My soul was asbestos when it came to magic, and I just sucked it up, piling on the power until my ears rang and the world spun. Then, right before I passed out, I slammed the spell down, wrenching the crowbar-shaped magic between the metal girders holding up the walkway until the bolts snapped with a sound like gunshots, and the whole thing broke free.

The magic left me like a thunderclap. I almost hurled when it was gone. The rush of its sudden absence felt like it was turning my stomach inside out. My grip was sliding as well, my numb fingers losing their hold on the anchored railing, the only part of the walkway that was still attached to the Skyway. The rest of it was falling toward the pavement fifty feet below, including the chunk under my feet. But just as I started to fall after it, something grabbed me around the waist and clenched down like a metal vise. I was still reeling from the sudden stop when Nik hauled me up.

"*Are you crazy?*" he yelled in my face. He was hanging from the knob of the magnetic door we'd failed to open, pinning me to his body with his right arm, which felt as metal as his chest. I was idly wondering if that was because his arm was fake too or if he was just absurdly hard bodied when he forced my head back up. "Are you all right?"

"I'ms fines," I slurred. "Especially now they're not shooting at us."

I finished with a shaky smile Nik did not return. He just cursed under his breath and started swinging us, using his body weight to rock us back and forth until he got high enough to kick a leg through the metal anchor I'd grabbed and then failed to hold onto. Once his knee was securely locked around the bottom of the U-shaped loop, he lifted me so I could grab on as well. When I had both arms looped around the metal, he let me go and swung himself as deftly as an acrobat, ending up perched with his hands on the anchor in the ceiling and his feet pressed against the metal wall of the building beside the door we'd been trying to open.

"What kind of mage are you?" he grumbled as he walked himself sideways toward the still-closed magnetic door. "I've seen plenty of people throw magic around, but none of them ever made themselves bleed for it."

"The bleeding was not intentional," I said, or thought I said. The ringing in my head was making it hard to keep track of words. "It was…I didn't properly account for…force it would take to break through steel."

That halting explanation definitely wasn't my greatest, but it seemed to satisfy Nik. Sibyl, however, was another matter entirely.

"You didn't 'properly account' for anything!" my AI screamed in my ear. "You didn't even look at the metal! You just grabbed whatever was slightly less than the amount of power needed to *kill yourself* and used that! You are seriously going to turn your brain into mush if you keep pulling stunts like this!"

I was feeling pretty punch drunk, but the fear that should have caused was lost in the euphoric glow of survival. I was beaming like an idiot when Nik finished kicking down the magnetic door. I was so drunk on the backlash, it didn't even occur to me how crazy it was that he'd kicked down a *steel door* until after he'd yanked me through, grabbing my hand and dragging me down a very red, very posh-looking hallway lined with glossy wooden doors and moving pictures of astonishingly beautiful people wearing not a lot of clothing.

"Where are we?" I asked, staring at the doors in confusion. "A hotel?"

"It's a brothel," Nik replied, kicking the closest door shut again the second it started to open. "An expensive one, which is why we're getting out of here fast."

It certainly looked expensive. Between the plush carpeting and the fancy wallpaper, you'd never suspect that this place was dangling from the bottom of the DFZ's busiest highway. The people sticking their heads curiously out of the doors behind us weren't quite to the caliber of human perfection my father had demanded back home, but they were the prettiest I'd seen in the DFZ. Good variety, too. There were men and women and others on the spectrum between. Some of them looked to have impressively inventive cyberwear, which struck me as really going the extra mile. As someone who'd grown up among hundreds of women vying for one man's attention, I knew how much work it took to stand out, and I was professionally impressed. I was also—as I was beginning to realize from Nik's increasingly tight grip on my hand—not nearly as stable on my feet as I'd thought.

"Huh," I said, reaching up to touch the blood that was still dripping from my nose. "Maybe I *did* turn my brain into mush."

"What was that?" Nik demanded.

Before I could even try to explain, a dark shadow stepped in front of us, cutting off the red light from the room at the end of the long hall, which I'd just realized must have been the front parlor. A very *big* shadow that arranged itself into a very big man. He was dressed in a suit and wearing sunglasses indoors at night, the universal signs of an expensive security guard, but what really caught my attention was the glowing spellwork on the shirt he wore under his suit. Spellwork I actually recognized for once because those were the same markings that I had on my poncho.

That sobered me up real quick. I blinked hard, clearing the fog from my head as I realized just how screwed we were. There was a giant man covered in anti-bullet wards standing between us and the doors out of here. We couldn't turn around because I'd blown the bridge behind us, but the way forward was looking more and more like suicide as the security guard raised his hands—his *glowing* hands—and pointed them at us.

In the part of my brain that wasn't panicking, that made a lot of sense. You didn't want to fire guns in a nice place like this. Magic was much less damaging to property, especially if you weren't too picky about what you did to people's insides. I didn't know what kind of mage this guy was, but the magic condensing in his ham-sized fists already felt like it wasn't going to be fun. When I tried to yank in some magic of my own so I could do something about that, though, all I got was a flash of pain.

"I told you!" Sibyl yelled when I gasped. "You can't keep doing this to yourself, Opal!"

There was more to the lecture, but I didn't hear it. I was too busy flipping back and forth between the fear that I'd broken my magic and the realization that we were running head first into our gruesome death, and I couldn't do anything to stop it. But just as I was starting to panic in earnest, Nik lifted his arm and shot something.

It wasn't his gun. I knew the sound of Nik's sleek pistol pretty well by now, and the near-silent *whir* that came this time was nothing like it. It was also too small. The little black object in Nik's gloved fist barely extended past his fingers, but it dropped the big mage like a stone, sending him flailing to the carpet. I was still staring, dumbstruck, when Nik jerked his wrist to reel back in the two metal electrodes he'd shot into the mage's stomach.

"Taser," he said before I could ask. "It's cheap, so they always forget to ward against it. Screws magic up good. Now let's *go.*"

He didn't have to tell me twice this time. We jumped together over the still-twitching mage and sprinted for the doors. Back in the brothel, a beautiful older woman in a very expensive dress was yelling for someone to stop us, but if anyone was listening, we'd already left them behind.

I'd never run so fast in my life. We flew down the suspended walkway, bouncing off the drunks until we reached the ramp that led to the warehouse roof. I was so disoriented by this point I had no idea if this was the same warehouse we'd come up from originally or a different one entirely. The staircase reeked the same either way, but it didn't matter much in the end, because we came out in sight of Nik's car.

And the half dozen tattooed, cybered men surrounding it.

I skidded to a halt, sending Nik's lead-filled jacket sliding over my face as my feet dug into the dusty gravel. I was about to wheel and start running again when Nik grabbed my arm.

"Opal, wait!"

I froze, looking over my shoulder just in time to see him smile. "They're on our side." His smile turned cocky. "I paid protection, remember?"

There was no *way* twenty dollars bought all of that. That wasn't how money worked. I was trying to explain this to Nik when he let me go and walked away, strolling over to his car as if this was totally normal. "Thank you, gentlemen," he said as he unlocked his door. "I appreciate it."

"You pay, you get," the nicest-dressed of the men replied, rolling his wide shoulders. Then he leaned in on Nik. "But don't cause trouble here again. I own the streets and the parking, not the ramps, so it ain't my business who breaks what. But the next time your lady feels like smashing something, take her to the arena."

He turned his glare on me, and I gulped.

"She won't do it again," Nik promised, waving for me to get in the car. As I scurried to my seat, the nicely dressed man put out his hand again, rubbing his fingers together. With a look of physical pain, Nik reached into his wallet and pulled out another bill. A much bigger one.

"Glad we could do business," the man said, pocketing the money with a smile. "Have a good night, man we never saw."

"You too," Nik grumbled, slamming his body into the driver's seat. He revved the engine like he was trying to murder it, and we drove away with the headlights off, sliding into the quiet traffic behind the glittery tourist vice-land like a fish into the river.

"You are very expensive," he said through clenched teeth.

"Look on the bright side," I said, sliding his coat off my shoulders and tossing it into the backseat. "At least this bounty proves the thing we're after is worth a lot."

"It had better be worth a mint," Nik growled, glancing at his mirror. "Madame's going to have my head for kicking in her back door and tasing her mage."

"Desperate times, desperate measures," I said, looking out the window. "You'll just have to find another brothel."

"I don't go to brothels," he snapped. "If you have to spend money on sex, you're doing it wrong. But there's a lot of people who *do* go to Madame's, and they're all going to be pissed at me."

"Sorry to inconvenience you by saving your life," I grumbled. Then I snapped my head around. "Wait, why are you mad at me? You were the one who decided to go through her place!"

"I'm not mad at you," Nik said, tightening his hands on the steering wheel. "I'm just *mad*. This has turned into a fiasco. I got into Cleaning specifically so I could make money without this kind of trouble."

I could only shrug at that. "Gotta eat the risk to collect the reward."

Nik sighed as though I'd spoken a great truth, and then he reached back to grab something from behind my seat. "Here," he said, dropping a first aid kit in my lap. "You're bleeding."

I jumped and reached up to touch my face. He was right. I hadn't noticed in all the life-or-death excitement, but I was still bleeding like crazy from my nose and ears. I'd only gotten a few drips on my shirt, which was a miracle, but I looked like an angry ghost when I checked myself in the visor mirror.

"What did you do to yourself?" he asked as I started mopping my face clean with a square of gauze.

"Went too hard," I said, wincing as I scrubbed my tender ears. "But I don't regret it. If I hadn't dropped that walkway, we'd be heads on a platter for Kauffman right now."

"Kauffman wouldn't kill us," Nik said quickly. "He needs us alive to find out what we know."

"We'd still have lost," I snapped. "Same difference."

"I don't want to lose to Kauffman any more than you do," he said. "But you almost died back there."

I rolled my eyes. "I didn't almost die."

"You looked like you did," Nik said quietly, giving me a look that made me very uncomfortable. "I'm not a mage, but I don't think you should do that again."

"*Yes!*" Sibyl said triumphantly. "Listen to him!"

"Fine, fine," I said, slumping in my seat. "I won't do it again."

At least not that hard. But it was now several hours into Tuesday morning, which meant I was a day closer to my deadline. Even if Rena was absolutely accurate about the hack taking eight hours, I no longer believed finding Dr. Lyle's circle would be easy. If we'd had this much trouble just getting this far, the end was bound to be worse, but I couldn't go back. I needed that money like I needed air, and I'd do anything it took to get it.

"'Anything' is a lot, Opal," Sibyl said nervously. "As your emotional support AI, I feel I should caution you against making these kinds of ultimatums. They're not good for your—"

I poked my finger through her mute button, sliding my goggles down to my neck so I could finish cleaning my face. I was scrubbing off the last of the blood with a sanitizing wipe when Nik cleared his throat.

"So," he said as I repacked his first aid kit. "We've got several hours before the hand is done. I'm going to go home and sleep. Where do you want me to drop you off? Do you have a safe house?"

"Safe house?" I could barely afford my normal house. "Nope, sorry."

"A hotel you trust, then? Anywhere you can lie low for a few hours will work, because you can't go home."

"I know that," I said, frustrated. "I just haven't had time to think of an alternative."

"I know some good places that don't ask questions," he offered.

I was sure he did. I was also sure none of them were in my price range.

Stomach sinking, I clicked the AR icon for my bank account, but no miracles had occurred. I still only had sixteen bucks. That was enough to buy dinner and breakfast if I wasn't picky, but it wouldn't cover even the cheapest coffin motel. I technically owned Dr. Lyle's house right now, but going back there was an even stupider idea than going home. It also had no furniture and no door, not exactly a fun place to spend what was left of the night. I supposed I could have sold some of my stuff from the box in Nik's trunk to cover it, but all the good auction places were closed right now, and I'd rather walk in circles until dawn than sell the last of my treasures to fix what was ultimately a temporary problem. In eight hours, we'd have the information from Dr. Lyle's hand and be on the way to our prize. One third of a day, that was all I had to hold out for.

"Just take me back to the Cleaners' Office."

Nik frowned. "You sure? There's nothing over there."

There was a neighborhood I knew and a bookstore that was open 24 hours and didn't kick you out so long as you bought at least one cup of coffee. "It'll be fine."

Nik sighed and changed lanes. Then, without warning, he changed back, pulling off the road into the parking lot of a fast food joint.

The sudden switch in direction caused me to drop the first aid kit on the floor. "Geeze," I said, leaning down to pick it up. "If you were hungry, you could have just said…"

I trailed off when I saw Nik staring at me, his gray eyes hard. "You don't have anywhere to go, do you?"

I could have lied. Covering up has always been my default reaction, but after everything that had happened tonight, I just didn't have it in me. Even if you didn't count what I'd just done to my magic, I was a mess. I'd been awake for nearly twenty-four hours now. I hadn't eaten, hadn't showered, and my poncho's anti-bullet ward was drained yet again. I was running on empty in every category, and fighting Nik to save my pride suddenly felt like a bridge too far.

"Not really."

His glare turned irritated. "Why didn't you just say so?"

"Because I don't want your pity," I snapped, glaring back at him. "You might be some kind of Underground super-soldier of fortune, but I'm not. I'm just a Cleaner. I don't have safe houses and gang connections, but that doesn't mean I can't take care of myself."

"Normally, sure," he said. "But you have a bounty on your head, and Kauffman's throwing money around looking for you."

"Then I'll go to places where people who take that sort of money don't hang out," I said stubbornly. "The DFZ isn't entirely made up of criminals, and we've only got eight more hours to kill. I'll just kick back in a coffee shop or something. It's not a big deal."

I didn't fully appreciate how sad that sounded until the words were out of my mouth. I really was homeless now, wasn't I? Next thing you knew, I'd be living out of my rental truck. The one I couldn't move because the tires were still slashed and I couldn't afford to buy new ones.

"Opal," Sibyl whispered from my lowered goggles. "I think this has gone too far."

Not now, I thought at her.

"*Yes* now," she said, not even bothering to hide that she was reading my mind anymore. "I've gone along with everything so far because I'm your AI and it's my job to support you. But I'm also programmed to protect your mental well-being, and you're being very self-destructive. You nearly killed yourself tonight. There are dangerous people after you right now, and your plan is to wander the streets because you can't afford fifty dollars for an hourly hotel. Surely you can see why I'm concerned."

I wasn't planning to wander the streets. I was going to sit in a quiet cafe, drink a coffee with free refills, and catch up on episodes of—

"I think it's time to call your father."

"Absolutely not," I said out loud, making Nik jump.

"Absolutely not what?" he asked.

"Stop being stubborn," Sibyl said at the same time. "Maybe you can't see what you're doing to yourself, but worrying about you is why I exist, and this is too much, Opal! You made a good try at it. You lived as a Cleaner for a lot longer than anyone expected, including yourself, but enough is enough. This is your *life* we're talking about! Mr. Kos might be bulletproof, but you're not. It doesn't matter how much money Dr. Lyle's stash is worth if you don't survive to get it!" She heaved a recorded sigh. "It's time to face reality. You're out of money, you have nowhere to go, you're being hunted by a career criminal, and your only ally is a guy who barely let you into his car and bullied you into giving him sixty percent of your prize. This is not winning, Opal! This is *really* bad, but it doesn't have to be this way. You can fix everything right now. All you have to do is let me stop blocking your mom's calls and tell her you need help. She won't even gloat. All she wants is for you to be safe. I bet your dad can have a car out here to pick you up in five—"

I yanked my goggles off my head, breaking the mental connection. I turned my phone off as well, pressing the power button before Sibyl could switch her voice to the speakers. I was not listening to this. I'd let Kauffman string me up by my toes and force-feed me Dr. Lyle's hand before I gave my father one inch of leverage over me. Not a phone call. Not a peep. I didn't care if I was hungry. I didn't care if I was tired. I was going to make that damn payment on time. I'd sell a kidney if that was what it took, but I would *never* bow my head to him again.

Just thinking about it made me shake in rage. I was shoving my goggles and my powered-down phone into my bag to cover it up when I realized Nik was still watching me.

"Are you okay?"

"No," I said angrily. "But I will be. Just drop me off wherever. I'll make it work."

Nik nodded and settled back into his seat, but he didn't get us moving again. He just sat there scowling at his hands on the steering wheel. Then, as though he'd come to a decision, he put the car in reverse and pulled out, turning around in his seat to look out the rear window as he backed us into traffic.

"You can stay with me."

My head whipped around. "What?"

"You can stay with me," he repeated. "My place isn't great, but it's safe, and Kauffman doesn't know where it is. If you don't mind roughing it, it should be fine for eight hours."

Roughing it, nothing. Compared to my plan to squat in some poor cafe owner's least expensive chair, anything with a roof and a door sounded like paradise. But while I was touched that he'd offered, I couldn't. Nik had barely let me into his car. I couldn't invade his home as well just because I was short on cash.

"I can't," I said, shaking my head. "Thanks for the offer, it means a lot, but I don't want your charity."

"It's not charity," he said sharply. "The bounty's for both of us, so it makes more sense to stick together. Also, I can't stand the idea of you wandering around until morning. You look like you're about to fall over."

That sure sounded like charity to me, but my resolve on this matter was quickly fading. I might have been ready to go through hell to make this work, but that didn't mean I was jumping at the opportunity. It galled knowing I was relying on Nik to save me, but Sibyl had been right about one thing. It *was* time to face reality, and as much as I wanted to stand strong and fight, I was at the end of my rope. I'd have a much better chance of pulling this off if I could get a few hours of sleep, and Nik *did* have a good point about sticking together.

It was a thin straw, but I grasped at it anyway, lowering my head like the charity case I was desperately trying not to be. "Thank you."

Nik shrugged and kept his eyes on the road, driving us silently through the pre-morning rush hour as the flickers of sky visible between the cracks in the Skyways began to brighten with the first light of the false dawn.

CHAPTER 8

Nik's apartment was at the southernmost tip of the DFZ. He lived just half a mile from the airport, in a neighborhood that was a Tetris stack of extended-stay hotels, industrial office space, car rental agencies, and self-storage units. He actually parked inside one of the latter, driving his fancy car into a self-storage locker and locking the rolling metal door, which was a pretty cheap alternative to renting a private garage.

His apartment was right next door in the basement of a nondescript building that seemed to be a mix of office space and closet apartments aimed at business travelers. The stairs down to his unit reminded me uncomfortably of the subbasement where I'd found Dr. Lyle's body, but at least there was no unidentifiable sticky stuff or black mold. Quite the opposite; the stairs down to Nik's door looked like they'd just been pressure washed, and the security light was so bright it made my veins glow blue-green under my skin.

Since it was basically underground, there were no windows, just a metal door set into a wall at the bottom that Nik opened with a key code. This was *not* an apartment you could sneak up on, in other words, and while I didn't normally appreciate the military-industrial vibe, that was something I could get behind tonight.

"You can put your stuff wherever," Nik said, turning on the light as we walked in. "Don't mind the mess."

Given that I was an unexpected guest at a bachelor pad, that comment had me braced for horrors, but the room I walked into wasn't messy at all. It couldn't be, because it didn't have anything in it.

The bunker ambiance from outside didn't stop at the front door. Nik's apartment looked like the inside of a gray cement box. There was no carpet and nothing on the walls, just a high-efficiency ceiling light and smooth-poured cement top, sides, and bottom. One wall had a shelf built from cinder blocks and wooden boards stacked with what appeared to be Nik's daily necessities: cleaning supplies, ammunition, weapons maintenance kits, a giant box of zip-ties. There was a single metal folding chair and a plastic card table set up in the opposite corner, but otherwise the room was empty. There was no couch, no television, not even a closet for coats. And to think I'd been embarrassed to show him my place. My picked-over apartment was a decadent palace compared to this bleakness.

"You can use the shower first," Nik said, draping his armored coat over the back of the folding chair and then placing it against the wall so it wouldn't topple backwards from the weight. "I'll get dinner."

"I think it's breakfast now," I said, setting the trash bag I'd stuffed full of my clothes down in one of the empty corners. "And I'll buy the food. It's the least I can do since you're putting me up."

I couldn't afford much, but I'd spotted a Zip Kabab on the drive over. It was the lowest form of fast food, but you got a lot for your money. When I mentioned the idea to Nik, though, he wrinkled his nose in distaste. "Save your money. If we want to eat garbage, we can get it off the street for free. Don't worry about food. I'll cook."

I gaped at him in amazement. "*You* can cook?"

"Only one dish," he said, giving me a rare smile. "But I do it very well."

"Sounds great," I said, and I meant it. It had been ages since someone had cooked for me. "Do you cook a lot?"

"I cook every meal," he said, walking over to turn on the light in the tiny kitchen, which was tucked away in its own little cement hole at the back. "It's cheaper than packaged stuff when you average it out, and it's the only way to know what's actually in your food. Never forget: this is the DFZ. It's not like we have food safety laws or health inspectors."

My eyes shot wide. I'd lived in this city for three and a half years now, and the idea that no one was checking the food had never occurred to me before this moment. My stomach did a double flip remembering all the cheap takeout I'd eaten over the years. It was a miracle I wasn't dead.

"Well then," I said, trying not to look as nauseous as I felt. "Thank you for saving me from salmonella." I moved a little closer, hanging awkwardly by the kitchen door while he pulled a very well-used frying pan out of the cabinet. "Can I help with anything?"

"Not enough room in here for two," he said, which was absolutely true. I hadn't even stepped through the doorway, and I already felt like I was crowding him. "Just go clean up. I've got this."

"Okay," I said, stepping back. Then, because I felt the need to say *something*, I added, "Thank you."

He waved my thanks away and put the pan down on his tiny one-burner portable electric range, whistling as he grabbed a head of something green out of the fridge and started chopping it straight on the counter with a chef's knife that had been sharpened so many times the blade had been worn down to a metal spike. Duly dismissed, I crept back to my trash bag, dug out some clean clothes and the toiletries I was so glad I'd remembered, and made my way to the only door in the tiny apartment I hadn't been through yet.

The door to Nik's bedroom.

My heart started fluttering when I grabbed the doorknob, which was stupid. I wasn't a teenager anymore, but despite going on a lot of dates in college, the number of guys' bedrooms I'd entered could be counted on one half of one hand. I wasn't overly picky or anything like that. It was the guys. For some reason, every man I showed interest in always ghosted on me after the first week. It had gotten so frustrating that I'd eventually given up on dating entirely, which had left me a little rusty at the whole "I'm so cool, I totally don't care that I'm walking into your private space" song and dance.

Not that this situation was anything like that, of course. I was here as a shameless couch crasher, not a date. But now that he'd taken his bulky jacket off, it was impossible to ignore that Nik was, well, a *guy*. A very well-put-together guy, which was only to be expected given that parts of him had been literally put together. But the stupid fluttery parts of me didn't seem to care that the solid shoulders and back muscles I could see through his T-shirt had been shaped with a band saw. They just liked the way he moved, and that made walking through his bedroom to get naked in his shower *super awkward.*

I stood there tapping my fingers nervously on the doorknob for a good thirty seconds before I realized what an idiot I was being. Nik was cooking me dinner because I was broke, and he'd asked me to shower because I probably still smelled like dead guy. There was nothing to be fluttery about in this situation. A shower was the only thrill I was getting tonight, and I was wasting time I could have spent under blessed hot water feeling awkward about things that were entirely in my head.

Thoroughly disgusted with myself, I shoved the door open and marched inside, turning on the light only so I wouldn't trip over any piles of dirty laundry only to find that there was nothing of the sort. Nik's bedroom was as empty as the rest of his apartment. That shouldn't have been a shock at this point, but for some reason the twin mattress on the floor with its single blanket and military-style unfitted sheets hit me a lot harder than the furniture-less living room. It just looked so...lonely. There was nothing personal, no pictures or books or knickknacks. He didn't even have boxes in his closet. Just more jeans and plain black T-shirts on cheap wire hangers.

It was so sterile and practical that I was starting to wonder if he'd taken me to a safe house to keep me from knowing where he actually slept. That would have been suitably Nik-level paranoid, except that I'd seen him pull fresh produce out of the fridge. Perishables didn't seem like something you'd stock in a place you only visited when you needed to hide, but I couldn't imagine Nik lived in this spotless mausoleum of an apartment all the time. There wasn't even soap scum in the shower of his tiny bathroom. You couldn't be a Cleaner without developing a certain level of neat-freakiness, so I hadn't expected it to be *that* bad, but this looked like he'd just moved in.

It was all very strange, but I was in no position to look clean bathrooms in the drain. I stripped off my filthy, bloody clothes and dove in, turning the water as hot as I could stand it. Nik's soap was predictably horrible, one of those super-cheap, abrasive bulk bars that could double as dish soap or laundry detergent in a pinch. But in a rare stroke of good fortune, everything from my bathroom had fit into one plastic bag, which meant I had my own soap, shampoo, and conditioner. I even had my loofah, and I used it to scrub myself raw, scouring my skin until every bit of death and blood had been washed down the drain.

When I was bright red and wrinkly and my hair was so clean it squeaked, I turned off the water and stepped onto the cool linoleum floor, the only floor in the entire apartment that wasn't bare cement. I had to use two towels from the stack in the plastic bin that served as a linen cabinet to get properly dry, but once I was in clean clothes, I felt like a new woman. Even my magic felt better. It barely hurt at all when I pulled a little into my palms to dry my hair so that it wouldn't curl. Satisfied that my life had finally turned at least the first hint of a corner, I put on my socks and padded back out to the living room. Which smelled like *heaven*.

"What did you make?" I asked, hurrying over to the card table, where Nik was placing a plate in front of the apartment's only chair.

"Pork and chicken sausage patties, buttered shredded cabbage, and pan-fried potatoes," he replied.

I nearly bowled him over in my rush to sit down. I'd been getting increasingly hungry over the past several hours, but it had been easy to ignore in the face of all the other impending dooms. Now, though, I was certain I would *die* if I did not eat in the next sixty seconds. But as I sat down and grabbed my fork to dig in, I realized there was only one place set at the table.

"Aren't you going to eat?"

"I ate already," Nik said, walking around the table to lean against the wall where he could look at me. "Not trying to be antisocial, it's just that I only have one plate."

"Oh," I said, pushing aside one of the perfectly fried sausage patties to get a look at the cafeteria-style hard plastic plate beneath it. "You should try a restaurant surplus store. Sometimes they have whole matching sets for less than the price of one normal plate."

"I know, I just never saw the point," he said with a shrug. "I don't exactly have many guests."

Given his single chair, single plate, single bed, and single everything else, it didn't look as if Nik had *ever* had a guest. That made me feel a strange mix of special and sorry, because Nik wasn't a bad guy. He deserved to have more company, especially with food like this.

His earlier bragging was justified. I had no idea what was in the sausage patty other than pork and chicken, but it tasted incredible. Everything did. Maybe it was the starvation, but I'd never enjoyed a plate of food so much in my life. I couldn't even talk while I ate; I was too intent on getting everything into my mouth as fast as possible without choking. Nik waited quietly until I was finished, but though his gray eyes were constantly moving like always, they kept coming back to my face.

"What is it?" I asked when my plate was spotless and every molecule of food was in my stomach. "Never seen someone vacuum up food like that before?"

It was supposed to be a joke, but Nik's expression was serious. "Actually, it's your hair. I've never seen you wear it down before. I didn't realize it was so long."

It *had* been a while since I'd had a haircut. I glanced down at my black hair, which was already curling up against my collarbone despite my best efforts. All the ends were splitting, too. Yet another thing I needed to take care of if I ever got money again.

"It is a bit out of control, isn't it?"

Nik shrugged and dropped his eyes. "I think it looks nice."

"Thanks," I said, shifting awkwardly in my chair as I scrambled for a return compliment that wouldn't be an admission of the fact that I'd been checking him out earlier. "Your food was delicious. Thank you very much."

He shrugged again. "Everything tastes better when you're hungry, and you looked pretty hungry."

Now it was my turn to look away. "Yeah, well, it's been a rough few months. And I never was much of a cook." I certainly hadn't had the chance to learn at home. I didn't even think my mother knew what a stove *was*.

Nik nodded as if that wasn't much of a surprise, and then he looked up again. "Can I ask you a question?"

"Sure," I said, tilting back in the chair. "I'm your guest. The least I can do is be entertaining."

His eyebrows shot up at that, but his voice was as serious as ever when he asked, "What happened to you?"

"Which part?" Because there'd been a lot.

"Any of it," he said, looking me up and down. "You're one of the best Cleaners. I've seen you buy units guys like DeSantos dismissed as junk and turn them into piles of money. Out of all of us solo sellers, I would have bet money that you were making the most, so what happened? How did you get so broke?"

The confusion in his voice made me cringe, because I remembered the Opal he was talking about. There'd been a time when I could turn a profit just by looking at a unit. Now, five months later, I was homeless, starving, and dependent on Nik's charity to keep me off the street. No wonder he was curious. It was quite the precipitous fall. I just wished I had an explanation to give him, but I didn't, because even though I was the one who'd lived through it, I wasn't entirely sure what had happened either.

"I've had some bad luck."

"No one's luck is that bad," Nik said, pushing off the wall so he could face me directly. "What happened, Opal? Where did your money go? Did someone shake you down? Are you in debt to the mob? You don't look like you have a raging drug habit, so what is it?"

Under any other circumstances, that interrogation would have been insulting, but I actually liked Nik's bluntness. It made him sound as if he cared, which was something I didn't get a lot of these days. "Nothing so dramatic," I said with a shrug. "I've just had a long spell where none of the units I bought Cleaned for enough to earn my money back. Spend five months putting out more than you take in and you go broke."

"It can't be that simple," he pressed, leaning closer. "I saw what you did to yourself up on the railings. Why did you push so hard?"

"Hey, you were getting shot at, too," I reminded him. "I didn't see you surrendering."

"Because I'm used to this sort of thing," Nik said, reaching up to tap the metal part of his chest. "I've been risking my life for money for years. I'm made for it. You're not. Like you said in the car, you're a Cleaner. We're all looking for the next big score, but you're acting like you're going to die if you don't make this work. Why? What's got you so desperate?"

That was none of his business, but I didn't get the feeling Nik was pushing to be rude. He looked really concerned, and that was touching enough to convince me to tell him what I hadn't told anyone since I'd come to this city.

"I'm in debt."

"Thought so," Nik said with a sharp nod. "Who is it? Loan sharks? Gangers? Someone who's going to break your kneecaps if you don't pay?"

"It's nothing like that," I said quickly, and then I took a long breath. "It's my dad."

Now he just looked confused. "You owe money to your dad?"

"For college," I said, nodding. "I got a graduate degree in magical art history from the Institute for Magical Arts. It was really expensive."

Nik dragged a hand over his face. "Let me make sure I've got this straight," he said. "You've been risking your life and dodging bullets so you can get money to pay your *dad* back for college?"

"Well, technically, I was Cleaning to get money to pay him back for college," I said. "The bullets are a new development. But yes, that's more or less correct."

"Why?" he demanded. "Why even go into Cleaning if you have a graduate degree? Even when you're not running afoul of guys like Kauffman, it's a dirty, dangerous job. What sort of father lets his daughter put herself at risk just so he can get his money back?"

"He doesn't *let* me," I said angrily. "I chose Cleaning because I was good at it and because it was the only work I could find that paid enough to cover my expenses. Everything was going great until my luck went south. That's why I need this job so badly. I haven't missed a payment yet, but if I can't get ten thousand dollars by midnight on Friday, I'm toast. If we can find Dr. Lyle's cockatrice eggs, though, I'll be saved."

"I get that part," Nik said, his voice frustrated. "But…he's your *dad*. This is a college loan, not a gambling debt to a mob boss who's going to drop you in the river if you don't pay. I'm guessing asking for an extension is out or you would have done that already, but it can't possibly be this bad."

I almost laughed at that. "You don't know my father."

"I don't think I want to," Nik said bitterly. "What kind of man is all right with his daughter risking her life to pay back his money on time?"

In fairness, my dad didn't know about that part. If he had, he would have put an end to it at once, but not for the reasons Nik was implying. He would have made me stop because damage would lessen my value, and if there was anything in his treasury that couldn't take a price hit, it was me. *A pretty gem of very little worth.*

"No offense," Nik said darkly. "But your dad sounds like an ass."

"Oh, he is," I agreed. "But happy as I am to lay all the blame at his feet, the loan was actually my idea. He didn't want me to leave home at all. The only way I could convince him to let me go away to school was if it was something I couldn't get in Korea. That was why I chose IMA. It's the best magical arts school in the world, which was the level it took to make him say yes. He only considers things worthy of his attention if they're world class." And he'd thought I was doing it for him, that I was trying to bring myself up to his level at last. It had been a dirty trick, but it was the only way I could think of to escape.

"When I graduated, he came to collect me," I went on. "But I refused to leave the DFZ. When he tried to force me, I made him a deal. If he let me stay, I'd pay back all the money he'd spent to send me here. If I paid it all off, he'd let me go. If I failed, I'd go home."

"Why would he agree to that?" Nik asked. "From what you've said so far, your dad doesn't sound like someone who takes no for an answer. Why didn't he just make you go home?"

"Because he wanted me to go willingly." I could still see the anger on his face. His fury at my defiance was the most terrifying thing I'd ever faced. Scarier than being shot at. Scarier than even the Empty Wind. The only reason I hadn't crumpled was because I'd known it was my only chance. "He could have dragged me home kicking and screaming, but then he would have had to lock me up to keep me from running away. That would have made him look bad, which is the only thing he's *actually* afraid of. That's why I offered him the loan. He thought he was making a safe bet, that there was no way I could pay back so much money and I'd be forced to retreat with my tail between my legs. He didn't know when we agreed that I'd already discovered Cleaning."

"I get it," Nik said, his face breaking into a grin. "You tricked him."

"Oh yeah, I played him *good*," I said, grinning back. "I let him believe that I had no idea how much money I owed and that I was planning to work some entry-level museum gig. I even had a job lined up so the ruse would look legit. He was furious when he found out I was making real money somewhere else, but by then it was too late. The deal had already been made."

"And you think he'll keep his end?" Nik asked.

I nodded. "My dad's an ass, but he's an ass of his word. He has a very high opinion of his honor, so if you can get him to make one, he *always* keeps his promises. That's why he usually only makes deals that are grossly in his favor, but I *got* him. It took me years to set it up, but I played him for a fool. Now I just have to see it through. I'm almost there, too. You were right earlier, I *was* making bank as a Cleaner. If I hadn't hit this stupid bad-luck streak, my debt would already be paid off. That's why I need to see this job through no matter what. If I can just get that money, I can pay my dad the rest of what I owe, and then I'll be *free.*"

Just saying that word made my whole body tingle. I'd been working on this plan for so long now, I couldn't remember a time when it hadn't been on my mind. That was why I was so desperate. I'd invested so much already, put so much on the line. I couldn't stumble here at the finish line. I *couldn't.*

"At least this explains why you're so gung ho," Nik said, rubbing the back of his neck. "It was bothering me. The world is full of people who'll do really stupid things for money. Most of them live in the DFZ, but you didn't strike me as the 'sell your mother' type."

"Don't give me too much credit," I warned him. "My mother's worth a lot of money."

Nik gave me a scathing look. "Don't even try. If you were only in this for the money, you would have sold all those collectibles we moved out of your apartment. You wouldn't even have brought them home." He held up two fingers. "There are two kinds of Cleaners: those who are in it for the stuff and those who are in it for the money. You're a stuff Cleaner."

"And you're a money Cleaner," I said, looking pointedly around at his empty apartment.

"Absolutely," he said. "That's important. If you don't know what people want, you can't trust them. That's why I asked what had happened to you. I wasn't trying to be nosy. I just had to be sure I knew what was driving you, because as soon as Rena cracks that hand, we're going right back into the fray, and I don't want to be caught by any more surprises like the one on the walkway."

In fairness, that had surprised me as well. It wasn't like I'd planted my feet and chosen that ramp to die on. I'd just done what I'd needed to do to win at the time, and things had gotten out of hand. So, pretty much the story of my life, in other words.

"What about you?" I asked, tilting my head back so I could see his face better. "That's my story, but why are you fighting so hard for this? I mean, it can't just be for the money."

"Why not?" Nik asked sharply. "Money's the reason people do most things."

"Yeah, but not take a bullet."

"Depends on the bullet."

"Come on," I said. "Me being crazy is one thing. I've got my freedom riding on this. But you can't spend your money if you're dead."

He flashed me a cocky look. "It takes a lot more than a few thugs to kill me. Tonight was hairy, sure, but I've gotten through way worse for a lot less. This is my first chance at a big payout in a long time. Of course I'm going to chase it hard."

That made a Nik-ish amount of sense. "Good to know you're all in on this."

"If you're not going all in, why go at all?" he said, leaning forward. "The important thing, though, is that we're *both* in. That makes us business partners, at least until this job is done, so from here forward, *please* tell me what you're going to do before you do it. I really hate surprises."

"I'll try," I said. "But I'm a 'make it up as I go' kind of mage, so no promises. If I'm going to be telling you my plans, though, the same has to go for you. No more taking me to weird places without explaining why we're there or what parts of the infrastructure I'm not supposed to blow up."

"I didn't think that was going to be an issue," Nik said grudgingly. "But fair enough. We share information and work together until we both get rich. Deal?"

"Deal," I said, putting out my hand.

Nik took it with his left hand, squeezing my palm tight with fingers that felt like real, warm flesh through his thin glove. I was wondering if that meant they were actually real or if I was just experiencing some really good cybernetics when Nik let me go. "That's better," he said, letting out what sounded like a relieved breath. "Now that we're both on the same page, let's get some sleep."

Sweeter words had never touched my ears. "Do you have a blanket or something I could borrow?" I asked hopefully. "It's nice to be somewhere with working AC, but your floor looks hard."

"You don't have to sleep on the floor," Nik said. "I have a cot."

It was a sign of just how low my life had sunk that that statement made me genuinely excited. I jumped out of the chair and took my plate to the sink to wash it off while Nik pulled a folded camp cot I hadn't noticed before out of the back of his closet. I would have done the rest of the dishes, too, but Nik had already taken care of those while I was in the shower. I took the time to brush my teeth instead while Nik went out to his car. When he came back, he was carrying a black sleeping bag stuffed into a sack the size of a bowling ball.

"You never know when you're going to need to sleep out," he said in response to my funny look, shaking the silky bag out of its sack and spreading it over the cot. "Are you good?"

"I'm great," I said without a trace of irony, grinning down at the cot and sleeping bag like they were a king bed at the Ritz. "Thank you so much again for putting me up."

He shrugged. "We're business partners now. I need you alert and not exhausted."

"It's still very kind of you."

Nik looked a lot less comfortable with that comment than he had with the helping-a-business-partner angle. "It's nothing," he muttered, keeping his eyes down as he picked up his gun off the table and strode a little too quickly into his bedroom. "Knock if you need anything."

I knew better than to knock on the door of a man who took a gun to bed, but I told him I would and lay down on the cot, which creaked like an old rocking chair. I barely heard it. Now that I was fed and washed, I was so tired I could have passed out on the floor. I didn't even bother getting inside the sleeping bag. The moment I stopped being vertical, I was out, falling asleep on top of the silky fabric before Nik could finish closing his door.

CHAPTER 9

I woke to the sound of someone knocking.

I sat bolt upright, cursing under my breath as my back twinged painfully, reminding me that cots, though better than cement floors, were still not beds. I was trying to get my spine working again when Nik burst out of his bedroom with his gun.

He must have been in the middle of a shower, because his dark hair was dripping wet. He'd managed to throw some jeans on, but his feet were bare. He also wasn't wearing a shirt.

That made me gasp, but not for salacious reasons. I was staring because, now that his shirt wasn't in the way, I was finally able to see just how *much* cyberwear Nik was packing. He'd shown me his metal shoulders on the walkway, but I saw now that his entire right arm was fake as well. It was covered in synthetic skin, so it wasn't obvious like his metal chest, but there was no hiding the articulated joints on his right hand, which explained why he always wore gloves.

His left arm looked real, at least below the shoulder, but he had flesh-colored metal plates protecting his ribs on both sides that went all the way down into his jeans, making me wonder just how much of himself he'd replaced. His bare feet were legit, though, leaving a trail of wet footprints on the floor as he ran silently to press his back against the wall beside the front door—the source of the knocking.

It sounded again as he got into position, snapping me out of my gawking. Heart pounding, I grabbed Nik's armored jacket off the back of the chair where he'd left it last night and tossed it at him. He caught it with his left hand, eyes flicking pointedly to my poncho, which was still on the floor where I'd dropped it.

I shook my head. Idiot that I was, I hadn't recharged my wards last night. I'd been too focused on food and sleep and showers and other things that felt petty and frivolous right now. As a result, what should have been my most expensive and reliable magical safety device was just a giant tarp, so I left it lying on the floor and pulled magic into my hands instead.

The first flux didn't hurt too bad, but the flow started to burn like hell once I reached serious levels. Clearly, whatever I'd done to myself yesterday was still hanging around. I could still move the magic, but it felt like trying to run on a pulled knee. It was all I had, though, so I gritted my teeth and pushed through. It might have been nothing—a door-to-door salesman, a Jehovah's Witness, a lost delivery person—but given that one knock had been enough to bring Nik running out of the shower with gun in hand, I didn't think he got many idle visitors down here. With my luck it was probably a mercenary team come to drag us back to Kauffman, so I braced for the worst, pulling as much magic as I could stand into my glowing fists before I nodded at Nik.

With a sharp nod back, Nik zipped his armored jacket over his wet torso and placed his free hand on the doorknob. Then, moving so fast my eyes could barely follow, he yanked the door open and shoved his arm out, pointing his gun into the face of the person on the other side.

By this point, I'd smashed the magic I'd pulled into my hands into a ball for throwing. I was hauling back to lob it at our attacker when I forced myself to stop short. The person standing in the doorway wasn't a mercenary or even a thug like the ones who'd shot at us yesterday. It was a lovely Korean woman only a few years older than myself. *Stunningly* lovely, with a face so perfectly symmetrical it scarcely looked real. Nik's gun actually bobbed for a split second when he saw her. To his credit, he recovered almost immediately, but not before the young woman spotted me standing behind him.

Her dark eyes lit up with a cruel delight that made my stomach curdle, and then she bowed respectfully, folding her hands over the skirt of her demure but *extremely* expensive blue silk skirt. "Lady Opal," she said, her lovely voice speaking the words in English with only the slightest trace of an accent. "Your father requests the pleasure of your company."

Gun still up, Nik turned slightly and flicked his gray eyes back to me. *Father?* he mouthed.

I was too panicked to be subtle. "Shut the door!" I yelled. "Shut it *now!* Before—"

Nik was moving to do as I asked when a pale hand reached out from the stairwell to grab the door. The long, elegant fingers didn't push, didn't strain at all, but they stopped Nik cold, leaving him shoving futilely against the metal door. When he realized it wasn't going anywhere, he backed up to stand guard beside me as the beautiful woman shuffled to the rear of the stairwell, making room so that the man who'd caught the door could step forward.

The moment he appeared in the doorway, I heard all the breath leave Nik's body. In hindsight, I should have expected something like that. I'd grown up with my father, so I was used to his presence, but this was the first time Nik had seen him. The resulting shock hit him full force, sending him gasping to his knees.

I thought no less of him for it. Mortal terror is a unique experience. It's not like being spooked by something in the dark or even having someone shoot at you. This was a primal malfunction, the same deeply wired fatal flaw in judgment that makes a mouse seize up when it hears the hawk instead of running. Every human had it, but just like any sensation, it lost its edge the more you were exposed. Before I had come to the DFZ, I'd felt it almost every day of my life, which was how I was able to stay on my feet, looking my father in the face as he stepped into the room.

That turned out to be a mistake. This was the longest I'd ever been apart from him. The distance hadn't lessened my resistance to his terror, but his beauty was another matter entirely. There was no earthly parallel to how my father looked. On the surface, he resembled a tall Korean man wearing an immaculately fitted business suit that cost more than most cars. He didn't look young, but he wasn't old either. He was timeless: a cold, perfect marble statue that the centuries couldn't touch. His face was such that men and women had written poetry about it, comparing his pale skin to the moon and his long black hair to a waterfall of night. All of that was accurate enough, I supposed, but the bit I always got stuck on was his eyes. They were the same color as the Hwanghae Sea, a mix of deep blue and yellow-green so beautiful, you couldn't help but love it even as it drowned you.

There was nothing human in those eyes. The rest of him might fool idiots who didn't want to see past what was in front of their face, but even if you were foolish enough to ignore the scent of the fire that clung to his clothes, no one could look my father in the eyes and not know what he was. Nik did. I could see it on his face, read it in the shape of his lips as he mouthed the obvious at me with increasing panic.

Dragon, he said silently. *Dragon!*

I nodded and gave him a stern look that I hoped he'd interpret as *stay down.* My father hadn't said anything yet, but he didn't have to. I could feel his silent demand that I bow, cry, beg his forgiveness, all the usual things humans did in his presence.

"How did you find me?" I said instead.

The girl he'd brought with him—probably so she could get shot instead and thus avoid putting a bullet hole in his expensive suit—gasped at my disobedience. Proof that she was new.

"How dare you?" she cried. "You speak to the sublime Yong! The dragon of all Korea, master of a thousand—"

My father twitched his fingers, and the girl snapped her mouth shut, dropping her eyes at once.

I rolled mine. "How did you find me?" I demanded again.

My father blew out a long line of smoke. "What does it matter?"

His voice was the essence of apex predator, deep and menacing enough that even Nik trembled. I shook too, but for a different reason. I could hear the anger hidden beneath the deadly, iron calm. A smarter mortal would have heeded that, but I've never been smart when it came to my family, and I barged right ahead.

"It matters because you don't belong here!" I yelled at him. "My own apartment I could understand. I've lived there for over a year, I'm sure I made mistakes. But this place was hidden, and you just barged right in! I want to know how."

Because it was certain to be my fault. I was the only reason the great and snooty Yong would deign to set foot in a place like this. He didn't enter the DFZ unless forced to, and even then he stuck to the luxury hotels near Dragon Consulate. If he'd come all the way down to Nik's doorstep at the bottom corner of the Underground, it was because I'd screwed up, and dammit, I was going to know how.

"Actually," said a sheepish, computerized voice from behind me. "It's my fault."

I whirled around, grabbing my bag off the floor. Sure enough, the phone I'd switched off last night was back on and blinking, its screen displaying a detailed map with our location clearly marked.

"Sibyl," I whispered, my voice cracking. "How? You're *my* AI. I bought you! *How did this happen?*"

"Sorry, Opal," she said. "I didn't have a choice. I got hacked last December during that big security update fiasco. The guy who got in set your dad as the parental control, giving him admin power over all your accounts. He's been forcing me to hand over your info for months."

By the time she finished, my hands were shaking so badly I dropped my phone on the cement floor. "You hacked my AI?"

"Of course I hacked your AI," my father said, his sea-green eyes narrowing. "I promised I'd let you attempt to pay the loan back. I didn't say I'd let you scamper about without supervision."

"I don't need supervision!" I shouted at him. "I'm an adult! You don't get to run my life!"

"Someone needs to," he said, eyes flicking to Nik. "Look at the mess you've made of it."

He waved his hand, and my bank balance appeared on the cracked screen of my phone. It happened so fast, I could have easily believed it was magic, but the answer was far more mundane. The bastard had an AI of his own, and it was running my Sibyl like a puppet.

"You're out of money," Yong said scornfully. "You've got a bounty on your head that's drawing every lowlife in this disaster of a city to you like flies to honey. You almost died yesterday because of it, and now you're squatting in the home of a man who answers his door with a gun. It's obvious that your life here is a failure. You've made it abundantly clear that you don't care how your actions reflect on my name, but even selfish creatures care for their own futures. Have a care for yours. It's time to stop being stubborn and come home."

I clenched my fists. "No."

His jaw tightened. "Opal—"

"*No!*" I yelled at him. "So long as I pay my debt, you leave me alone. That was our deal! You gave me your word."

"And I keep my word," he snarled. "It's not my fault if you don't pay attention to yours."

For a terrifying moment, I had no idea what he was talking about, which was catastrophically bad. If you let a dragon get you in a trap, you were lost. I was still scrambling to figure out how screwed I was when Sibyl cleared her nonexistent throat.

"I, um, might have entered the wrong payment date for the debt on your calendar."

I snatched my broken phone off the ground. "*What?*"

"I'm sorry!" she cried. "He ordered me to do it! I didn't want to lie!"

I was so furious I couldn't see straight, but there was no time for that. "When's the real deadline?" I demanded.

"Today," Sibyl whispered.

I closed my eyes with a hiss as I realized just how hard I'd been set up. How *long* I'd been played. "Is this why you tried to get me to call my dad last night?"

"No, that was legitimate concern for your welfare," Sibyl said earnestly. "You were seriously considering wandering around homeless while there were thugs trying to kidnap you. Of *course* I told you to stop! And if you weren't so crazy about this debt thing, you'd see I was right! I refuse to apologize for trying to help you."

That was almost enough to make me feel bad. Almost. "But you still wanted me to go home to my dad even after he had you hacked so he could keep secret tabs on my life? You thought *that* was a better alternative?!"

"Well, yeah," Sibyl said. "It's not the healthiest relationship, but he only had me hacked because he wanted to protect you."

Bullshit. He wanted to control me. I could see it in his smug smile. He already thought he'd won. That was all *he'd* ever cared about: winning, dominating, crushing anyone who opposed him. I couldn't even blame him for it. It was draconic nature to demand obedience, but that didn't mean I had to give it.

"You played your hand too early," I said, shoving my broken phone into my pocket as I turned on my father. "If you'd waited until tomorrow, you'd have had me hook, line, and sinker, but now I know my debt isn't due until midnight. That means I still have time."

"Given your current trajectory, if I'd waited until tomorrow, you'd be dead," my father said flatly. "You're no use to me picked apart by Underground dwellers. This isn't some childish treasure hunt. Even if you do find whatever it is your dead mage made, you still have to turn it into a form of currency I'll accept. You know how long it takes to auction anything really valuable. If this ritual is worth as much as you seem to think, it could take weeks to find a buyer. Even if you slashed the price to the bone to find a buyer tonight, it still takes twenty-four hours to transfer that much money. You could sell it right now, and you'd still be too late." He smiled at me and switched to Korean. "Face it, little dog-girl, you've lost. There's no shame in being defeated by a greater opponent, but it's time to stop running and come back to your kennel."

If I'd been mad before, I was seeing red now. The old bastard even had the audacity to pat his leg, *literally* calling me like a dog, and I clenched my fists so hard I drew blood.

"Get out."

He heaved a long-suffering sigh. "Opal—"

"Get. Out." I said again, forcing the words through my bared teeth. "You gave your word. I'm not beaten until tonight. Honor that, or the whole world will know the Sublime Yong is an oath breaker."

"No one would listen," he said, but I knew I'd gotten him. There was nothing my father cared about more than his pride. Attacking it now was a low blow, but he was the one who'd brought me this far down. He could live with it.

"Everyone," I said, repeating the word in every language I knew. "You do anything before midnight, and I swear, I will spend the rest of my life making sure *everyone* knows that the Dragon of Korea is a liar and a cheat."

His chest expanded, and I knew I'd gone too far. I could already smell his fire building, the carbon reek of his magic filling the air. I stared back defiantly, daring him to burn me. The pain would almost be a relief after everything else he'd done. In the end, though, my father was an old dragon. An old, *honorable* dragon, famous the world over for his self-control. He got himself back together in the space of a single breath, but his eyes were still terrifying when he looked down on me again.

"Have it your way," he said idly. "Enjoy your day of running wild. It will be the last you ever get."

"We'll see," I growled back, lifting my chin high. "Now get out of Nik's apartment."

He would have left faster if I hadn't challenged him. He'd clearly been ready to storm out on his own, but I wanted to make him leave on my terms. It was the same stupid power game I was always accusing him of playing, but power was the only language dragons understood, so I spoke it loud and clear, planting my feet as if Nik's cement floor was the hill I'd chosen to die on. For a moment, I thought the Great Yong was actually going to take my challenge, but it must have been too far beneath his vaunted dignity, because in the end, he stepped back into the stairwell, leaving his accessory mortal to close the door behind them.

The moment the lock clicked shut, Nik collapsed on the ground. "Christ, Opal," he gasped, sucking in air like he'd been waiting all this time to breathe. "You didn't tell me your dad was a dragon!"

"I told you he was an ass," I said. "Same thing."

"*Not* the same," he insisted, turning to stare up at me. "Are *you* a dragon?"

I rolled my eyes. "Of course not. I'm human. I've done human magic in front of you."

"How do I know it's human?" he said, suddenly suspicious. "I've never seen dragon magic."

"Trust me, you'd know," I replied, reaching down to help him up. "Dragon magic involves a *lot* more fire."

"If you aren't a dragon, how is your dad one?" Nik demanded, taking my hand. Then his eyes went wide. "Are you a half dragon?"

"Humans and dragons can't interbreed," I informed him, determined to nip this in the bud before he got any other wild ideas. "The Dragon of Korea isn't my actual father. We all just pretend that he is. It's part of his fantasy of playing head to a respectable family." A fantasy I still—*still*—couldn't seem to shake myself free of, even in my own mind.

"I'm one of his mortals," I continued. "Every big dragon has some, but Yong is a collector. He was up to almost two hundred when I left home."

"Two *hundred*?" Nik repeated, shocked. "You mean there are two hundred people willing to be owned by a dragon?"

"There's a lot more than that," I said. "Those two hundred are the choicest specimens selected from thousands of applicants from all over the world. And you're not safe once you get in, either. My father is constantly switching humans out as they get too old or lose his favor. You can imagine the competition that creates. They're crawling over each other for his attention, backstabbing and fawning at his feet in their desperate attempts to curry his favor. It's disgusting."

Absolutely disgusting. Something I knew for a fact because, before I'd gotten old enough to know better, I'd been the same.

"He must really like you, though," Nik said. "He wouldn't have gone through all this trouble if he didn't."

I shook my head. "He likes my mother. She's the queen of his menagerie. She's been First Mortal for thirty years now, and she's still going strong. Her only flaw is that she's not a mage. Yong couldn't stand the lack, so he made a breeding agreement with one of the European dragons to fix the problem."

"Wait wait wait," Nik said, putting up his hands. "A *breeding* agreement? He *bred* your mother with another human?"

"Not actual sex," I said quickly. "My mother belongs to Yong, and the first thing to know about dragons is they don't share. It was all done by mail, the way you breed expensive cattle. He got samples from the best specimens he could find and then hired a lab to blend all the genetics into the best possible combination. The goal was to recreate my mother, except even better and with magic, but the reality was me." I chuckled. "Huge disappointment, as you can see."

Nik looked legitimately confused. "How are you a disappointment? You're a hell of a mage."

"I'm a *terrible* mage," I corrected. "As for the rest, well, you've seen the caliber of human beauty my father runs around with." I pointed at my face. "Even the best genetics don't actually guarantee results. Mom was praying for puberty to work a miracle, but it never panned out. There's a reason Dad's nickname for me is 'dog girl.'"

"You're not a dog-girl!" Nik said fiercely. "You're—" He stopped suddenly, gritting his teeth. "You're *not* ugly," he said at last.

I shrugged. "Maybe not by human standards, but that's not what I'm judged by. That's okay, though. I don't have to live up to the Great Yong's expectations anymore, because I'm done being his pet."

It was what I'd always been to him: a puppy, a toy, something he paid attention to when it gave *him* joy. We were all his playthings, but unlike everyone else in Yong's household, I wasn't okay with that. I refused to worship the ground he walked on, which was why Yong refused to let me go. It didn't matter that I was a dog-faced girl who couldn't dance or sing or master the magic he'd paid so much for me to be born with. I was the one human who didn't act as if he was my moon, sun, and stars, and that stung his pride. He wouldn't stop until he'd put me back in my place, which was why I had to win no matter what. I'd risked everything to get into this game. If I couldn't play as dirty as he did, I'd *never* be free.

"We need to get moving," I said grimly, checking the time on my cracked phone. It was ten minutes past nine a.m., just over the eight hours Rena had said she'd need to crack the security on Dr. Lyle's hand, and fifteen hours away from my father's midnight deadline.

"It *is* midnight DFZ time, right?" I asked Sibyl, digging into my bag for my goggles, which had also turned themselves back on just like my phone. "You're not screwing me over again, are you?"

"I didn't mean to screw you over at all," my AI said, her voice hurt. "I can't help it if I'm hacked! And it wasn't as though I did anything *really* bad. I put the wrong dates in your calendar, sure, but your father was only trying to get you to come back before you did something you'd really regret. He just wants what's best for you, you know."

I made a disgusted sound, and Nik shook his head. "I *told* you AIs were a liability. She's totally compromised. You'll have to do a factory reset."

"That'll take all day," I said. "And it'll completely wipe her personality."

"Better than carrying a mole around with you."

I looked down at the goggles in my hands. I knew Nik was right, but I'd had Sibyl for three years now. Even compromised, she was the closest thing I had to a best friend. I was fully aware of how pathetic that sounded, but it didn't change the way I felt. No matter how cold and practical I tried to be, resetting Sibyl felt like killing a sister, and I just couldn't bring myself to do it.

"Thank you, Opal," Sibyl whispered. "You're a good person."

"Yeah, yeah," I muttered. "But you are going into the shop for a full security reset the moment I get some spare cash."

"I can't believe you're still going to trust that thing," Nik said as I slid the goggles onto my head.

"I *don't* trust her," I said, smiling in relief when my AR heads-up display appeared in front of my eyes again. "But I need her. She's still my second brain, and it's not like she can make things any worse. I've already been hung out to dry. What else is my dad going to do? Follow me around all day and trip me?"

From the sour look on his face, it was clear Nik thought that was *exactly* what was going to happen and I was being an idiot for enabling it, which, to be fair, I was. To my relief, though, he didn't keep arguing. He just shoved his dripping hair out of his face and turned around. "Your funeral," he said, walking back to his room. "You do what you want. I'm going to go finish my shower. Since you've got a hard deadline now, I'm guessing you want to leave as soon as possible?"

"Yes, please," I said, digging my poncho's collapsible charging circle out of the trash bag I'd shoved all my stuff into.

He nodded. "I'll message Rena then. She should be done with the hand soon if she's not already. It's still too hot for us to pick up at her place, so I'll get us a midway location. Anywhere you prefer?"

I thought about that for a moment. "Somewhere I can get breakfast." Because if this was ending tonight, there was no point in hoarding my money anymore, and if I was going to make a last stand, I wanted to do it on a full stomach.

Nik nodded. "I'll see what I can do."

I smiled my thanks at him as he shut the door.

"Aww, he's a nice guy after all," Sibyl said in my ear.

"Shut it," I growled at her, spreading my poncho's charging circle out on the bare cement floor. "Just because I decided not to erase you doesn't mean you're out of the dog house."

"I really am sorry," she said contritely. "What can I do to make it up to you?"

"You could tell me which of my files my dad has rummaged through."

"Ooo, sorry," she said. "The admin permissions he enabled explicitly forbid me from giving you that information. But he did leave his current number in case you want to surrender early."

"Good to know," I said flatly as I dropped my poncho into the circle and started shoving magic at it. When the spellwork was glowing at what I judged to be the correct level of brightness, I left it to cook and moved on to the rest.

Determined to be a polite charity case, I packed up Nik's cot and tidied everything in the living room. When no sign of my presence remained, I dug a fresh set of clothes out of the bag, changing out of the soft shorts and T-shirt I'd slept in for my thickest pair of Cleaner jeans and a heavy cotton button-up. I'd nabbed my tall boots out of Nik's car last night, so I washed them off in the kitchen sink and put them on as well, pulling the protective rubber up to my knees and shoving the legs of my jeans into the tops so that I was completely covered.

I was sweating by the time I finished. From the weather app on my heads-up display, I knew it would be even worse once we stepped outside, but I didn't change into something cooler. I'd learned the hard way to never leave bare skin exposed when I was dealing with strange magic, and given how much spellwork I'd seen in Dr. Lyle's places so far, strange magic was a given. I just hoped it was the sort that could be turned around for a very quick profit.

I hated to admit it, but my dad had had a good point about the trouble of finding a buyer. He would know, too, because humans weren't the only thing he collected. He had a whole lair full of priceless treasures that he was constantly adding to. Years ago, before I'd woken up to the fact that I was being used, he used to take me with him to auctions to train my eye. His logic was that if I couldn't be beautiful, I could at least be useful, which was how I'd gotten him to let me go to school for art history. I'd fed his arrogance and greed, letting him think he'd be getting a world-class expert to curate his hoard if he'd just take the risk of letting me go overseas. The fact that I was legitimately interested in ancient magical art just gave the story more validity.

It had been *such* a good plan, but it wasn't over yet. The DFZ was very different from the international auctions my father traded in. If something had value, you could always find someone to buy it here. Maybe not at the price you wanted, but that was the cost of being in a hurry. First, though, I needed something to sell. I was about to knock on Nik's door when it opened on its own, and Nik burst into the living room.

Like me, he was dressed for trouble in heavy black jeans and black combat boots. His armored jacket was zipped up to his neck, and he was wearing his gun on his hip rather than hidden under his jacket. He had a messenger bag over his shoulder as well this time, and he walked straight past me to the wood-and-cinder block shelf to start filling it with all manner of things: nylon rope, zip-ties, boxes of ammo, blocks of something gray and clay-like that I *really* hoped wasn't C4. Not that I'd say anything if it was. This job had jumped the shark on danger ages ago. If he wanted to bring explosives, the only thing I wanted to know was when to duck and cover.

"That should do it," he said when his bag was full. "Ready?"

My poncho wasn't quite done, but I was tired of waiting. "Ready," I said, hauling the protective spellworked plastic over my head. "Where are we going?"

"I'm not saying in the presence of your spybot," he replied, opening the door.

"Aww," Sibyl whined.

"Fair enough," I said over her, shoving my charging circle into my trash bag before throwing it over my shoulder and following him out into the stairwell. "So long as Rena has our stuff and there are pancakes, I don't care if we're going to Canada."

"It's not in Canada," he assured me as we climbed the steps. "But there are definitely pancakes."

That was all I needed to know.

CHAPTER 10

Since he refused to give me an address on account of Sibyl, I couldn't do a thing to help Nik navigate the DFZ's morning craziness. And it was *crazy*. In addition to the usual work rush hour, there was some sort of huge dragon event going on, which, in hindsight, was probably the "business" my mom had been referring to when she'd told me my dad was in town. We weren't even near the Peacemaker's Consulate, but with so many dragons flying in, every Skyway ramp in the city was choked with rubberneckers gawking as giant monsters of legend flew over their heads. Even Nik poked his head out the window when we drove under a gap in the bridges, his eyes going wide at the winged shadows silhouetted against the bright-blue sky.

I stayed firmly in the car. It wasn't that I didn't appreciate the wonder, but after this morning's events, I was totally fine with never seeing another dragon for as long as I lived.

Thankfully, other than the jam-ups at the ramps, we didn't have to shove our way through the upper city's traffic. For someone who refused to use an AI, Nik had a strangely encyclopedic knowledge of the Underground's roadways. He made a few wrong turns at intersections where bits of the DFZ had rearranged themselves recently, but for the most part he drove perfectly from memory, pulling us into the tiny parking lot of an old-style Americana diner that stood like an island at the heart of a five-way intersection.

"What's this place?" I asked, squinting at the neon sign, which was so cursive and curly I couldn't actually read what it said.

"Martina's," Nik replied as we got out of the car. "I'm not vouching for the quality of the food, but I know the owner, so I'm pretty sure you won't get poisoned."

"A ringing endorsement," I said, breathing in deep. "It smells good, though."

It smelled like grease and fried potatoes. Exactly as a diner should, in other words. It was busy, too. We'd gotten the last parking spot in the back by the dumpsters. The place was a wall of noise when we walked inside, but it looked like mostly office workers and maintenance crews grabbing breakfast on their way to work. Plenty of people still looked up when we came in, though, and I moved closer to Nik.

"Shouldn't we be lying low?" I whispered as we pushed past the crowded bar area toward the booths at the back. "Not that I've ever had a bounty on my head, but going into crowds doesn't seem like a smart move."

"Depends on the crowd," Nik whispered back. "This isn't like where we went last night. These are normal people, which means they're too busy to care about us."

He seemed to be right. Every head that had popped up when we'd come in was back down, too preoccupied with food or conversation to care about two more people. What really shocked me, though, was that no one was staring at Rena.

She was sitting in a circular booth at the back, taking up the entire swath of the red-plastic covered seat with various toolkits and bags. Her white lab coat was gone, replaced by a black tank top that only served to highlight the artificiality of her chased-silver body. I would have stared like crazy if she'd walked into my restaurant, but either she'd been waiting long enough that the novelty had worn off, or the people here really didn't care. Normally, I'd have bet on the former, but there was nothing on the table in front of her, not even a cup of coffee.

"You'd better have a damn good reason for dragging me out to this grease pit," she snapped when we got close. "Do you know how hard it is to get the smell of fry oil out of synthetic hair?"

"Can't say that I do," Nik said, moving her boxes to make room for us to join her in the booth.

"I know this neighborhood is well away from Kauffman's sphere of influence," she went on. "But a *diner*, Nikki? Really? You never eat out, and you know I can't eat real food anymore. Why couldn't we just meet on a corner like usual?"

Nik shrugged. "Opal wanted breakfast."

I blushed at Rena's look of scorn. The automatic apology for causing inconvenience was already on the tip of my tongue when I came to my senses and swallowed it back down. This was *not* my problem. Wanting to eat breakfast was a perfectly normal thing to do, and I refused to let a sleazy robot lady who'd given up *food* make me feel guilty about what might well be my last meal eaten in freedom. She and Nik could sit there and be weirdos who didn't eat together. *I* was going to enjoy my breakfast.

With a belligerent glare at Rena, I grabbed the old-fashioned plastic menu and started thumbing through it. Since we were at a diner, pancakes were right on the first page. After doing some quick menu-fu, I figured out how to work the combos in order to land a full stack of five plus bacon, ham, and coffee while staying within my budget. I even had money left over for the tip, which was good, because the waitress had my coffee out within seconds of Sibyl putting my order into the diner's AR. No one deserved money more than people who brought coffee quickly. I was sipping in bliss when Nik leaned over the table.

"Do you have it?"

"No," Rena said, waving at the pile of kits and boxes on the seat beside her. "I just decided to bring my entire installation set to a place that sells nothing I can use for funsies."

Nik gave her an exasperated look, and Rena rolled her eyes. "It's been a long night," she muttered. "I got interrogated by every bigwig in the Heights about who knocked down their ramp."

I froze mid-sip. "You didn't tell them about us, did you?"

"Of course not," Rena said, her electronically augmented voice insulted. "Tight lips are the most critical component of our business. I'd lose all my customers if word got out that I'd squealed, but that doesn't mean people won't try."

"It'll blow over," Nik assured her. "People are always getting into fights up on the ramps."

"Not ones that destroy the infrastructure. The Heights aren't exactly built to code, you know. You could have brought the whole place down!"

Considering we'd been under fire and no one up there had done a thing to help us, I was having a hard time finding sympathy for the business owners of the Heights. Saying as much to Rena didn't seem like a savvy move, though, so I kept my mouth shut. At least until my pancakes arrived.

The pictures had not done them justice. My plate took up the whole table, and it was stacked high with five fluffy, golden, buttery pancakes the size of my head. The sight almost made me cry. It felt silly, but I'd been so broke for so long that getting to splurge and eat something I was *really* excited about felt like New Year's and my birthday rolled into one. I was painstakingly soaking them in the perfect amount of warm syrup when Rena dug into the biggest bag sitting on the bench beside her.

"Here," she said, setting Dr. Lyle's hand on the opposite side of the plastic table from where I was elevating syrup to an art form. "Everything's cracked and ready to access, as requested."

"Excellent," Nik said, reaching out to take the hand. "What does it hook in to?"

Rena's synthetic lips quirked. "You, I'm afraid." She reached out to tap the base of the hand where the layer of synthetic skin gave way to the naked circuitry that connected it to the wrist. "The entire point of hard coding something into a cyberwear unit's VCI is that it can't be accessed externally. I've cracked the DNA lock for you, but nothing can change the fact that that information can *only* be reached via direct interface." She slid her silver finger over to tap lovingly on Nik's own artificial hand. "If you want whatever's hidden inside, you're going to have to put a hand in it, so to speak."

Nik winced. I did, too. "Wait," I said, swallowing my bite of pancake. "You mean he has to physically put on the hand? Like on his own wrist?"

"That's why I brought my stuff," Rena said, waving her hand at the tool kits on the bench beside her.

I paled. "But it was on a dead guy."

"So what?" she said. "I sterilized it."

Considering I regularly resold cyberwear I found while Cleaning, I knew there had to be a sterile way to transfer synthetic limbs between people, but I knew where that hand had come from. I'd seen Dr. Lyle's black, rotting corpse on the floor of his apartment and in the morgue. It wasn't an image that got out of your head easily, or one you wanted associated with things that were going anywhere near your body, let alone *into*. From the look on his face, I knew Nik had to be thinking the same thing. When he spoke, though, his complaint was about something else entirely.

"I can't," he said. "It's a left hand."

My eyes shot to Nik's synthetic arm, which was indeed his right, but Rena just waved the concern away. "Please," she said, pulling a small electric screwdriver out of her kit. "Who do you think you're dealing with? I can put a foot on a head. A left hand on a right arm is no trouble at all."

"No trouble for *you*," Nik said angrily. "But I'm talking about me. How am I supposed to drive or shoot with two left hands?"

Rena shrugged with a soft, mechanical click. "No idea. Not my problem. You wanted the info in this hand, I've told you how to get it. What you do with that is up to you, but I still expect to be paid in full."

My whole body tightened at the mention of money. I'd forgotten we hadn't paid for Rena's work yet. Nik had mentioned she'd be expensive, but I'd just spent my last fifteen dollars and twelve cents on pancakes, which meant I was even broker now than I'd been yesterday. I was panicking trying to figure out what I was going to do when Nik's face broke into a wicked smile.

"Consider it paid," he said. "You still owe me for what happened last year. This should make us even."

Rena's fake eyes went wide. "You're calling in your favor for *this*? Really?"

Nik shrugged. "I know how much it costs to run a crack, and you don't get rich by spending money. Besides, what's the point of a favor if you don't use it?"

Rena gave him a nasty look. "And you couldn't have mentioned this before I did the work?"

"If you'd known you were doing it pro bono, you wouldn't have worked so diligently. Or agreed to meet me all the way out here," Nik said, his smile going wider. "Fair is fair, Rena."

That didn't sound fair at all to me, but to my surprise, Rena chuckled. "You really are a cheap bastard," she said, shaking her head. "But fine. Have it your way." She put out her hand. "Arm, please."

Nik dutifully stretched out his artificial right arm, and I nearly choked on my pancakes. "You're doing it *here*?" I cried. "At the table?"

"Actually, I was planning to do it down on the bench, but anywhere is fine." Rena gave me a superior smile. "That's why cybernetics will always beat flesh, kitten. You can switch them out and change them around however and wherever you want without worrying about fluids or infection or any other nasty biology. If you replace enough, you don't even have to eat. You just keep your batteries full and your nutrient tank topped off and you can go for days." She reached down to rap her knuckles against her flat metal stomach. "It's so efficient. You really should start upgrading."

"No thank you," I said, bending low over my half-eaten pancakes, which now seemed more precious than ever.

Rena shrugged. "Suit yourself." She grabbed Dr. Lyle's hand off the table and turned around in the bench. "Ready, Nikki?"

Nik nodded and scooted around the circular booth until he was sitting directly next to her. "Just make sure I can get it off again."

"Don't worry," Rena said, pushing his sleeve up and moving her small electric screwdriver into place. "It'll be easy as one." She undid the hidden screws that held his hand to his wrist. "Two." She twisted his hand sickeningly back and forth until it popped off, leaving only the connective stump. "Three." She fit Dr. Lyle's left hand onto Nik's wrist and slid it around until all the electrodes were connected. When things were more or less in place, she put one screw—the only one that would fit in the new configuration—back in.

"Voila," she said proudly, reaching for a roll of electrical tape, which she used to finish securing the new hand to Nik's wrist. "It's not in very tight since I didn't want to ruin my creation by drilling new holes, so don't be rough with it. But that should do well enough to reference the information."

"That was fast," I said, impressed. Then my eyes went to all the stuff on the bench beside her. "Wait. If screws were all you needed, why did you bring all that other stuff?"

"In case screws *weren't* all I needed," Rena said with a smile. "Always be prepared!"

Considering she had a defibrillator pack in there, I didn't want to know what kind of disaster Rena felt we needed to be prepared for. I didn't have time to worry about it, either. Nik was staring at his new hand as if it held the secrets of the universe, and I was desperate to know what he saw.

"Can you access the info?"

"I don't know," he muttered, looking horribly confused. "Give me something to write with."

I blinked, confused. "You mean like a pen?"

"I think I've got one," Rena said, digging into her bag. "Here."

Nik took the cheap ballpoint and pressed it against his paper napkin. He started to write a second later, but I knew from the way his hand jerked that Nik wasn't the one controlling it. Nik's movements were always precise, like a finely tuned machine. These were small and janky, writing a series of numbers across the paper napkin in the same chicken-scratch cursive I'd seen in all of Dr. Lyle's notes.

"Nice trick," Rena said when he lifted the pen at last. "What does it mean?"

"I have no idea," Nik said. "The hand wrote that, not me."

I scowled at the numbers. They looked familiar, but I couldn't put my finger on where I'd seen the pattern before.

"I know!" Sibyl said in my ear, her voice desperate to prove that she was still useful. "Those are three-dimensional coordinates."

"They're coordinates," I said out loud so the rest of the people at the table would know what was up.

"Coordinates to what?" Nik asked.

"A location in the city," Sibyl said, bringing up a map of the DFZ. "Here."

She lit up the spot in question, and I shook my head. "That can't be right."

"What can't be right?" Rena asked eagerly, getting into it. "Where is it?"

Since Rena had AR, I had Sibyl put the map up in our shared space. Nik still wouldn't be able to see it, but at least I'd only have to explain this insanity to one person. "The point is straight down," I said, flicking my fingers to scroll the map down until I reached the red dot marking the spot. "Almost a mile underground. There's nothing that goes that deep in the DFZ. You'd hit the water table."

Nik took all of that in with a stoic frown. Then he winced. "Wait," he said, moving his new hand—or, more accurately, letting the hand move him—back to the paper, where he wrote down a second string of numbers in the same chicken-scratch cursive. "How about that?"

Sibyl put the numbers in as soon as they appeared. Sure enough, it was another set of coordinates, but it didn't fix the problem. "It's still underground," I moaned, sliding the map down even further this time. "Just in a different place."

"Can you try again?" Rena asked.

"No," Nik said, sounding as frustrated as I felt. "I wasn't giving it a second try before. The pressure just moved, and then the numbers were different."

"Pressure?" I asked. "What kind of pressure?"

Nik shook his head. "I'm not sure how else to describe it. The hand's a hand. It feels weird because it's not mine, but it doesn't move unless I tell it to. Even when I'm holding it still, though, there's a pressure in the palm that keeps shifting, like string on a balloon."

"Or a needle in a compass," Rena said excitedly. "That hand's not built to plug into an artificial brain enhancement, so it doesn't have a complex input array. It still has to communicate the information somehow, though, and pressure-point feedback is a classic. I bet it's pointing you at those coordinates!"

"Well, if that's what it's supposed to do, then it's broken," Nik said angrily, clutching his new hand. "Stupid thing keeps jerking around."

"Maybe it's not jerking around," I said, staring at my map. "Maybe the thing it's pointing at is *moving*."

"That's impossible," Rena said. "Even the DFZ doesn't move that fast."

"The DFZ doesn't," I agreed. "But the Gnarls do."

Nik arched a skeptical eyebrow in my direction. Rena was less polite. "Don't be so gullible," she scolded. "The Gnarls are an urban legend. The whole thing was made up to sell overpriced maps to tourists."

"No, they're not," I said sharply. "They're a real phenomenon."

I couldn't fault them for their skepticism. The Gnarls did sound pretty sketchy, and knowledge of them *was* horribly abused by the tourism companies. But while almost all of the stories about a secret network of ever-changing tunnels below the sewers were false, the Gnarls were a concept that was firmly rooted in spirit theory, which also happened to be the *only* magical theory class I'd actually done well in.

"Okay, so everyone knows that all spirits have a domain, right?" I said, looking around the table to make sure they were following. "A domain is whatever they're the spirit of, the place or concept that fuels all their power. For a spirit like Algonquin, it's pretty obvious. She's the Lady of the Great Lakes, so her domain is the lakes. It gets more complicated when you're talking about conceptual entities such as the Empty Wind, but the general idea is always the same. Whether it's a physical location or a concept like 'the forgotten dead,' every spirit has a core that binds them together, somewhere all the magic that makes them tick can pool together. But the DFZ is a little different. Like the Empty Wind, she's a concept: the *idea* of a city where nothing's illegal and anything is possible. But she's also a physical place, which is the city we're in right now. That duality means that the DFZ has both a physical domain *and* a conceptual one. Everyone following so far?"

"I think so," Nik said. "I just don't understand why it matters."

"It matters because she's a blend," I said. "Spirits of the land are rooted in the land. With them, what you see is what you get. But the DFZ was born from humanity. She's the sum of all our conceptions about what the DFZ is. That's why she's able to move buildings around like puzzle pieces instead of relying on geological forces like other physical spirits. She's god of both the physical city *and* our ideal of the city. When you shove the physical and the conceptual together, you get an area of overlap, and that place is the Gnarls. The University of Michigan has three whole labs dedicated to studying the phenomenon. It's *totally* legit."

And a fantastic place to hide a ritual. I'd never been to the Gnarls myself, but according to the papers I'd had to read for class, they were an ever-changing labyrinth where the physical and magical worlds had been squished together during the DFZ's awakening as a spirit. They were locked in a state of constant magical flux, which meant that no matter how much magic *you* cast, no one would ever be able to trace it through all the background noise. It was the perfect hiding place, so much so that I felt like an idiot for not thinking of them earlier.

"This is great," I said, looking at Nik. "Normally the Gnarls are unnavigable, but your new hand points to where we want to go. That must be how Dr. Lyle didn't lose his ritual site every time the Gnarls moved. He put a compass in his hand!"

"That *would* explain the weird spellwork I found on the inside," Rena said, nodding sagely.

I stared at her. "There was spellwork inside it? Why didn't you mention that earlier?!"

"Because it's very common in cyberwear that belonged to a mage," she said with a shrug. "Every spell slinger with a fake limb tries to jimmy that thing with spellwork to improve the magical throughput. I thought this was just a really bad attempt, but a compass makes *way* more sense."

"So I just follow this pressure," Nik said, staring at Dr. Lyle's hand as if he was afraid it was going to start punching him. "And this thing will take us to what we're searching for?"

"That's my theory," I said, nodding.

"Great," he said, sliding over in the booth until he was bumping into me. "Let's go."

He was clearly in an enormous hurry. So was I, but I couldn't go just yet. "*Please* let me finish my pancakes first," I begged. "I already paid for them."

Nik gave me a scathing look, but he settled back into the booth, waving at me to go ahead.

I ate in a fury. Honestly, I was already full to the point of discomfort, but I'd spent the last of my money on these, and there was no way Nik would allow a to-go box full of pancakes covered in syrup into his car. They went into my stomach or they'd go into the trash, so I ate until I was bursting, shoveling pancakes into my mouth until the smell of syrup started to make me nauseous. Only then did I stop, dropping my head against the cushy back of the bench with a groan.

"That was impressive," Nik said. "Horrific, but impressive."

"Do you want the last few bites?" I asked, nodding at the final half a pancake swimming in the syrup of its fallen brothers.

"No," he said firmly. "After that, I don't think I ever want to see a pancake again."

I was also okay with never seeing, smelling, or even hearing the word "pancake" again, which I took as a sign I'd gotten my money's worth. Satisfied that I'd spent my last dollars in a fit of excess truly worthy of the DFZ, I hauled myself up and started waddling toward the door with Nik hot on my heels.

CHAPTER 11

The next thing we had to do was figure out how to get *into* the Gnarls.

It wasn't a simple question. Like the name suggested, everything about the Gnarls was tricky. According to the Thaumaturgical research papers Sibyl looked up for me, the entrance to the Gnarls moved to a different spot in the city every few minutes. According to the forums for conspiracy theorists who'd turned finding the Gnarls into a competitive sport, though, those locations tended to repeat. The closest one was only a few miles away, so that was the address I gave Nik as we got into the car.

And discovered a new problem.

"Ah, come *on*," he growled, baring his teeth as he attempted to grip his steering wheel with both of his left hands.

I bit my lip. "Do you want me to drive?"

Nik shot me a look so blistering I swear I lost skin.

"Sorry, sorry," I said, cringing back into my seat. "It was just an offer."

"A ridiculous one," he muttered. Then his gray eyes snapped back to me. "*Can* you drive?"

"I've played driving games." Mostly of the crash derby variety, but I understood the basic mechanics of physically piloting a car. You know, in theory.

He grimaced. "I'll stick to my two left hands. You freaked the first time you watched me drive through DFZ traffic without a computer. I don't even want to be in the car when you try it yourself."

Couldn't argue there. "Is there another way I can help?"

"Yes," he said, placing his right-left hand on the stick shift. "Be patient."

I was patient as a saint. I sat in my seat without a word for ten full minutes while Nik figured himself out. Finally, after he'd adjusted his hands for what had to be the millionth time, Nik started the engine and pulled us out, driving us very, very cautiously into the wreath of roads that surrounded the diner.

According to the internet, the closest entrance to the Gnarls was beneath the Second Renaissance Center, a fourteen-tower complex that was part office building, part convention center, and part corporate hotel. It was also the busiest tourist district in the city at the heart of the downtown portion of the riverfront. Naturally, then, parking was hell. We ended up in an auto-sorted magazine deck four blocks away from our destination, much to Nik's chagrin, but there was no other choice. Unless we wanted to circle for hours stalking the ten spots where street parking was allowed, magazine decks were the only option in this part of the city.

As the name suggested, they worked just like magazines, except instead of being packed with bullets, they were packed with cars. You drove your vehicle onto a metal plate, and the machinery picked it up and stuffed it into a metal chute full of other cars on plates. When you wanted it back, you put your ticket into the machine and waited for the magazine to cycle back around to your car.

I didn't blame Nik for hating it. It was a rough-and-tumble way to park with no way to get your car back quickly if you needed it. If his new hand hadn't been tugging on him so hard, he probably would have demanded we go somewhere else. But I could see the twitches in the synthetic muscles on the back of his hand going crazy, which I took as a good sign.

"We have to be getting close," I said, securing the strap for my messenger bag with Dr. Lyle's notes across my chest beneath my poncho.

"I just don't understand why it would be *here*," Nik grumbled, slinging on his own bag full of combat supplies, which now included his right hand. "This place is a zoo, nothing but overpriced tourist nonsense. I thought the Gnarls were supposed to be the DFZ's heart. Why would she choose to open it *here?*"

That was a good question. The Second Renaissance—or 2R, according to the souvenir T-shirt carts that lined the sidewalk—was classic

DFZ tourist trap at its most exuberant. It was still divided between the Skyways and Underground, but there were more connecting escalators, stairways, and elevators in these few blocks than anywhere else in the city. The convention complex even had a big ground-level entrance with a courtyard so guests could experience the famous DFZ Underground without technically having to leave the hotel. The Skyways above were full of boutique stores and fancy restaurants with expense account pricing, while Underground blocks surrounding the center looked like they'd come right out of a movie set.

There were no cheap concrete squares here. This was what was known as a Free-build Zone, a place where people could build their own buildings instead of renting space in whatever DFZ decided to push out of the ground. Since these zones only seemed to be in super-hot areas, the result was always pure capitalist insanity, and the 2R was no different. We walked past structures made of shipping containers that had been welded together and buildings that had been built out over the street, turning the sidewalk into a tunnel in an effort to expand their floor space. There were buildings built to look like they'd come from Old Detroit, complete with fake damage and painted-on weathering, and buildings that were nothing but stairs leading to single-person-wide alleyways filled with even more shops. One block had abandoned even the pretense of structures and simply built scaffolding so they could stack as many street carts onto the lot as possible, using giant AR projectors to beam advertisements down into the river of customers that was constantly flowing by.

"This can't be right," Nik said angrily, swatting at the dancing images of souvenir plastic beer steins projected from the cart suspended on steel cables above our heads. "This place is so far down the rabbit hole it's practically a parody. It's not the *real* DFZ."

"Who are we to say what's the real DFZ?" I asked, grabbing onto his arm to keep from getting squished against the wall of European tourists eagerly taking pictures to our left. "Spirits are defined by their domains, remember? You're right when you say this place is solid stereotype, but I think that's exactly why the Gnarls open here. I mean, just look at it."

I swept my hand across the glaringly bright street. We were almost to the base of the 2R, and the crowds—and the commerce—had only gotten denser. Cars couldn't even drive on the streets down here. It was just an ocean of people surrounded by a neon- and LED-lit canyon of closet casinos, souvenir shops, vending machine bars, single-use joy parlors, and card-operated VR brothels. There were pawn shops with human organs for sale in the windows and pet stores full of animals that were banned everywhere else in the world. There were fight bars, topless bars, drug bars, bars where you paid interesting people to pretend to be your friends. The whole place was a chaotic, unregulated, booze- and drug-soaked nightmare of greed, hedonism, and reckless ambition. It was simultaneously the worst of humanity and the height of human ingenuity and creativity as shopkeepers fought to one-up each other and corner the rich flow of gullible tourist money. If you said "DFZ" to someone who didn't live here, this was exactly what they'd envision, and that made my heart pound with anticipation.

"This *has* to be it," I said, pulling up my map and zooming in as far as I could. "Sibyl, show me the entrance locations."

A smattering of red dots appeared across my augmented vision. "Here's all the ones reported in the last two months," my AI said, flipping my map into 3D to show depth. "They're almost all below your current position, though. You'll have to find a way down."

That wasn't hard. There was a giant flashing "down" arrow right next to us with a sign promising even more shops on the lower levels. I wasn't aware this street *had* a lower level, but given that there were shops suspended on cables above my head, nothing surprised me anymore.

"Come on," I said, tugging on Nik's armored jacket. "Let's go down."

Keeping his actual left hand in his false pocket where his gun was, Nik helped me push through the gawking crowd to the stairwell, which turned out to be a storm drain someone had ripped the cement cap off and replaced with a spiral staircase lined with flashing string lights. With no small amount of trepidation, I made my way down, pausing to put on my Cleaning gloves before I grabbed the sticky-looking railing.

Unsurprisingly given the entrance, we came out in the storm water system. Or, rather, what *had* been the storm water system. Someone had bricked over the upstream pipe to divert the runoff into another drain, leaving the ten-foot-diameter pipe running below this street dry enough to convert into an underground mall. The pipe itself was just the main drag. Individual shops had dug further, cutting through the pipe's cement wall and into the dirt behind it to create spacious caves. It was mostly gambling, sex shops, and bars, but there were plenty of normal restaurants, too, along with barber shops, nail salons, dry cleaners, and capsule hotels.

That last part surprised me. After the terrifying stairwell, I'd expected the stuff down here to be *extra* salacious. Now that I thought about it, though, the choice was actually pretty practical. When nothing was illegal, it made sense to put the really shocking stuff right out in front for maximum impact. The rest of it—the normal everyday stores and services—was swept down to the cheaper real estate. This was probably where the shopkeepers who ran all the craziness up top went for lunch and drinks after work. The base layer of the 2R's commercial ecosystem.

It was also not deep enough.

"There's another way down to your left," Sibyl whispered in my ear. "Beside the synth-sushi shop."

I nodded and motioned for Nik to follow me, turning sideways to squeeze down the maintenance tunnel where the restaurant stored its trashcans. Once we got past that, the tunnel started going down, taking us away from the blocked-off storm pipe into another system of tunnels. One that wasn't on Sibyl's map.

"Where are we?" Nik asked, looking at the curved, water-stained walls.

I switched on the lights on my goggles so I could see. "I think it's one of the old train tunnels," I said, pointing at the metal rails that were still embedded in the crumbling floor. "There were a couple that followed the river in Old Detroit so freight could move through the city without turning it into a train yard. I'm not sure if this is part of the Windsor Tunnel or the old Michigan Central Line since things down here have gotten pretty shuffled in the last eighty years, but it's got to be over a hundred and fifty years old."

"How do you know all this stuff?" Nik asked, jogging up beside me. "I've lived in the DFZ since I was thirteen, and I've never heard anything about underground train tunnels."

I shrugged. "I read about it. I like history, and Detroit's was fascinating even before magic and spirits got involved. This city is full of hidden places. Just make sure you watch out for eyes in the dark. There's a lot of magical beasties who live down here."

That wasn't a joke. Judging from the size of the tracks in the mud on the tunnel's floor, this place was a highway for some pretty big specimens. I wasn't a good enough tracker to say which ones exactly, but I'd seen every season of *DFZ Sewer Hunters,* so I knew all that stuff about giant alligators and lampreys and rats the size of dump trucks wasn't just made up to sell tours. Hunting the things that lived under the DFZ was big business. How else did all those illegal pet shops get their mana-eater larvae and giant alligator eggs?

"I know better than to let my guard down in the dark," Nik said, looking over his shoulder to keep an eye on the tunnel behind us. "I've fought the sort of stuff that lives down here before. It's not fun."

"Did you used to be a hunter?" I asked.

Nik shook his head. "No, never."

"Why not?" Given Nik's metal coating, skill at violence, and love of money, hunting monsters for cash seemed like it would be a natural choice, but he just winced.

"I don't like being underground."

I gaped at him. "But you live in a hole in the ground."

"I live in an *apartment,*" Nik said sharply. "That's a far cry from this."

"Fair enough," I said, looking up at the rounded ceiling dripping with water that was seeping down from the city above. "But are you going to be okay?" Nik was jumpy enough under normal circumstances. I didn't want to think of what would happen if he really freaked out.

"I'll be fine," he said stubbornly. "I don't have to be comfortable to be effective. I'm just saying I wouldn't want to be down here all day. And speaking of, are we close? My hand is getting really jumpy."

"That's a better indicator than I've got," I said, checking my map. "We're in the middle of the thickest cluster of recorded sightings for this area. According to the information I've got, the Gnarls can open anywhere along here. Assuming they even appear in this part of town today, of course."

"We'll just have to hope we get lucky," Nik said, pulling a flashlight of his own out of his bag.

Going by my last five months, that wasn't a good hope, but there was no point in being a downer. This was where we'd chosen to make our play, so I turned up my lights and started searching down the tunnels, muttering a prayer to the DFZ under my breath.

Please, I whispered. *Please, great city, I need this to work. I just started my life here. I don't want it to be over. Please help me out. I don't want to lose.*

I didn't want to go back under my father's claw.

I was still whispering different variations of my fears to myself when I felt something move behind me. There was no sound, no flicker. It was more like a change in the air. Nik must have felt it too, though, because he whirled around even faster than I did only to stop cold. When I finally managed to turn around, I saw why.

There was a cathedral behind us.

I'm fully aware of how nuts that sounds. It looked even crazier. The entire span of the old train tunnel we'd been walking down for the last five minutes was now completely blocked off by what could only be described as the ornate front of a Gothic cathedral, complete with weathered stone steps, rusted iron railings, and red-painted doors. It looked as if the whole building had been teleported into the ground, and we were just looking at a tiny sliver of it that happened to contain the front door. Even the stained-glass windows were still intact, though very scratched up. Whatever this place was, it was old, and it had been through a lot. But despite the damage, it was still standing strong, lighting up the dark tunnel with the warm glow of light through its windows.

"What the hell is that?" Nik said.

I had no idea. Fortunately, Sibyl did. "That's the Wandering Cathedral!" she said excitedly. "The one from the urban legends!"

"You're going to have to be more precise," I said shakily. "The DFZ has a lot of urban legends." So many even I hadn't read them all.

"This one's special," my AI promised, filling my augmented reality with pictures showing the Gothic cathedral in the middle of a highway or shoved into an underpass or in the middle of a parking lot and lots of other places a giant historic church wasn't supposed to be.

"According to the internet, it's one of the few cathedrals from Old Detroit that survived Algonquin's initial flooding. It made it sixty more years through the first DFZ Underground only to be destroyed during the Second Mana Crash. Apparently, the DFZ was so upset, she rebuilt the whole thing brick by brick and added it to her private collection. There's all sorts of theories about why it surfaces when and where it does, most of which are crazy, but everyone agrees that it's one of the best entrances to the Gnarls."

"Why didn't you say that part first?" I yelled at her, grabbing Nik's arm. "These things only stay open for a few minutes!"

"I was just trying to answer your question," Sibyl said, but I wasn't paying attention. I was too busy running up the cathedral steps. The door was locked when I tried the handle, so I banged on it with my open hand, making the wood rattle against the metal frame.

"Hello?" I cried. "We need to get inside. We're looking for the Gnarls. It's very important!"

"Who are you talking to?" Nik hissed, pulling back his leg for a kick. "Just break it down."

"*No!*" I shouted, throwing myself between him and the door. "This is one of the DFZ's personal buildings! You don't get into the Gnarls by breaking things that belong to the god who controls them!"

"Then what are we supposed to do?"

"I don't know," I said, turning back to the door. "It's not like there's instructions..."

My voice faded. Now that I was no longer running at or beating on the door, I could see there were, in fact, instructions in the form of a small slip of paper pasted to the wall beside the doors. *Entry fee required,* it read. *Please pay below.*

"What the—" Nik said, pushing past me to read the sign for himself. "There's an entry fee for the legendary magical tunnel system?!"

"This *is* the DFZ," I reminded him with a sigh. "Nothing's free here."

I just hoped I wasn't screwed.

I glanced down at the battered plastic pay pad attached to the stone below the sign, sorely regretting my decision to spend the last of my money gorging on pancakes. Still uncomfortably full stomach sinking, I reached out to touch the pad, blinking in real surprise when a perfectly normal payment interface popped up in my AR. There was no amount listed, but I didn't have a lot of options. My bank account consisted of exactly eighty-eight cents, so that was what I paid, dropping every last virtual penny into the receptor.

The moment I touched the *Pay* button, I felt something bump into my foot. When I looked down, there was a red paper ticket lying on the stone floor with my name printed on it. I picked it up with shaking fingers, not in the least surprised when I felt the bite of magic through my gloves. If the magically appearing cathedral hadn't been a big enough tip-off, this was proof that we were dealing with *serious* power, which meant there was no room for shenanigans.

"Get your ticket," I told Nik, stepping aside so he could access the payment pad. "Hurry."

"How much was it?" he asked, pulling out his battered phone.

"Eighty-eight cents."

His expression brightened enormously. "That's not bad," he said, tapping the number into the payment interface, which appeared on his phone screen since he was a savage who didn't have AR. "I was worried it was going to ask for my soul or my firstborn or—"

He cut off with a curse as a bright red error message appeared on his screen. "'Eighty-eight cents is insufficient!'" he read in a furious voice. "Why? That's what you paid!"

I shrugged. "Maybe it's different based on the person."

"Why would that be?"

"It's a magical moving cathedral," I said helplessly. "I don't know, just keep trying."

Muttering angrily under his breath, Nik did as I asked, entering higher and higher numbers into the payment screen. Finally, when he got to one hundred dollars, the button turned green, and a ticket just like mine but with his name on it appeared at our feet.

"This is extortion," Nik growled, snatching the ticket off the ground. "Why did mine cost so much more than yours?"

"Because she paid more than you."

We both jumped. The voice was as creaky and old as the cathedral itself, but it wasn't in my head like the Empty Wind's had been. A few breathless seconds later, I realized it wasn't a spirit at all. It belonged to a short, pale figure with a stooped back, stringy gray hair, gray skin, and white eyes that reminded me of a blind cave fish's that blinked at me when the cathedral door opened.

"Opal paid all that she had," the person went on, their voice so old and scratchy, I couldn't tell if they were a man or a woman, or if it even mattered. "Be glad the cathedral did not charge you the same, Nikola Kos."

Nik took a step back. "Right," he said meekly. "Thank you for the discount, then."

"Can we come in?" I asked nervously. The way into the Gnarls was only supposed to appear for a few minutes, and we'd wasted most of that trying to pay Nik's entry fee. It would be just my luck if the cathedral vanished just when we got the door open.

Rather than answer, the cave-fish person stepped back, which I took as an invitation to rush inside. Nik was right behind me, getting through just before the cathedral doors slammed on his back. A heartbeat later, I felt the same sensation of movement I'd noticed earlier, only now it was all around me, making my stomach roll as the Wandering Cathedral left the tunnel and went who knew where.

"Um," I said, looking around at the cavernous church. "So now that we're in, could you please tell us what this place is, exactly?"

"And who you are?" Nik added with a glare.

I elbowed him in the ribs for being rude, which I'm pretty sure hurt me way more than it bothered him. His armor plating was *hard*. I was rubbing my bruised elbow when the bent figure laughed.

"Death gods aren't the only ones who've picked up priests," they said, hobbling up the aisle toward the place where the altar would have been if this had still been a functioning church. Now, the space between the choir pews was decorated like a living room, complete with a couch, where, after a bit of groping around to find the right spot, our host sat down.

"I am Nameless," they continued when they'd gotten comfy.

Nik arched an eyebrow. "Is Nameless your name or a description?"

"Both," Nameless said. "Sexton of the Wandering Cathedral and Blind Priest of the DFZ." One of the white cave-fish eyes winked at me.

"The 'blind' part was my own addition. I like to differentiate myself from the others."

"Others?" Nik said. "How many more of you are there?"

"Quite a few," Nameless replied. "It *is* a city of millions. The DFZ can't do everything herself, so she outsources. You should be familiar with that since you're both Cleaners. The priesthood's the same. We take care of the idiots who are always trying to worm their way into the city's secret spaces, and in return, the city gives us a cut of the entry fees." The priest's wrinkled face broke into a toothless smile. "It's good business for everyone involved, but between you and me, I have the best office."

"You absolutely do," I assured Nameless, speaking quickly before Nik could say anything to antagonize our host further. "But I promise we're not here to steal the city's secrets. We're actually looking for something that was hidden in the Gnarls by someone else, a man named Dr. Theodore Lyle."

"I have no idea who that is," Nameless said with a shrug. "But you're welcome to search all you like. Understand, though, that everything in the Gnarls is property of the DFZ by default. Even if you find what you're looking for, unless you can prove ownership, you won't be able to take it out."

I started sweating bullets. I hadn't counted on ownership being an issue. Before I could come up with something, though, Nik answered for me.

"That's no problem," he said, pointing at me with his thumb. "When she bought Dr. Lyle's safe house at a Cleaning auction, his dead body was still inside it. Rather than issue a refund, Broker told her she could take her fee out of stuff inside, but all she found was a bunch of papers. They aren't worth a twentieth of what she paid for the place, which means she's still short. Since the DFZ has already formally declined to offer her a refund via the Cleaning office, I feel it's reasonable to say that everything related to those papers belongs to her as valid compensation for services rendered."

By the time he finished, my jaw was on the ground.

Nik scowled. "Why do you look so shocked?"

"Well," I said, scrambling. "That was, I mean…I didn't expect you to go all lawyer on me."

"I'm not a lawyer," he said. "I'm a Cleaner. The DFZ doesn't have a lot of laws, but a lot of the ones it does have apply to our business, so I made it *my* business to learn them. That's just common sense."

Not common enough, apparently, because it had never occurred to me. I hadn't even considered that I might have a legal claim on Dr. Lyle's ritual, but I was so, *so* glad that Nik had.

"Yeah!" I said enthusiastically, turning back to Nameless. "What he said!"

Nameless scratched the wispy white hairs on their chin thoughtfully. "It sounds plausible enough," they said at last. "But it's not my call. The DFZ will make the final decision, but so long as there's no one with a stronger claim, I'd say you're safe."

"My claim is the strongest," I said confidently, pointing at Nik's second left hand. "We're here with the blessing of the deceased as communicated by the Empty Wind. Finding Dr. Lyle's ritual and reclaiming it is the best way to honor his memory. It's practically a religious rite."

That was stretching the truth a bit, but Nameless didn't seem to care. "The Empty Wind is none of my concern," they said. "My business is with the living city, not the dead. If you want to go into the Gnarls, be my guest. You've already bought your tickets, so I couldn't stop you even if I wanted."

"All right," I said nervously. Then, because it seemed like something I should ask, I added, "Are there any rules we need to follow? Things we should know before we go in?"

The priest burst out laughing. "Where do you think you are, girlie? You're stepping into the heart of the DFZ! There's no *rules* here, though if you want to survive, you'd do well to remember that the city is not, and never will be, your friend."

Nik snorted. "Why would we ever think that?"

"People think all kinds of things," the priest said with a shrug. "Including that calling a city their home is a two-way street. But the DFZ doesn't work that way. She's not kind. Not moral or fair. She has no compassion, no sympathy for the plight of those who live within her. That's not her fault. She doesn't have the freedoms we mortals enjoy. Her mind, her soul, even her body does not belong to her. She is not an individual. She is a spirit, the soul of a living city. She can only be what we've made her. Do you understand?"

I wasn't sure that I did. I'd always thought of the DFZ as a whimsical god who did whatever she liked without caring how it affected the ants she crushed under her moving buildings. To hear Nameless say it, though, the city sounded almost pitiable. A prisoner of other people's expectations. "What *does* she care about, then?"

"Opportunity," Nameless said, giving me a smile. "From the moment it rose from the soggy ruins of Old Detroit, the DFZ has been a city where anything is possible. A city of freedom where people can be as horrible or as wonderful as they wish with no authority standing in their way. It's a place where everyone's an outsider, anyone can start afresh, and nothing can be taken for granted. *That* is the DFZ. She's not an easy god to love, but you must understand her at least a little, because you're both still here."

I didn't know about that. I'd come to the DFZ because it was across the ocean and because my father hated it. He thought it was a callous, dirty pit that humanity had dug for itself and deserved to wallow in. Honestly, when I'd first moved here, I'd agreed. I knew I was moving into hell; I'd just preferred this hell to the one I'd left back home. Now, three and a half years in, I still didn't think my father was wrong, but I understood the nuances better. The DFZ *was* cruel and chaotic, but there were times when it was wonderful, too. That wasn't enough to make me worship her as Nameless did, but I finally felt like I understood what the Gnarls were. They were the DFZ in her purest form, and if that was the case, then I knew how to survive here.

"Okay," I said, looking at Nik. "Ready?"

"I've been ready for the last five minutes," he said irritably. "I just don't know how to get out of here." He nodded at Nameless. "You seem friendly with the talcum-powder priest. Ask how we get to the Gnarls."

"Actually, you're already there," Nameless said while I sputtered. "The Gnarls are why the Wandering Cathedral wanders. If you want to reach them, just turn around and walk out. The ticket you bought is good for one round trip, so don't lose it, or you'll never come back."

"Good to know," Nik said, putting his ticket in his jeans pocket as he walked back to the door. "Opal?"

Shoving my ticket into my pocket as well, I hurried after him. "Thank you for your help!"

"Just doing my job," Nameless said, leaning back on their couch. "But do feel free to leave a tip on your way out if you enjoyed the service."

I was *definitely* going to tip big the moment I got money. This had been very educational. "Helpful" was still up in the air, but at least I no longer felt like I was flying blind as I followed Nik out the door and into an absolutely wild world.

CHAPTER 12

I was wrong. I was *not* prepared for the Gnarls. I shrieked the moment I stepped through the door, grabbing on to Nik as if my life depended on it. Which it did, because we were *upside down.*

Thank God Nik had faster reactions than I did. He took one look at the swirling abyss we were falling into and grabbed the wall, anchoring us in place as the floor became the ceiling and my feet lost contact with the ground. I flipped twice before he yanked me back onto something firm. When I finally pried my eyes open again, I was standing on the arch at the top of the cathedral's doorway, staring out into the strangest landscape I'd ever seen.

The only word I could think of to describe it was "suspended." We were standing at the entrance of the Wandering Cathedral, which was floating in the space between two terrifying extremes. Below us, in the place I'd thought of as "up" when I'd stepped out of the cathedral, was the terrifying abyss Nik had saved me from falling into. Above us, off the steps of the upside-down cathedral, were the roots of the city itself.

"Wow," I whispered, clutching even more tightly onto Nik's coat.

The bottom of the DFZ was suspended above us like a chandelier. From this angle, there was no dirt at all. I could see every pipe and tunnel and basement in the city all tangled together like the roots of a tree or the wires of a machine. It was hard to say which it resembled more closely, because the city above us was both: manufactured and organic, inanimate and animate, dead and alive. It was cement that moved like water and trees that stood firm as anchors. Both seemed equally important, because the bottom of the city above us was moving quite a lot, pivoting around the solid points like muscles around a joint. Just in the time I stood there gawking, I saw two roads and a support beam slide beneath a building to push it up, adding a few floors to the bottom. At the same time, the foundations of Highway 94 wiggled a bit to the left, adjusting a hard curve ever so slightly wider while the buildings on either side leaned away to make room.

"Wow!" I said again, my face breaking into an awestruck grin. "Look at that! It's like we're in the DFZ's backstage."

"Yes, yes, it's very impressive," Nik said quickly. "But how do we get *down*?"

Considering "down" was an endless abyss, that struck me as a funny question, but we had to go somewhere. The cathedral we were clinging to was basically an asteroid slowly revolving through the emptiness between two worlds. Not exactly a great starting spot for a search.

"What does your hand say?"

Nik scowled at his right-left hand, which I'd only just now realized was still resting on my waist from when he'd grabbed me earlier. I was no longer in danger of falling, but he didn't seem to be in a hurry to move it, tapping his fingers softly against my bunched-up poncho as he considered my question.

"It's actually calmed down a lot since we got in here," he said at last, leaning out slowly to get a better look at the nothing below us. "It's not jumping around anymore. It's just pointing down."

Down was *not* a direction I wanted to go. "Great," I moaned. "Dr. Lyle dropped his spell into the abyss."

"It's not all abyss," Nik said, leaning further over the edge. "Look."

I did not want to look. I wasn't normally afraid of heights, but clinging to a cathedral floating above an endless void was definitely extenuating circumstances. Now that I was no longer jacked up on the fear of plummeting to my death, I could feel the magic rising out of the void in waves. It was as thick as cement and stronger than anything I'd ever felt on the surface. The only thing I could compare it to was dragon fire, and I'd only had the misfortune of feeling that once. But that fire had been brief and directed. This magic was everywhere at once, a waterfall of power pouring up from the abyss toward the city. Even with the cathedral blocking some of it, the power of the magic roaring by was enough to rattle my soul inside my body like a nut in its shell, and Nik wanted me to stick my head over the edge?

Just the thought made my stomach lurch. If I hadn't paid so dearly for them, I would have vomited up every pancake I'd eaten. But I had, so I didn't, gallantly keeping my breakfast down as I took off my goggles and held them out over the edge to see what Nik was talking about.

Even secondhand through my cameras, the void was all I could see at first. There was just so *much* of it, an endless swirling darkness that was bigger than the sky. Bigger than anything I'd ever seen. Just trying to fit it all in my head made me feel like something was going to break, so I stopped attempting and focused instead on finding something that *wasn't* boundless nothing.

That went much better. It took a while, but once I started ignoring the void, other things began to take shape, and I realized that Nik was right. There *was* stuff down there: roads and bridges, buildings, city parks with playgrounds in them. Whole portions of the DFZ were floating in the space between the city and the abyss like lost puzzle pieces. They looked like independent islands, free-floating objects similar to the cathedral we were clinging to. The longer I stared, though, the more I realized that wasn't entirely true. There was a cloud of smaller debris connecting the larger masses, a root-like network of old pipes and steel rebar that formed a definite, if very twisty, path.

"I see why it's called the Gnarls now," I said, returning my goggles to the top of my head. "Think we can get down there?"

"We'll have to," Nik said, releasing his grip on my waist at last to point his right-left hand at a particularly dense cluster of discarded landmasses. "It's that way."

"You sure?"

"*I* have no idea, but the hand is absolutely positive. The thing we're looking for is two point three kilometers in that direction."

I gave him a puzzled look. "Breaking out the metric now?"

"It's not my fault," he said angrily, shaking Dr. Lyle's hand. "It's this stupid thing. It wants me to be precise, and it thinks metric is the superior system."

"Well, to be fair, it is," I agreed. "But I thought that hand didn't have an interface you could communicate with?"

"So did I," Nik growled. "But apparently it doesn't need words to make its opinion known now that we're used to each other."

I couldn't help myself. "So you're saying you can *talk to the hand?*"

The look Nik gave me then was absolutely scalding, but I didn't regret a thing. No matter how serious the situation, a good pun is never a waste. It certainly cheered me up, which was good, because I'd been clinging to Nik like a wet napkin this whole time. If we were going to make any distance, much less 2.3 kilometers, I needed to get myself together.

"Okay," I said, releasing my death grip on Nik's jacket. "Let's do this."

It took almost half an hour to figure out how we were going to get down. To my enormous surprise, Sibyl's signal wasn't bad down here. In hindsight, it made sense that wireless internet would be part of the DFZ's heart—she was a modern city, after all—but it didn't actually help our situation. I found plenty of guides online, but they all turned out to be useless since the Gnarls were apparently different every time you went in.

That wasn't too out there considering we were inside the magical heart of the god of an ever-moving city, but it meant there was no easy solution to our current predicament. After a bit of watching, though, we noticed that the Wandering Cathedral had its own path through the chaos, almost like an orbit. It wasn't much, but with Sibyl's ability to keep track of multiple relative positions and a lot of patience, I was able to chart a course.

After that, it was just a matter of waiting for the right moment. We spent the time climbing down (or up) the cathedral's ornate face to the bell tower, which was much closer to the floating islands below (above) us.

We sat there for a while, watching the islands moving like clouds above the void. Then, when one of the biggest pieces of disconnected highway was directly below us, we jumped, falling together through the chaos.

Much, much later than I'd anticipated, we landed on the pavement. I didn't actually break my leg, but from the horrifying crunch my knee made, it was a near thing.

"*Ow,*" I groaned, sinking to the ground. "That was a lot farther than I thought."

"I just hope we can get back," Nik said, holding out his actual left hand, the one that wasn't cybernetic, to help me up. "Jumping's a lot harder than falling."

"We'll cross that bridge when we get there," I said, hauling myself to my feet. "Now, which way do we go?"

Nik pointed to his right without hesitation, and we set off, walking down the stretch of floating highway as though it were a normal road, not a slowly rotating plane of asphalt hanging in air over an abyss that was pouring itself up toward the city like an upside-down magical version of Victoria Falls.

"You know," I said, staring at the void that was now above us again thanks to relative orientation, "when they said the Gnarls were the overlap between the DFZ's physical and magical domains, I didn't think the truth would be quite so literal. I'm pretty sure that's the *actual* Sea of Magic above our heads. As in the realm of spirits, source of all magic, and the place our souls go when we die."

"I don't want to think about dying right now," Nik replied, keeping his eyes firmly on the asphalt. "I just want to get what we're here for and get out of this madhouse."

"I wonder what would happen if we fell into it," I went on. "I've always heard that humans can't take the other side. The magic is too intense, so our souls get ripped to shreds. We're still technically inside the DFZ, though, so do you think we can actually fall out? Like, is there a bottom we're not seeing, or would we just plummet endlessly until the magic dissolved our—"

"*Opal*," Nik said sharply, his face pale and tight. "Not helping."

I apologized at once, but the questions stuck with me. It wasn't every day you found yourself face to face with the literal Great Beyond. The Sea of Magic was where all the magic in the world originated and eventually returned to, including the magic inside of us. The soul of every person who'd ever died was somewhere in that darkness. Staring at it, I was glad that Peter had committed Dr. Lyle to the Empty Wind. Spending the rest of eternity tumbling with other forgotten souls on a grave-cold wind didn't exactly sound like a party, but what did I know? I'd never been dead. At least he had someone who cared watching over him. That had to be better than falling into that void alone.

True to their name, the Gnarls were incredibly confusing. Everything was always spinning, and the connecting lines of pipes and cement never seemed to lead where you thought they would. Even with Nik's unerring sense of direction, we had to backtrack a lot, a frustrating complication that was only made worse by Nik's habit of constantly looking over his shoulder.

"Would you *stop*?" I pleaded, pointing at the broken archipelago of spinning oak trees we were currently trying to navigate through. "This is complicated enough without you constantly throwing off my sense of which direction is forward."

"Sorry," he said, rubbing the back of his neck. "It's just…"

"Just what?"

"Nothing," he said with a sigh. "This place messes with me is all. I keep getting the feeling that we're being followed."

He said that like he was embarrassed about it, but I'd always trusted my instincts, and Nik had saved my bacon enough times recently that I was developing a near-religious faith in his. If he said someone was following us, I absolutely believed it. When I turned to search, though, all I saw was the empty corkscrew of pipes and wires we'd followed to get here.

Scowling, I pulled my goggles down from my head. "Sibyl—"

"Don't ask me," my AI grumbled as my augmented-reality filled with error icons. "This place is a nightmare. I've still got internet somehow, but there's no GPS, and the magic's so thick it's messing with my electronics. I feel like one giant glitch."

"Sorry," I said automatically, walking back to the last bend we'd turned. "But this isn't complicated. I just need you to play back the last few minutes of footage from my rear cameras. Anything you've got will be—"

I stopped. I couldn't say what had set it off, but I had that prickly feeling on the back of my neck again, the one that meant I was being watched. It was the same feeling I'd had yesterday, the one that had come seconds before my anti-bullet ward had caught the shot aimed at my head.

That was enough for me. I hit the deck without thinking twice, diving face first into the piebald grass of the small patch of park we'd been walking through. Above me, I heard Nik curse and draw his gun, which would have been a good move if we'd been looking in the right direction. But we weren't. Our eyes were level with the chunk of grassy field we'd been walking across, but the threat came from above—something we discovered the hard way when it landed right on top of us.

"*Oof,*" I grunted as something heavy and wearing boots landed on my back. Nik's sound of surprise was a lot more profane as he was knocked to the ground beside me, gun wrenched out of his hand by a very large man in the distinctive black body armor of a professional mercenary. I had no idea which company the small logo on his arm was for—I only paid attention to body armor when I was trying to resell it—but I recognized a pro when he was shoving my face into the dirt. Considering we had bounties on our heads, the fact that we'd been jumped by mercs wasn't actually what surprised me. *My* big question was how had they found us *here?* Fortunately—or unfortunately, as it turned out—I didn't have to be curious for long.

"Well, well, Mr. Kos," said a familiar voice. "You *certainly* lived up to your reputation this time."

I groaned, grinding my face into the grass. Of course. *Of course.* Who else could it be? I didn't even know why I'd bothered to wonder as I craned my neck back to see Kauffman standing on a chunk of floating cement above us. The only thing I still didn't understand was "How?"

Kauffman reached into his pocket and pulled out a plastic baggie holding a tissue stained a dull, coppery red. "You should be more careful where you bleed, Miss Yong-ae," he said, his normally dazzling smile spreading into something much more sinister. "You did a good job burning off your material links, but it's all for nothing if you're going to drip bits of yourself all over the Heights." He tsked at me. "Absolutely amateur."

The truth of those words burned like a hot poker in my gut. How could I have been so stupid? I'd been bleeding like a faucet after I'd blasted that scaffolding last night. Of course I'd dripped something on the ground, which meant I'd basically handed Kauffman a leash and invited him to yank it. Blood was the strongest of all material links. You could trace a person from anywhere in the world with it, including, apparently, through the Gnarls. That wasn't the only way Kauffman had outmaged me, either. While he was gloating, I noticed that the floating cement chunk he was standing on was covered in spellworked circles.

Now I *really* felt like an idiot. Kauffman and his hired muscle hadn't just floated over our heads by accident. He'd used spellwork to catch the magic that was roaring up from the void and tie it to the rock he was standing on. No wonder he'd been able to catch up with us! He'd turned that hunk of cement into his own private sailboat. While we'd been wandering the Gnarls, he'd been flying wherever he liked, riding the constant roar of magic like a sailor at sea.

If it hadn't screwed us so epically, I would have been impressed by his inventiveness, but I mostly just wished I'd thought of it first. Now we were sunk, stuck on our stomachs with four mercs on our backs and Kauffman floating over us smirking like he was the Spirit of Bad Winners.

"I don't suppose the offer to buy us out is still on the table?" Nik asked, turning his face against the boot the merc on top of him was pressing into his cheek.

Kauffman shook his head. "I'm afraid that ship has sailed, old friend. The only deal I can offer you now is the chance to get out of this alive. Now." His eyes flicked to me. "Let me speak to Dr. Lyle."

Nik and I shared a confused look. "What?"

"Let me speak to Dr. Lyle," Kauffman repeated, his voice growing frustrated. "I *know* you have to be in communication with him, because it's the only way you can know where you're going. Coordinates don't work in this place. The only way to find a fixed point down here is with a beacon spell, and that's tied to Dr. Lyle's magic. I know this because he showed me how he was planning to do it right before he bolted with our employer's investment, so stop playing stupid and let me talk to him. If he agrees to guide me to the ritual location, we'll have no more reason to quarrel. I'll tell my men to stop hunting for his safe house, our employer will recoup his investment, and you get to avoid having a bullet put through your skull. Everybody gets what they want. Now hand him over."

He ended with a deadly glare at me, but all I could do was gape. *My god*, I thought, *he still doesn't know*. Kauffman had only come after me when his goons had seen me Cleaning Dr. Lyle's robbed house, but he'd never found out about the first apartment. I'd thought for sure he must have figured it out by now, but apparently he hadn't done much digging into my past, because he still didn't know Dr. Lyle was dead. He thought the poor man was still cowering in his basement safe house, guiding us by remote.

I snapped my mouth shut, holding Kauffman's eyes as I scrambled to think this through. I couldn't do as Kauffman wanted because Dr. Lyle was dead. If I told him that, though, it would only take a few educated guesses for him to figure out Nik was using Dr. Lyle's hand. Once he knew that, he'd just take it for himself. We'd already done the hard work of cracking the security, and while Kauffman probably didn't have any cybernetics as a mage, one of his mercs almost certainly did. He'd take everything if I let him, but unlike Nik, I wasn't in this for the big score. I just needed enough money to pay my dad, which meant I had room to bluff.

"How about this?" I said, giving Kauffman a sweet smile from under the merc's boot. "Dr. Lyle is never going to tell you where he hid his ritual because he hates you, but if you get your guys off us, I will. Let Nik and me go, and we'll guide you straight to the ritual site, where we'll split what we find fifty-fifty. That way everyone gets a piece, and no one has to get nasty. Deal?"

"*No* deal!" Nik yelled, shooting me a furious look. "Don't offer him my money!"

"Why would I split anything with you?" Kauffman said at the same time. "I have all the power, and that ritual was financed by my employer, which means everything it created belongs to us. You had your chance to cash out, but you threw it away. Your window for negotiation ended yesterday. The only options left to you now are my way…or that way."

He pointed over the edge of his rock down at the swirling abyss, and my stomach curled into a knot. Before I could think of another angle, though, Nik spoke over me.

"So what you're saying is it's all or nothing."

"You get to keep your lives," Kauffman said with a shrug. "That's not nothing. But if you keep trying to stall, I'm not above killing someone to speed things along. Probably you, since if Theo Lyle was going to entrust a stranger with his life's work, he'd be far more likely to pick the pretty mage." He smiled at Nik. "Nothing personal, Nikola. Just business. You know how it is."

The look Nik gave him then made me sink into the ground. I'd seen him get angry plenty of times now, mostly at me, but I'd never see him look like that.

"I do know," Nik said in a voice so cold even Kauffman flinched. "Glad we have an understanding."

"Yes," Kauffman said, reaching up to wipe away the drop of sweat sliding down his temple. "But this can all be avoided if you'll just—"

He never got to finish. He'd barely started talking when Nik ripped his right arm out from under the mercenary's metal-toed boot and swung it up, rotating his shoulder an inhuman ninety degrees in its socket to shoot the man holding him.

Since Nik's gun was still on the grass beside him, I didn't see how that was possible. Then I saw Dr. Lyle's hand hit the dirt, and I understood. Nik had a secret gun *inside* his false arm. He'd ejected Dr. Lyle's hand so he wouldn't destroy it, and then he'd shot the man holding him down by surprise.

I could still see the wisp of smoke rising from the stump of his wrist as the merc fell sideways, screaming and clutching his shoulder, which was bleeding from the bottom where Nik had nailed him in the armpit, threading the needle through the tiny gap where the chest and the arm portions of his body armor came together. It was a perfect shot, one I couldn't have made if I'd had an hour to aim, let alone in a snap shot from the ground while I was trapped on my stomach. I was still marveling at it when Nik kicked straight up off the ground like it was nothing to plant his boot in the second guard's knee, dislocating the joint with a sickening *pop*.

Again, it was perfect. He'd done the whole thing in one lightning-fast motion, ending up on his feet before either of the men who'd been holding him could hit the ground. I'd never seen anyone move that fast aside from my father, but Nik was no dragon. He was worse. The Dragon of Korea fought with dignity and grace, always giving his opponents at least the pretense of a chance. Nik didn't even give the guard on my back time to gasp before he launched forward and punched him in the throat, sliding his left hand deftly between the man's helmet and chestplate to nail him in the windpipe.

The weight on my back vanished as the merc holding me down flew backward. To my left, the man who'd had his gun pointed at my face snatched it up in an effort to catch Nik. He must have been wired something fierce, because he almost managed to get a shot off before Nik slammed the stump of his cybernetic arm into the merc's clear plexiglass faceplate, crushing it into the man's nose.

By this point, I was shaking all over from a cocktail of emotions. Fear was there, definitely, and triumph, but what I felt most was awe. I'd known Nik was good, but I'd had no idea he was *that* good. What I'd witnessed went way beyond street-tough Cleaner. I didn't even have words for the way Nik moved. "Beauty" almost fit, as did "grace." But those words were too clean, too nice for the savage, tyrannical efficiency of the way he continued the punch past its natural end, slamming the man into the ground beside me with so much force that the whole floating island tilted.

But even that wasn't enough. When the last merc dropped his gun, Nik snatched it off the ground with his remaining left hand and fired, planting a bullet in the mercenary's dominant hand before he could even get it to his bleeding face. He did the others next, turning and shooting the soldiers-for-hire in the hands they'd used to hold their guns so they couldn't pick them back up again. He'd just finished the last one when something fell over me.

It felt like an avalanche. We'd been in the Gnarls for a while now, and while my body would never get used to the constant pounding magic here, it had stopped taking up all of my attention. Watching Nik during the fight, I'd been too awestruck to even think about it. A stupid blunder, in hindsight, because there was one enemy Nik's perfect storm of violence couldn't reach, and his magic grabbed me like a giant hand, yanking me off the ground and ten feet straight up, where Kauffman was waiting with a gun of his own.

"Stop," he ordered, shoving the short pistol's steel barrel into the hollow below my chin. "Now."

The words cut through the violence like knives, and Nik stopped, kicking the groaning merc at his feet one last time before craning his head back to glare at Kauffman.

"You don't want to play this game with me," he said quietly, slinging the blood off his fingers. "Let her go."

"I'm not the one playing," Kauffman snarled back, grimacing at the soldiers Nik had so efficiently taken out. "It seems the rumors were wrong. You haven't gone soft at all, have you, Mad Dog?"

"Don't call me that," Nik snarled. "And your hired muscle is still alive. I'd say that's pretty soft."

"Maybe by your standards," Kauffman said, his gun shaking against my skin. "But you're not the only one after a big score."

His eyes flicked down to Dr. Lyle's hand on the ground. Nik's did, too, and his body tensed. For the first time, though, he wasn't fast enough. I barely had time to recognize the suffocating feel of Kauffman's magic before it reached out and crushed the hand on the ground, breaking it into a million pieces.

"*No!*" I screamed, lurching against his hold.

Kauffman yanked me right back. "The next one will be your head," he said, keeping his gun on me while his eyes watched Nik, who was staring at the destroyed hand as if he couldn't believe what had just happened. "Are you listening to me? Let me talk to Dr. Lyle *now*."

"You idiot!" I yelled, kicking him in the shins as hard as I could. "That *was* Dr. Lyle!"

He dug the pistol harder into the underside of my jaw. "Shut. Up," he growled. "I have more riding on this job than you can possibly know."

"Then you should have paid more attention to current events," Nik said furiously. "Your doctor is dead. We've been following what's left of his location spell, which was inside the hand *you* just destroyed!"

I felt Kauffman's body stiffen, and then he squeezed my neck so hard he almost choked me out. "You're lying!"

"When have I ever needed to lie to you?" Nik demanded, crossing his arms over his chest. "You just played yourself, jackass! Now we're all screwed!"

"We'll see about that," Kauffman said, his voice taking on a final, lethal-sounding edge. "I'm not going to be led around by the two of you again." I felt the gun click as Kauffman tightened his finger on the trigger. "Even you're not fast enough to beat a bullet," he growled at Nik. "So if you care about the well-being of your new partner in petty crime, you're going to drop the act and take me to Dr. Lyle's ritual site. You have five seconds."

Nik's jaw tightened. Mine did, too, but not for the same reason. He looked frustrated and scared, but I was *furious*. Furious at these idiots for attacking us. Furious at Kauffman for destroying my only shot at getting free of my dad. Furious at this whole stupid situation.

Most of all, though, I was furious at myself. I'd been doing nothing but screw up since yesterday when Nik had had to save me from getting shot. I'd lost all my money, been played by my dad, and sacrificed my very last penny only to lose it all because Kauffman was too stupid to know when a bluff wasn't a bluff. Now he was *princessing* me to get back the very thing he'd just destroyed, and I couldn't do anything about it. I was the weakest link in this whole fiasco, the reason Kauffman had found us in the first place. I hadn't felt this powerless since I'd left my father's house. Unlike back then, though, I was free to do something about it here. The only question was what.

Even shaking with rage, I wasn't stupid. Kauffman had a gun, and he was hands down the better mage. Now that I was inside his circles, I could feel why he'd yet to leave his floating rock. In addition to the inherent advantage of height, he'd ringed this thing with a fortress's worth of wards. Even if Nik decided I wasn't worth the trouble and shot at him, the bullets would never get through. So long as he stayed inside his circles, Kauffman could probably take a missile to the face and come out okay. But though he'd outmaneuvered, outgunned, and outmaged me in every possible way, there was still one place where I was still champion. One thing *no one* could beat me at.

I could outcrazy anybody.

"Opal," Sibyl whispered in my ear. "Opal, *don't!*"

Opal did.

With zero concern for my body or the gun pushing into it, I threw myself forward and reached with everything I had, diving into the roaring magic like I was diving off a cliff. The resulting shock of power nearly fried me on the spot. If I'd been trying to channel it or grab it or any of the things mages normally did, it would have, but I wasn't. I'd given up even the pretense of proper magic. I had no circle, no spellwork, no careful logical system to bend the magic to my will. All I cared about was volume, so I turned my soul into a conduit, letting the magic flow through my soul as fast as it liked into the carefully constructed circles Kauffman had been stupid enough to bring me inside.

As it happened, my only regret was that, due to the way I'd lunged forward, I couldn't see Kauffman's face anymore. I would have given anything to see his expression as the uncontrolled magic crashed into his circles like a fire hose into a teacup. If they'd been my circles, they would have popped instantly, but Kauffman was a legitimately skilled mage. His finely wrought chain of interwoven circles lasted a good five seconds before the whole thing blew apart, sending out a shockwave that set every island in the Gnarls spinning.

Including the one we were standing on.

Reeling from the backlash, I dropped to the ground, clinging to the rough cement as the rock Kauffman had made into his battle station whirled like a top. Normally, that would have been enough to make me lose my pancakes, but what was going on inside me hurt so much I didn't have space for anything else. I'd *never* had that much power through me before. It had only been a few seconds, but my magic still felt like a snapped rubber band. I hadn't known it was possible to hurt in so many ways. From the darkness dripping into my eyes and the distant clamor of Sibyl screaming into my ears, I knew I had to be bleeding bad, but that felt like the least of my worries at the moment. I'd deal with the blood loss later, if there was a later. Right now, it was taking everything I had to keep myself together. Not my body, but what lived inside it.

It was funny. I'd been aware of magic for all of my life that I could remember. Most mages didn't come into their power until nine or ten, but my parents had been determined to breed a prodigy. They'd packed me full of the best genetics and hired a fleet of experts to train me in how to recognize and grasp magic before I could speak. I hadn't been able to actually cast anything until I was six, but there wasn't a time in my life when the power hadn't been there. Until this moment, though, when it was closer than ever to sputtering out, I'd never realized that the power I could feel constantly inside my head wasn't just part of being a mage. It was *me*. My magic, my soul.

That should have made me feel even worse about being so bad at using it, but I was too drained to work up the usual bitterness. All I felt was relief that it was still there, flickering inside me. I was cupping my mental hands around it to keep it safe when another pair of hands—real, crushing ones—grabbed me by the shoulders.

Even dulled, the pain was enough to knock me out of my stupor. Groggy and reeling, I got my head up just in time to see Kauffman. He was as bloody as I was. His handsome face was a mess, and his whole body was heaving with the aftershocks of the backlash I'd brought down on us both. But even though he had to be as out of it as I was, there was hatred burning in his bloodshot eyes—real, killing fury that had nothing to do with the business he was always going on about.

"Go to hell," he whispered, the words coming out in a spray of blood and spittle as he shoved me with all his might, sending me sliding off the still-spinning rock and into the void beyond.

CHAPTER 13

I fell like a stone.

There was magic rushing past me, but I couldn't grab it. My soul was too weak, too battered to reach out.

"This is why I told you not to do it!" Sibyl screamed in my ear. "You *idiot*! It's not winning if you blow yourself up too!"

She was probably right, but I was having a hard time regretting it. It had felt good to backlash Kauffman, to *finally* hit back at even one of the things that was constantly shoving me down. I was powerless against my father, no more respected than the little yapping dog he was always comparing me to, but for five seconds there, I'd been a nuclear weapon. A true force to be reckoned with.

Too bad it was probably going to cost me my life.

"There's no 'probably' about it!" Sibyl yelled as the backstage view of the bottom of the DFZ grew smaller and smaller above us. "You are going to fall into the abyss if you don't do. Something. *Now!*"

For all that she was an AI, Sibyl's voice programming had always been top notch at conveying emotion. Her design team had won all kinds of awards for it, which was the big reason I'd purchased her over the more practical virtual assistants. I'd liked that she'd sounded alive, like a real guardian angel sitting on my shoulder. Listening to her now, I could almost forget that her concern was part of a learning algorithm designed to make her more sensitive to my needs. All I heard was the fear, the terror and sadness over what was about to happen. Happen to *me*.

That was finally enough to snap me out of my backlashed stupor. I came to with a gasp, my whole body going rigid as my physical state finally caught up with my mental one and realized what was happening. I was falling. Falling to my *death* if I didn't take Sibyl's advice and do something.

Unfortunately, there wasn't much for me to do. I was well below any of the islands, and I couldn't even see Nik or Kauffman anymore. My poor abused magic was as useless as a broken limb. I couldn't even flex it, let alone reach out and grab something. That should have been cause for panic, but I was too busy to care right now, so I shoved it down and moved on to my next option, which was flipping myself around.

Folding my arms and legs tight against my body, I rolled in midair, flipping my body to look down rather than up. I was hoping that there were more floating islands down here that I hadn't been able to see from above. If I could catch one, I could break my fall. Or my arm, but that was still a step up. But while the plan was good, the reality was very much not, because the moment I rolled over, I came face to face with the void.

It was a lot scarier when you were falling into it. There was no cathedral holding me up anymore, no islands or paths. Just yawning blackness so dark and vast, the only way I knew my eyes were open was because of the wind that was stinging them. There was nothing to cling to, nothing to catch. Just the dark and the cold, hard understanding that I was going to die. I was going to *die.*

I did start to panic then. Truly panic like I never had before in my life. I was vaguely aware of Sibyl saying something soothing and reasonable in my ear, but I was past processing words. The animal part of my brain had taken over, leaving me clawing the air as I fell and fell and *fell* into magic that got thicker and thicker and *thicker.*

The light vanished. I stopped being able to see my body. The magic was starting to move now, swirling around me in eddies that quickly grew into crashing waves that were big enough to throw me around. The power was thick as water now, making me feel more like I was sinking than falling, but I still didn't stop. I just kept going deeper and deeper, farther and farther. And then, just as the pressure started to crush me, something brushed my face.

It was a wind. A grave-cold wind that came from everywhere and nowhere, tossing me up like a leaf on a gale. I was still spinning when it swallowed me whole, replacing the endless dark with something else entirely.

***

The next thing I knew, I was in a bedroom.

I had no idea how I'd gotten there, if I'd died or passed out or hallucinated the whole thing, but I definitely recognized the place. It was the bedroom in Dr. Lyle's basement apartment. The one where I'd found his body.

"Hello."

I jumped a foot in the air, whirling around with my fists up. To do what, I had no idea. I've never thrown a punch in my life, and my magic was thoroughly useless. It must have looked threatening, though, because the man behind me jumped as well, putting up his own hands—or rather, *hand*—in self-defense.

"Stop! It's me!"

I blinked. "Me who?" Because I was certain I'd never seen this man in my life. He looked stereotypically professorial—fifties to sixties, bushy graying beard, slight pot belly, button-up shirt and khaki Bermuda shorts. The only thing he was missing was a pair of horn-rimmed glasses. That and his left hand, which was gone at the wrist, and I let out a long breath.

"You're Dr. Lyle."

It wasn't a question, but the man nodded anyway, head bobbing excitedly.

The blood drained from my face as the implications of that sank in. "Oh god," I said, dropping to the bed. "Am I dead?"

"I certainly hope not," Dr. Lyle said briskly. "If you are, then I just stuck my neck out for nothing. You wouldn't believe what I had to do to convince the Empty Wind to save you."

That explained the cold wind that had caught me. Even so. "Why did you save me?"

"For the same reason I gave you my hand," he said, showing me the stump. "You're the only one who can save my babies."

I blinked. "Babies?"

"My work," he clarified, looking at me very intently. "You have to understand, I didn't know what Kauffman was going to do. I only took his money because I thought he was a fellow alchemy enthusiast and because no one else would give me funding. When I found out what he really wanted, I grabbed all my notes and ran. I'd already cast the ritual, but this kind of power takes weeks to build, and I was the only one with the location spell. I thought it would be a simple matter of hiding in my storage apartment and waiting it out, but then…"

His rapid-fire speech gave out, and I sighed. "But then you died."

He nodded sadly, looking around at his windowless bedroom, which looked exactly as it had when I'd found it, minus the dust and the death. "I woke up here. This little room is all that's left of my life, and the only reason I have this much is because of you. Even if it was just for profit, you looked through my life. You remembered me. That's why I stuck my neck out to save you. You're the only one who can save my legacy now. If Kauffman gets it, I'll have done the greatest evil a man can. You have to stop him."

"Already done that," I said smugly, lifting my arm to flex my muscle. "I fried him good."

"So I heard," Dr. Lyle said. "But he wouldn't be much of a combat mage if he couldn't recover from a backlash, and he won't stop until he wins. He made a lot of promises when he found me, and our employer isn't the forgiving type. He'll spend his whole fortune to bribe your partner if he has to. You're the only one I can trust to stop him."

"But why me?" I asked. "I'm in this for the money too."

"No, you're not," Dr. Lyle said, looking at me as if I was being very silly. "If you were in this for *money*, you would have taken Kauffman's first buyout. You wouldn't have kept going after they shot at you or blown yourself up just to spite Kauffman. Money's worthless if you're dead, and yet you keep risking your life over and over, being more and more reckless. That's how I knew money wasn't the point in your case. It's just a tool to get what you *really* want."

That was a lot more information about me than I was comfortable with a dead guy I'd never technically met knowing. "And what do you think I want?"

He smiled. "Freedom."

I shook my head in wonder. "How do you know all this?"

"Because you've had a piece of me," Dr. Lyle said, lifting up his stump. "Granted, I spent the majority of my time in a box while that terrifying woman was hacking my security, but the bits I did see told me plenty. Keeping the connection open put a huge strain on what's left of my soul, but it was worth it, because if I hadn't gone so far, I wouldn't know you, and I wouldn't have been able to use that information to save you. Your defiance of your father and determination to keep your free life in the city is what convinced the DFZ to let us in, by the way. She doesn't normally let the Empty Wind interfere with her domain. Spirits are *very* territorial. But we convinced her to make an exception."

"You convinced a *god?*" I said, shocked. "For *me?*"

"No, I did it for me," he said. "Don't get me wrong, you seem like a very nice girl, but I'm not risking my immortal soul for someone I've never met. I'm doing it because you're one of the few people left who knows who I am. And of those few, you're the *only* one with the skills and mindset necessary to save my life's work. *That* I would gladly die for as many times as it takes." He grinned at me. "Just as money is your tool, you are mine. I didn't get much choice in the matter, but now that I have you, I'll risk everything I have left to enable you to achieve victory, including saving you from the void. In return, though, you must *promise* you'll save my work."

"I promise, I promise," I said quickly. "If you get me back to the world of the living, I swear I'll save whatever you want. But..." I stopped, dragging my hands over my bloody face. "I *need* that money," I said at last.

"I want to help you, and I'm definitely down with keeping everything from Kauffman, but if I don't get at least ten grand, I go back to my dad *tonight*."

"I'll leave that up to you," he said. "So long as it doesn't go to Kauffman, I trust you to do the right thing."

I narrowed my eyes. That sounded suspiciously blasé from a man who'd put his soul on the line to save his work. "What do you mean you trust me? You don't even know me. How do you know I won't be as bad as Kauffman?"

"I don't," he admitted. "But that's a gamble I have to take. I'm dead. I can't do things for myself anymore. You're the only tool I have, so you're what I'll use. But I like to think I've learned a little about you through all of this, Opal Yong-ae. I'm sure that when you see the product of my labors, you'll feel the same way about it as I do."

Now I was *super* suspicious. "We *are* still talking about cockatrice eggs, right?" Because to hear him talk, you'd think this was a ritual to find the true meaning of friendship.

"You saw my spell notes," he said proudly as a breeze ruffled his thinning hair. "And I'll have you know everything worked perfectly on the first try. Better than perfect! But you'll see for yourself soon enough. We've been talking for too long already. It's time for you to go."

It must have been. The breeze that had ruffled his hair turned into a torrent as he spoke. Other than tousling his hair, it didn't seem to touch Dr. Lyle, but it was blowing me so hard I had to fight to stay upright.

"Wait!" I yelled as the wind lifted me off my feet. "How do I find it? Your hand got broken!"

"The same way you found me!" he yelled back. "Follow the wind!"

That sounded like some Pocahontas nonsense, but before I could say as much, the wind blew me away, sweeping me out of the room, through the dark, and up, up, up into the air. I was still flipping over when my back crashed into something solid, knocking the breath right out of me.

I opened my eyes with a gasp. I was lying on my back in the grass. Above me, the bottom of the DFZ hung like a galactic battleship while islands of disconnected city bits floated beneath it like clouds. I was staring at it in shock, wondering how I'd gotten here, when I heard Nik's voice.

"*Opal!*"

I'd barely managed to lift my head before he grabbed me off the ground and yanked me into his arms. "*I thought you were dead!*"

I pretty much had been. Before I could tell him what had happened, though, he hugged me tighter, burying his face in the crook of my neck as if he was trying to get as close as possible.

I jolted, eyes flying wide. I'd never been this close to Nik before, let alone seen him show affection. To be honest, it was a little alarming, but it was also nice. *Very* nice. It had been a long time since I'd been hugged, and Nik was surprisingly good at it. You would have thought being hugged by someone with that much metal in his body would have been uncomfortable, but he just felt solid and warm, like a sun-baked rock. That plus the feeling of his ragged breaths against my shoulder was deeply comforting in a primal, proof-of-being-alive sort of way, and the longer it lasted, the more I liked it. I was about to try lowering my head to his shoulder to see if I could hear his heart beating through all the plates when Nik suddenly jumped away.

"Sorry," he said quickly, putting a good two feet between us. "I didn't intend, that is…" He dropped his eyes, running his hands through his short-cropped black hair. "I'm sorry. That was out of line."

"You're gonna be sorry," Sibyl muttered.

"It's fine," I said quickly, turning down my AI's volume. "We all had a traumatic experience. I'm just happy you're okay."

Nik's head snapped up. "Happy *I'm* okay? You fell into the void!"

There was a raw edge on his voice that made me cringe. I wasn't used to thinking of Nik as a sensitive person, but I'd clearly scared him something fierce.

"I thought you were gone forever," he continued. "But then you just fell out of the sky behind me. It was like you'd gone in a loop!" He glared at me hard. "What happened? How did you get back?"

"I'm not entirely sure," I said, looking up at the city floating above us. "I fell for a long time. I'm pretty sure I did almost die, but then the Empty Wind saved me."

He gave me an incredulous look. "A *death* god saved your life?"

I nodded, which was a bit of a cop-out. I could have told him about the meeting with Dr. Lyle in a place that might or might not have been the afterlife, but that was all complicated and crazy sounding, and we still had a lot to do. Nik's answer was close enough, so I let it lie and started looking for my bag.

I found it right by my foot. Nik hadn't been exaggerating when he'd said I'd landed behind him. We were still on the same floating hunk of disconnected grassland where we'd gotten jumped, barely two feet away from where I'd been standing when Kauffman had grabbed me. The mercs were still there, too, moaning where Nik had dropped them. The only person who wasn't in the same place was Kauffman. The last time I'd seen him, he'd been shoving me off his spellworked rock. Now he was splayed on his back in the grass behind Nik with his face battered, his eyes closed, and his body very, very still.

"What happened to him?"

"I did," Nik said.

I cringed at the naked violence in his voice, and Nik stuck his chin out stubbornly. "He pushed you into the void."

"Um, well, thanks for avenging me," I said awkwardly. "Is he…?"

"He's still alive," Nik said darkly. "I'm not letting him off that easy after all the trouble he's caused. But we should get moving. Mercenary companies always have an emergency evac plan for teams in the field. There's probably a whole squad scrambling to come rescue these idiots right now."

"Really?" I said, turning back to the wounded rent-a-soldiers. "Even in the Gnarls?"

"You looked this place up on the internet," Nik reminded me. "It's not like it's a huge secret. I've never had cause to come down here before, but Kauffman and Dr. Lyle clearly planned to do their business in the Gnarls way before Lyle bolted. I bet people do shady stuff down here all the time, and wherever people are being shady, you find mercenaries. They've probably even got a special protocol for it."

"You know a lot about mercenaries," I said, sliding my bag onto my shoulder.

Nik shrugged. "I've worked a lot of jobs. But I'd bet you ten to one that backup's already on the way, and it's best if we're not here when they arrive."

"Good thinking," I said, looking around. "Just give me a minute to…Ah ha!"

I ran across the stretch of grass, dropping to my knees beside the pile of crushed scrap that was all that remained of Dr. Lyle's hand.

"What are you doing?" Nik asked.

"Keeping a promise," I replied.

Working as fast as I could, I unzipped the front pocket of my messenger bag and scraped all the pieces inside, taking care not to leave so much as a screw behind. When I was certain I'd gotten everything, I held my bag up to the gentle breeze blowing past my face. "See?" I whispered to the wind. "I didn't forget. I'm going to give it a proper burial just like I promised, and Nik and I are going to make sure that Kauffman doesn't get anything of Dr. Lyle's. I've done everything that was asked of me, so can you *please* guide us to the ritual site?"

I held my breath as I finished, listening for a sign, a word, some kind of proof that I wasn't just talking to myself, but the wind didn't reply. It just blew a little harder, sending my hair into my eyes. I pushed the strands away again with a frustrated huff. "Could you be a bit more specific?" I said as I rose to my feet. "Priests might be able to get by on signs and portents, but I'm a Cleaner, and I'm on a deadline. Can I get a big flashing arrow or something?"

I'd barely finished when the wind gusted so hard I was nearly knocked off my feet. I caught myself with a grin. "*Thank* you."

"Who are you talking to?"

I looked over my shoulder to see Nik behind me with Kauffman thrown over his shoulder like a bloody sack of potatoes. "Why are you bringing him?"

Nik snorted. "You think I'm going to leave him here to be rescued after what he pulled? He's the client. The merc evac team will grab him first, so I'm not going to give them the chance." He reached up to pat Kauffman on the back with his right hand—his original one, which he must have put back on while I was busy. "He's coming with me."

I did *not* like that Kauffman was coming. Not that I was worried about him giving us any more trouble—he wasn't even conscious, and his face looked worse than mine did—but given how many times Dr. Lyle had specifically warned me against him, bringing him didn't feel like a savvy move. Nik didn't look like he was going to budge, though, and my shoulders slumped in defeat. "Fine," I said. "But no making deals with him."

"I don't think he's going to be saying much," Nik said, then he gave me a funny look. "But what would we be making deals with him about? The hand's destroyed, and we're still half a kilometer from the ritual site." He nodded at the islands swirling around us. "This whole place shuffles itself like a card deck every few minutes. I'm not even sure which way we were headed anymore. There's no way we can find the ritual site now."

"Yes, we can," I said.

Nik sighed. "I know you're desperate to get money to pay your dad, but this place is dangerous on a really freaky level. You've already fallen into oblivion once. It's time to face up. We had a good shot, but it's over. We can't just poke around blindly, hoping we get lucky."

"It's not over!" I said fiercely. "And we don't have to get lucky. I know how to find it. All we have to do is follow the wind."

I pointed in the direction of the breeze, which, though no longer roaring, was still blowing steadily in a specific direction. Nik, however, was looking at me like I'd lost my marbles. "Follow the wind?"

"I know how it sounds," I said. "But you saw the Empty Wind blow me up here, so give it a chance. The worst that happens is we wander lost in the Gnarls for a few more hours."

"That's a pretty bad worst," Nik said. "Did you forget the part about how people get lost down here and never come back? And I'm not sure the Empty Wind is someone you should be taking help from. Maybe he wants us to get forgotten down here, too."

"That's not how it works," I said.

He arched an eyebrow. "You sure about that?"

I wasn't, really, but I needed this to be true, so I threw myself into it. "Let's just try," I said, looking him in the eyes. "Please."

Nik sighed and waved for me to lead the way. Flashing him a thankful smile, I pulled off my gloves, licked my index finger, and held it up to the wind. When I was certain of its direction, I turned and started walking, following the gusts through the loops and twists of the Gnarls toward what I hoped would be our prize.

***

After what felt like a lot more than half a kilometer of corkscrew paths and jumps between floating islands, the wind suddenly stopped. I stopped as well, looking around to see where it had brought us.

The answer seemed to be nowhere special. We'd just made it to a floating chunk of city that looked as if it had been part of a massive fire not too long ago. The whole thing was a maze of blackened cinderblock walls and big pits of rubble where buildings had collapsed. I could still smell the smoke on the air, but I didn't feel any magic aside from the flood that counted as normal down here. Not that it was easy to feel anything what with the geyser of power constantly rushing past me, but I should have sensed *something*. Big spells always left a presence, a hum in the air. That was what made them so hard to hide, and why Dr. Lyle had secreted his down here. Assuming the wind hadn't led me astray, he must have done a really good job, because I couldn't feel a thing.

I was about to suggest that we fan out to better search the burned buildings when Nik said, "Is that it?"

I whirled around to see Nik pointing down at my feet. When I looked down, I saw that I was standing on a manhole cover. Like everything else here, the round iron cap had been blackened by the fire, but on top of the ashy black was the deeper ink black of a marker, the marks forming a chicken-scratch spellwork I now recognized almost as well as my own name.

"This is it!" I cried, dropping to my knees on the pavement. When I tried to pull the manhole cover up, though, the spellwork sizzled, freezing it in place.

"Ugh," I groaned. "It's locked."

Nik arched an eyebrow. "Can you ask the wind to unlock it?"

I wasn't sure if he was making fun of me or not, and I didn't have the time or patience to find out. I was too busy glaring at the spellwork, attempting to work out the logic in my mind. Attempting and failing. This was why I'd taken the notes to Heidi. I'd never been good at wrapping my brain around Thaumaturgical logic, much less Dr. Lyle's crazy custom stuff. That was fine, though. The circumstances were wildly different, but when you boiled it down, this was just another lock, and cracking locks was what I did every day.

"Stand back," I said, placing my hands on either side of the circle.

"Are you sure this is smart?" Sibyl whispered as Nik got clear. "You nearly cooked yourself earlier. Should you really be using more magic now?"

"No," I said. "But I didn't come all this way just to look at it."

"Can you wait a little, at least?" my AI pleaded. "Your dad will delete me if I let you burn your magic out."

I couldn't care less what my dad thought of this, but she did raise a good point. "How much time do I have left before midnight?"

"Three hours," Sibyl said. "But that's still plenty of—"

I grabbed the magic and yanked it into my hands, ignoring the burning pain that came with it. When Sibyl started to lecture me about the dire ramifications of what I was doing, I shook my goggles off my head onto the ground behind me. I knew she was right, I just didn't want to hear it. What I wanted, what I *needed* was under this lid. It wasn't that I didn't care if I broke my magic—I cared enormously, so much so that I nearly dropped the power because my hands were shaking so badly—I just cared about my freedom more. I'd fought too hard and given too much already to lose at the last inch, so I gritted my teeth and pushed through, trying not to think about the very scary numbness that was starting to spread through my mind as I clumsily shaped the magic into the form I needed.

Thankfully, it didn't take much. The spellwork on the entrance seemed to be more of a seal than a lock, because it popped the moment I applied pressure, making the iron manhole cover jolt against its collar. As it moved, a rush of rich magic welled up from the dark, tingling across my skin like a thousand little feathers. Another time, it probably would have felt nice. In my current overextended state, though, it burned like hot needles, making me gasp as I jumped away.

"What?" Nik demanded.

"Nothing," I lied. "Let's see what we've got."

It took both of us to lift the heavy iron cover. When it was off, I put my goggles back on my head and flicked on my lights, ignoring Sibyl's grumbling as I scanned the metal rungs of the ladder down. They looked normal enough, so I put on my protective gloves and started making my way down. I wasn't entirely sure how manholes worked down here given that we were inside a floating hunk of unused city, but other than a slight swaying feeling, I noticed nothing out of the ordinary. After about ten feet, my feet hit solid ground. When I swept my lights around to see where we had come out, though, I realized the platform I was standing on was the only one.

"Wow," I breathed.

The manhole had led down into a storm cistern, one of those huge, circular wells designed to catch excess runoff before it became a flash flood. Now, though, the bottom of the tank was gone, leaving only the void beneath a golden mesh of pure magic that had been strung across the emptiness like a cargo net. And sitting *in* that net, cradled gently against each other like delicate fruits, were gold-and-crimson speckled eggs. Dozens of them.

"Are those what I think they are?" Nik asked, dropping Kauffman on the ground at the bottom of the ladder as he rushed in to get a better look.

"I think so," I said, eyes going round as I tried to count all the basketball-sized orbs. Tried and failed.

"There has to be a hundred of them!" Nik said, his eyes gleaming greedily in the glow of the magical net. "How much are they worth?"

"Thirty thousand," I replied breathlessly. "Each."

We stared at each other, our faces breaking into matching grins as we did the math. Thirty thousand times a hundred was three *million* dollars.

"We're *rich*!" Nik cried, grabbing me by the shoulders.

"We're *rich*!" I agreed, nodding so fast I made myself dizzy. "Sibyl!" I cried, too excited to do fractions. "What's forty percent of three million?"

"One point two million."

The rush of joy I felt then was almost too strong to take. One point two *million*. That was enough to pay back my dad multiple times over! Even if I had to sell a few eggs at rock-bottom prices to get the money before midnight, there was no way I could fail to raise at least ten thousand, which meant I'd done it. I'd *won*.

"I won!" I cried, grabbing Nik and jumping up and down. "We did it! We—"

A sound cut me off. It was loud and sharp, as though something had snapped. I was worried part of the infrastructure we were standing on was breaking off when it happened again. Then again and again. Within seconds, the air was full of cracking and popping, making my stomach knot as Nik and I slowly turned together to look our prize, our literal nest of golden eggs.

Which were now hatching before our eyes.

CHAPTER 14

"**O**h no," I moaned, running to the edge of the cistern. "No, no, no, no, *no*! You can't *hatch*!"

But the eggs didn't listen. They just kept going, the precious golden shells shattering before my eyes as little beaks pecked their way free.

"How bad is this?" Nik demanded, crouching down on the edge beside me.

"Bad," I said. "Cockatrice eggs are magical components, like chimera horns or dragon scales. That's what people buy them for, not for babies."

Nik's face grew grim. "Well, they're not going back in. How much are the chicks worth?"

I had no idea. I didn't even know if people wanted magical chicken lizards. But there was no point in crying over broken eggs. Cockatrice chicks were what we had, so cockatrice chicks were what we'd sell. But when I opened my mouth to ask Sibyl for a price check, a ragged voice spoke up behind us.

"I'll buy them."

Nik and I turned in unison to see Kauffman rolling himself over. "I'll buy them," he wheezed again. "I'll buy them all right now. Just name your—" He cut off with a hacking cough, spitting one of his formerly perfect teeth out onto the concrete with a wince. "Name your price," he finished feebly.

"Since when do *you* say 'name your price'?" Nik asked suspiciously.

"Since I'm out of leverage and trying to buy something that's worth more than money," Kauffman said, his bloody mouth spreading into a wry grin. "But maybe I shouldn't have told you that. You don't even know what you've got."

"Of course we do," I said, glaring at him. "They're cockatrices."

"But do you know why that matters?" Kauffman pressed. "Why they're worth so much?"

I glanced at Nik, who shrugged, and Kauffman's grin grew wider.

"Cockatrices are amazing animals. They're almost human-level intelligent, but even more vicious, and they have memories like steel traps. They're trainable, magical, and most important of all, baitable. Once you get one into a frenzy, it's capable of amazing feats of strength before it goes down. But due to their incredibly stupid breeding habits, they're highly endangered." He nodded down at the glowing pit. "Those eggs probably just doubled the world's cockatrice population. Do you know what that means?"

"They're rare," Nik answered. "And rare is expensive."

"This goes beyond expensive," Kauffman promised, his voice taking on that salesman's pitch he'd used on me back at my apartment. "You can't buy them for love or money, because there simply are none to buy. Even with his wealth and connections, my employer has only been able to secure two in the past year. Two! But that's about to change." He pushed himself up so that he was sitting against the ladder, looking us in the eye. "I'm willing to buy every one of them off you, right now." His eyes flicked to me. "I know you need money tonight. If you take my offer, I'll wire it straight to your account. No questions asked, no strings attached."

My mouth went dry. That was a very good deal. *Too* good.

"Hold up," I said, putting a hand on Nik's arm before he could accept. "Why are you doing this?"

"Because you've got what I want," Kauffman said, glancing down at the ropes Nik had tied around him so tightly, his hands were starting to turn purple. "And I'm not exactly in a position to bargain."

"I get that part," I said, frustrated. "But *why* do you want them? You don't seem like an environmentalist buying them to save the species. What are you going to do with a hundred cockatrices?"

Kauffman looked at me like I was a silly, naive little girl. "Fight them, of course."

I didn't need the icy wind that rose back up around me then to feel the chill in my gut. "Fight them?" I repeated. "You mean like dog fighting?"

"They're *so* much better than dogs," Kauffman said eagerly. "They're smarter, and they're armored. Once they go through their first molt, their feathers are like iron. They're highly social, brave, fierce. They love, they remember, they sacrifice. You couldn't ask for a better animal for the arena! The whole world went mad for them last spring when a pair took down a combat robot at an exhibition match in China. Naturally, we tried to get a stable going, but there were no cockatrices to buy. Everyone was trying, but it didn't matter how much money you put on the table; there are simply none to be had."

My scowl deepened. "So you hired Dr. Lyle to make them."

"We hired Dr. Lyle to create a resource," Kauffman said smugly, giving me a superior look. "This is about so much more than a handful of cockatrices. This is about creating a monopoly. The whole world wants cockatrices, but other than a few highly protected reserves, there *are* no cockatrices. It's the perfect storm of insane demand and no supply. Whoever can solve that problem will have the entire industry at their feet. That's *power*, Miss Yong-ae, and my employer is far more interested in power than in money." He turned to Nik. "I'll give you five million for the eggs, the ritual site, and the notes."

Nik set his jaw stubbornly. "Ten million."

"No!" I cried at the same time. The grave-cold wind was pushing at me now, but I batted it away impatiently. I didn't need supernatural help to know this was wrong. Down below, one of the chicks had made it out of its egg and was hopping around on the net. Like all newly hatched creatures, it was slimy and alien looking. It wasn't cute at all with its sharp, pointy beak and a lizard's tail, but its golden-rimmed eyes were clear when they met mine, gleaming with innocent curiosity as it started hopping toward me.

"No," I said again, looking at Nik. "We can't sell these animals to him."

"Of course you can," Kauffman said.

"No, we can't," I snapped, putting my hand down for the little chick, which turned out to be not so little after all. It had looked small down in the pit, but when it hopped up to me, the creature that landed in my arms was the size of a large cat. A cat with scaly chicken feet, a beak as sharp as a razor, and pin feathers that pricked like actual pins when it butted its wobbling, oversized head under my hand for a scratch.

"Now I see why Dr. Lyle ran," I said, turning my glare back on Kauffman. "He was trying to save them, wasn't he?"

"Theodore Lyle was a disgraced professor who developed an expensive obsession with creating alchemical life," Kauffman said coldly. "He didn't even ask *why* we wanted the eggs. All he cared about was funding for his experiments. It was only later, when he realized his theories actually worked, that he started asking questions, calling them his babies and other nonsense. I tried to make him see reason, showed him the projected profits and such, but once he realized we were going to be selling the cockatrices to arenas, he would hear none of it. He stole the eggs from the site I'd helped him prepare and hid them out here with a spell on the door to make sure they wouldn't hatch until he came to get them."

I was happy he had. I understood now what Dr. Lyle had meant when he'd said that without my help, he'd have committed great evil. He'd known what kind of man Kauffman was, but he'd still agreed to work for him because he'd needed the funding. He hadn't truly realized what he was attempting, what it meant to create life. By the time he *did* understand what Kauffman intended to do with his work, it was too late. The eggs were already made. All he could do was run away and try to protect the creatures he'd created from the man he'd so foolishly sold them to. But then he'd died. He'd died alone, with no one even knowing where his babies were.

No wonder he'd been desperate enough to accept the dubious help of a pair of money-hungry Cleaners, but at least I understood now why he'd been so adamant about not selling to Kauffman. This wasn't like selling unfertilized eggs to mages. It wasn't even like selling normal animals to be pets or even to the slaughterhouse. At least there, death was quick. If we gave the chicks to Kauffman, we'd be condemning them to slavery in an arena. It wasn't a question of *if* they would suffer. Their suffering was the point. It *was* the entertainment. They would be playthings, toys for cruel masters who put their backs against the wall for sport, and while there was a world of difference between our situations, I had some mighty strong opinions about that.

"We're not selling them to you."

"Don't be stupid," Kauffman said. "Of course you are. I'm your only buyer."

"We can get another," I said.

"No, you can't." He leaned forward. "I don't think you appreciate just how rare these animals are. They're *so* endangered and *so* magical that they've been given special protection under the Peacemaker's Edict. If you try to sell one out in the open, you'll bring the wrath of the Dragon of Detroit and all his allies down on your head. With that kind of heat, legality doesn't matter. No auction house in the world will touch those chicks. My employer is the only one audacious enough to defy the dragons in the name of profit and power. He is your *only* option, which is why I'm only going to give you six million."

"Eight," Nik said.

"Seven," Kauffman snapped back.

"No!" I yelled, glaring at Nik. "We can't do this."

Nik's jaw tightened. "They're just animals," he said stubbornly. "And seven million dollars is a *lot* of money."

"I'm not saying it isn't," I replied, putting my back to Kauffman so I wouldn't have to look at his hateful face. "You know how bad I need this cash, but this is *wrong*, Nik."

"So's everything else we do," Nik said. "You didn't complain when I shot those men. Or when we stole a hand from the morgue."

"I actually complained a lot about that last one," I reminded him. "But this is different. Everyone does bad things. Some of us do a lot of them, but there has to be a line." I held up the baby cockatrice, which was currently chewing a hole through my supposedly indestructible gloves. "You heard what he said. These things are near-human-level intelligent. They love, they fear, they grieve." I pointed into the glowing pit behind him. "There are a hundred innocent babies down there. It doesn't matter if they were made by magic or hatched by a toad. They don't deserve to be slaves who suffer for ticket sales. Yeah, seven million is a lot, but it's nothing compared to what he's asking you to give up in return. What's the point of money if you have to sell your soul to get it?"

"Spoken like a rich girl," Nik snarled, staring down at me with a fury I'd never seen from him before. At least, not directed at me. "What do you know about money? You've never been really poor. You're scraping by right now, but you could go back to your dad any time you want. Just walk right back into that life of private cars and jets. But while seven million might not be a big deal to you, it could change the world for me. Do you know how hard I've worked, the things I've done to get even a fraction of that? You think I *like* taking eviction jobs?"

I flinched at the reminder, and he bared his teeth. "That's right," he said. "You think I didn't see your face every time I raised my hand? You thought I was scum. But someone was going to get paid to evict those poor bastards. Might as well be me. Judge me all you want, but I took that money, and I made my life better."

"I'm not judging you," I said. "Maybe I did before, but now I know that I was wrong. You're not a bad person, Nik, and that's why we can't do this. Because if you take that money, you will be."

"Why do you even care?" he roared. "I thought you were willing to do anything to get free of your dad. Why did we go through all of this if you're just going to throw in the towel now that we're finally at the end?"

"Because I was willing to do anything to *me*!" I yelled. "*I'm* the one who's trapped, but just because I'm willing to gnaw my arm off to get free doesn't mean I'm willing to gnaw off someone else's! If the cost of my freedom is selling babies into slavery, then it's not freedom at all. I'm just trading one prison for another. A *worse* one, because I can hate my dad all day long, but I'm not willing to hate myself."

"Then don't," he said coldly, jerking his head back toward the glowing net, which was now filled with cheeping, hopping cockatrices. "You can take your forty percent and do whatever you want. Start a petting zoo, I don't care. But sixty percent of that lot is mine, and you can't stop me from selling them to anyone I want."

A lump formed in my throat as he spoke. A sad, hard lump no words seemed to be able to get by.

"He's right, you know," Kauffman said behind me. "You're wasting your breath. Nik's a stone-cold killer who'd sell his mother if the price was right. He keeps saying he's getting out of the business, that he's a *Cleaner* now, but I hired him just a few months ago to break a man's knees. I didn't even have to up my rates."

Nik closed his eyes. "Shut up."

"But Nik understands the power of money better than anyone," Kauffman went on. "There's nothing in this world he loves more, because money is the only thing keeping him alive."

"What does he mean by that?" I asked.

Nik turned away. "Nothing a rich girl would understand."

"Of course I can't understand if you won't tell me," I said angrily, smacking my hand against his metal chest. "But you keep saying 'rich girl' like it means ignorant, and that's as stupid as it is wrong. It's *because* I've been rich that I understand what money can't do. I've lived the luxury of never having to worry about food or clothes or if I could pay a bill, and I threw it away because the price of having all that wealth was giving up something I was worthless without. That doesn't mean I don't like money. I want to be rich just as much as you do! That's why I bust my butt as a Cleaner, but I also know that money isn't everything. I *know* this, because I tried to buy freedom and integrity and love, and I *couldn't*. But while you can't buy them, you can absolutely sell them. That's why I'm fighting you so hard on this. You're about to sell something that money can't buy.

That's a bad deal, Nik, and I'd be a worthless business partner if I let you take it."

By the time I finished, Nik's fists were clenched so tight that his metal hand was creaking. I wasn't sure if that meant I'd gotten through to him or if he was barely holding himself back from punching me. The reality was probably a little of both, but if there was one thing of value I'd learned from my father, it was that once you'd drawn a line in the sand, you could never step back. So I didn't. I stayed stubbornly put, meeting Nik glare for glare until he turned away with a curse.

"She's an idiot, Nikola," Kauffman warned. "Don't listen to her."

Nik said nothing. He just stood there, steadfastly looking at anything that wasn't Kauffman or me. Since the cockatrice chicks were the only other thing in the room, this meant he ended up watching them as they tussled and nipped and snoozed together in blissful ignorance of what was going on above their hideous little heads.

"Kauffman," he said at last, after the silence had stretched on for way too long. "Who are you working for?"

Kauffman rolled his bloodshot eyes. "He's spending millions of dollars to corner the market on rare animals for the purposes of fighting them in arenas. Who do you *think* I'm working for?"

I had no idea. Nik must have, though, because that tidbit of information seemed to push him over the edge.

"No deal," he said.

"Really?" I said excitedly.

"Have you lost your mind?" Kauffman yelled at the same time. "We're talking seven million—"

"I know exactly how much we're talking about," Nik said, putting his face in his hands. "And the answer is no."

"You can't possibly—" Kauffman cut off with a sputter. "Do you really think you're not for sale? *You?*"

"I'm always for sale," Nik snapped back. "But not to him."

The way he said that shut Kauffman down cold. It made me cower, too. There was a lifetime of hate buried under those words, but I didn't dare ask him about it. From the look on his face, Nik was going to kill someone in the next five minutes, and if I didn't want it to be me, I'd better make myself scarce. I did so by walking to the far edge of the cistern and bringing up my AR to see if there was such a thing as a cockatrice rescue.

"You should tell him he made the right choice," Sibyl whispered.

"I don't think he wants to hear that," I whispered back.

"Probably not," she agreed. "His body temperature and pulse rate are way up. Better let him cool down, figuratively and literally."

I nodded slowly, reading the mission statement of the Cockatrice Council of Canada to see if they were legit.

"You know," Sibyl said. "You don't have to give them to a rescue. Pet store isn't a bad fate, and unlike charities, they pay. Maybe not millions, but anything's better than nothing."

"Not in this case," I said, opening a new window to bring up the list of entities protected by the Peacemaker Edict. Sure enough, cockatrices were right at the top, which meant Kauffman had been telling the truth, the bastard. "Anyone who'll buy an animal protected by the Edict is either insane or a criminal. Either way, they're going to turn around and resell to the highest bidder, and unless cockatrices become the hot must-have celebrity pet in the next few hours, that means the arena. There's simply too much money on the table not to go there. The only people we *can* trust are the ones who already have cockatrices, because they're the ones who've already been offered millions and turned them down."

Unfortunately for me, all of those people seemed to live in secret locations. That was understandable when you were protecting animals that were worth gobs of money, but it made them really difficult to contact. That said, there was one group I knew would be interested that would be very easy to call. I actually already had their number stored in my phone, in case of emergencies. I wasn't sure if this counted, but if there was anyone who was interested in enforcing the Peacemaker's Edict, it was his office at the DFZ Dragon Consulate.

"Hoo boy," Sibyl said as I selected the number from my contacts list. "Your dad is not going to like this."

"Since when has that stopped me?" I muttered, holding the phone up to my ear. "Hi," I said when the operator picked up. "I think I've got something you want."

There was no faster way to get a dragon's—or a mortal who worked for a dragon's—attention. The moment the word "want" left my mouth, I heard her click on a recorder, all but guaranteeing the circus I knew I was about to bring down on our heads.

***

Two hours later, the cistern was swarming with men and women wearing the serpentine badge of the Peacemaker. We even got a legit dragon to oversee the transfer. To be fair, she was very young. She didn't have a fraction of the predatory menace my father could put out *and* she was a member of the Heartstriker clan, which is basically the bottom-shelf generic brand of dragon. But while she wasn't up to my dad's level, her human form was still unspeakably beautiful, and her burning magic was razor sharp, holding the ever-twisting Gnarls in place through sheer brute force so the retrieval team could work.

My father had always sneered at the Peacemaker for being weak, but so far, I was beyond impressed with his organization. They'd even persuaded the DFZ to open a special doorway between the Gnarls and the Dragon Consulate, which I hadn't known was possible. Clearly, the rumors about the city owing her local dragon big time were no joke. Then again, you didn't get to be the dragon of the most magical city in the world if you weren't something special.

"Thank you so much for this," I said, bowing low before the Heartstriker dragoness when the portal stabilized and she could finally release her magic. "And for coming so quickly."

"You have to be quick for these things," the dragoness said distractedly, her electric-green eyes locked on the virtual clipboard she'd brought up in her AR. "Cockatrice smuggling has been a major problem all year. If we don't move fast, we lose them, and we can't afford any more of that. The species is close enough to extinction as it is, though if it were up to me, I'd let them die. A species that unwilling to breed deserves to go extinct. But the Peacemaker's wife is friends with the Spirit of Cockatrices, so they go on the list and I do my job." She glanced back at the ritual circle in the cistern, where armored mages were carefully lifting cat-sized cockatrices into padded transport cages. "At least they're babies this time. The last one I had to save was the size of a horse. Nearly bit my arm off."

She shook her head with a sigh and flipped her floating clipboard around. "Sign," she ordered. "You put in the call, so that makes you legal guardian. Just sign here to surrender your rights, and we'll be out of your hair."

"Actually," I said quickly. "They're not all mine. I only own forty percent. My partner owns the rest."

She shrugged. "I don't care who signs."

"I do," I said, meeting the dragon's eyes. Never a smart move, but a vital one if you wanted them to actually listen to what you said. Some dragons would eat you on the spot for such insolence, but most respected mortals who didn't cower. Since she worked for the Peacemaker, I was betting this dragoness was one of the latter. Sure enough, after a good thirty seconds of dominance-staring contest, she waved me away.

"Do what you want."

I bowed again and scrambled up the manhole's metal rung ladder. Just like the cistern below it, the burned-out hunk of floating city was now full of people. There were DFZ cops, SWAT units, a Merlin Council mage team, city clerks, the works. It was the biggest show of civic authority I'd ever seen in this city, and I liked it. The huge response made me feel as if I'd done the right thing, and I *knew* Dr. Lyle was happy. After much prodding from the freezing wind, I'd given all his research notes about creating cockatrices to the mages, making very sure that they knew it was the work of Dr. Theodore Lyle, brilliant historical Thaumaturge and steadfast defender of the breed. I still had to return Dr. Lyle's hand to Peter, along with my apologies, but the Empty Wind must have thought I was good for it by that point, because the grave-cold wind let me be, finally letting me warm up again as I wandered the ruins in search of Nik.

I found him at the edge of the island, standing in the middle of a collapsed building that hadn't been collapsed when we'd gotten here. From the fist-sized holes in the blackened cement, I could guess what had happened, but I didn't say a word. Nik had given up more tonight than I had, and not just because he'd had the sixty-percent share. He deserved to be mad, though I did say a quick, silent prayer pleading to the DFZ not to punish him for taking it out on her buildings.

"Hey," I said when he finally noticed me standing behind him. "They're ready for us to sign off."

Nik took a breath so deep it moved his entire body. Then he dusted off his hands and walked over to grab his jacket, his bag, and Kauffman, who was still trussed up with rope and now sported a bloody gag.

"Um," I said as Nik threw the man over his shoulder. "Do I want to know what you're going to do?"

"No," Nik said in a monotone.

I swallowed my next question, leading him back to the dragon as quickly as I could go.

We signed the form without incident. I used my real name, but Nik put down a crypto ID, the blockchain-based anonymous identifier that anyone could use in place of their name in the DFZ. Add in the bloody man he was carrying on his shoulder, and I knew we had to look shady as hell, but the electronic form accepted his ID no problem, so the dragon didn't say a word.

"That's that," she said when all the authentications turned green. "Good work, everyone. Let's pack it in."

The crowd nodded and began collecting their things. Nik was already carrying Kauffman toward the portal, which, since it let out at the Dragon Consulate downtown, wasn't that far from where we'd parked his car. I was about to run after him when the dragon caught my arm.

"Wait," she said, squinting at the form we'd just signed. "Your name is Opal Yong-ae? That means you belong to the Dragon of Korea, right?"

I winced at the word "belong." "I'm part of his household, yes."

"Oh, well, that explains it."

"Explains what?" I asked nervously.

"The curse," she said, waving her hand in the general vicinity of my face. "You've got a dragon curse on you. I wasn't going to tell you since I didn't want to mess up anyone's plans, but the Dragon of Korea still hasn't joined the Peacemaker's Alliance, so he can choke on his tail for all I—"

"What does it do?"

She closed her mouth slowly, electric-green eyes narrowing, and I shrank in my boots. Interrupting a dragon was *never* good, but I couldn't help it. "Please, great dragon," I said, bowing my head in a flagrant display of deference. "I apologize for my rudeness, but I have to know. What curse am I under?"

"Nice groveling," she said, patting me on the head. "And it's a bad-luck curse. Not one of those cheap jobs that makes you stub your toes all the time, either. This is the real deal, the kind that hits you where it hurts the most." She grinned at me. "I bet you've had a *really* rotten year, haven't you?"

She had no idea. "Thank you, great dragon," I said through clenched teeth. "I can't tell you how much I appreciate your insight."

The dragoness cooed at me for being such a polite little mortal and sent me away, yelling at her team to hurry it up. Almost too angry to see, I turned and walked with the rest of the people flowing toward the portal to the Dragon Consulate.

Despite my upbringing, I'd never been inside the Consulate. Other dragons brought their mortals here all the time. It was one of the safest places in the world for them since the Dragon of Detroit did not tolerate violence between clans on his turf. But between his low respect for the Peacemaker and outright hatred of the dirt and savagery of the DFZ, my father had never brought any of us along the few times a year he was forced to come here. I got lost immediately and ended up walking up three floors when I should have gone down two. Finally, after much consulting with Sibyl and three stops to ask for directions, I walked out the front door of the massive Consulate's Underground entrance to find Nik waiting.

I hadn't realized how braced I'd been to never see him again until I spotted him. Even better, he was waiting in his car, which was another miracle, because I was seven miles from home and had no money for a cab. I still walked down the steps with trepidation, bending down to look at him through the window.

"Can I get in?"

"Only if you take off that damn spy camera," he muttered, keeping his eyes on the mirrors like he expected someone in the crowded pickup zone to start breathing fire. Which, to be fair, was a distinct possibility here.

I didn't wait to be asked twice. I ripped my goggles off my head and jumped in, turning off both of my devices and shoving them deep into my bag before putting it in the back seat.

"Where's Kauffman?"

"In the trunk," Nik said casually. "I'm saving him for later."

Twenty-four hours ago, hearing that would have terrified me. Now, though, I just nodded. "Give him one for me, please."

"He's already had several for you," Nik said as he pulled us out. "But there's always room for more."

We drove the next few minutes in silence. This was partially because I didn't want to distract Nik while he was navigating the swarms of tourists that always invaded this part of downtown, but mostly because I had no idea what to say. I felt as if I'd done him great wrong tonight, which sucked, because I'd been *trying* to do right. I didn't want to apologize for that, but I needed to say something. I wasn't sure when it had happened exactly, but at some point during the last day and a half, I'd come to think of Nik and me as being on the same side. Now, though, it felt like we were enemies again, and I hated that.

"Listen," I said when I couldn't take it anymore. "About what happened—"

"Don't."

I flinched like the word was a blow, and Nik sighed. "I don't want to talk about what happened down there," he said, keeping his eyes steadfastly on the road. "It is what it is. End of story."

"It's not the end," I said determinedly. "I still have to tell you that I think you did the right thing."

"I know *you* think that," he said, leaning his head hard against the driver's seat's padded headrest. "But all I can think about is the fact that I threw away sixty percent of seven million dollars."

A lot of replies ran through my head at that. I wanted to tell him he'd saved so much more, that I was proud of him, that he'd proven my faith in him. Those were my sincere feelings, but they all sounded too saccharine and sentimental when I imagined saying them out loud, so I kept my mouth shut, staring at my hands as the orange street lamps flashed past. Then, when we stopped for a traffic light, Nik spoke again.

"I'm glad I didn't do it."

My head shot up. "Really?"

"I still hate that I lost the money," he warned. "I'm going to be mad about that for a *very* long time. But that's the nature of opportunity cost. Sometimes you have to give up one thing to get something else."

The light changed, and he started us forward again, hands clenched tight on the wheel. "I've given up a lot of things I shouldn't for money," he said, his voice quiet, as if he was talking to himself. "What happened in that cistern has happened before. Never for that much, of course, but same basic situation. All the other times, I chose the money, and every single time, I regretted it. Not right away. Sometimes not for years. But sooner or later, I always missed what I'd sold, and I couldn't get it back."

I twisted my hands in my lap. "I—"

"But this time was different," he went on. "This time, you were there. And while I'm regretting the hell out of my choice right now, I think I'll feel different in the long run, which is the run that matters."

I blew out a long breath. Then, to my absolute mortification, I started to cry.

"What?" Nik said, looking at me in horror. "What did I say?"

"Nothing," I said, scrubbing at my face. "It's me. It's all me, not you. I just...I thought you were going to hate me, and I'm so relieved that you don't."

"How could I hate you?" he said, his voice frustrated. "You were just trying to help me. I'm *mad* at you, but it'll pass."

"I can accept that," I said, giving him a watery smile.

He nodded, and that was that. We spent the rest of the drive talking about little things—how fancy the Dragon Consulate had been, the idiot on the corner who was trying to wrestle a bucket of fried chicken away from a gutter nutria the size of a pit bull, how much longer we'd have to endure the heat before fall arrived to save us—but we didn't mention what had happened in the cistern again. I was still laughing about the chicken guy when we pulled into the lot for my apartment, and Nik cut the engine with a click that felt unaccountably final.

"So what are you going to do?" he asked the steering wheel. "About your dad, I mean."

I sighed. The clock had turned off with the car, but I didn't need it. I'd been secretly watching it the whole way back. I knew exactly how late it was and how screwed that made me.

"Nothing to do," I said at last, giving him a hapless shrug. "It's eleven thirty. The deadline's at midnight, and I have exactly zero dollars. So unless you know of a way someone with maxed-out credit and nothing to sell can get ten thousand dollars in thirty minutes, I'm pretty much sunk."

I knew why that was now, of course. My five-month-long bad luck streak hadn't been a streak at all. I'd been under a dragon curse, and I was pretty sure I knew which dragon was responsible. But that was a fury for my father, not Nik. We'd already met our negative-emotions quota for the night. I wasn't about to bring in more now, especially since this might be the last time I saw him.

"It won't be so bad," I said quietly. "Like you said, I'm going back to the land of private jets and chauffeured cars. It's hardly the Gulag. I lost this round, but there will be other chances. Even dragons can't think of everything. I'll just find a different way to win."

"I bet you can," he said, smiling at me. Then he glanced up at my apartment. "You think he'll come for you here?"

"That would make the most sense." I was certain Sibyl had already ratted out where I lived.

Nik nodded like that was a profound statement. "Need help carrying your stuff up?"

For a moment, I wasn't sure what he was talking about. I only had the one shoulder bag, and I didn't care what happened to my plastic trash bag full of Cleaning clothes and almost-empty bottles of shampoo if I was going back to Korea. I was opening my mouth to tell him not to worry about it when I suddenly remembered.

"My collection!" I'd *totally* forgotten about the box of treasures Nik had packed up for me when I'd had to flee my apartment, which made me feel terrible. How could I forget my darlings? "They're still in the trunk, right?"

"Actually, I moved them up here," Nik said, reaching back to pull the box out of the back seat behind me. "I didn't want Kauffman to bleed on them."

I could have hugged him then. He was just so thoughtful in the strangest ways. But it didn't seem appropriate, so I held back, distracting myself by grabbing the rest of my stuff and running up the stairs while Nik came behind me with my box. When I reached my door, though, I didn't know why we'd bothered.

"Great," I said, dropping my bags to the ground.

The door of my apartment was hanging on its hinges, the deadbolt shattered by what had to have been one hell of a kick. The inside was even worse. Kauffman must have brought in the same guys who'd destroyed Dr. Lyle's house, because everything that could be broken had been. They'd even taken the time to rip open every single paper cup in my Cup Noodle stash, which was just petty. If I hadn't been about to be kidnapped back home, I would have flown into a rage. As it was, all I could do was sigh.

"Please punch Kauffman a lot for me."

"I will," Nik promised, setting my box down in the middle of the living room floor, the only part of my apartment that wasn't covered in pulverized debris. "So," he said, rubbing the back of his neck. "I guess this is goodbye."

My heart started to sink. I'd known this was coming, but that didn't mean I wanted to hear it. "I'll be back someday," I promised, both to him and myself. "My dad hates this city, which makes it my favorite place in the world."

"Do you want me to tell the other Cleaners?"

"That I got sent home?" I snorted. "No way. Let them think I hit it rich and retired to a life of leisure. That's a good, happy ending to the life of Cleaner Yong-ae."

He nodded, then I nodded, and then we both just stopped and sort of stood there, staring at each other as the minutes ticked down.

"You should probably go," I said at last. "You don't want to be here when my dad arrives."

"No," he agreed, looking at me one last time. "Have a good life, Opal."

"You, too," I said, proud that my voice didn't shake. Honestly, this felt more like defeat than anything else had tonight, but I'd already been a weepy idiot once. I refused to do it again while he was here. There'd be plenty of time for crying and hating the world back at my father's lair in Seoul. For now, I was going to remember every moment, watching Nik as he waved goodbye and slipped silently out my broken door, shutting what was left of the splintered wood behind him.

I stood staring at the place where he'd been for a long time. It was a sad, mopey thing to do, but what else did I have? My apartment didn't even have a place to sit down anymore. In my bag, I heard my goggles turn themselves back on, which I assumed meant Sibyl was sending my location to my dad. I could have marched over and turned her back off, but there didn't seem to be much point. Whether it happened now or an hour from now, I was finished. I'd challenged the Dragon of Korea, and I'd lost. I was trying to be stoic about it when a knock sounded on my door.

Like a condemned prisoner walking to her noose, I trudged the four feet across my splinter-strewn carpet. I didn't want my father to see me beaten, though, so I forced myself to straighten up. When I'd squared my shoulders and pulled myself to my full height, such as it was, I grabbed the hole where my doorknob had been and yanked the door open, defiant scowl ready on my face.

And nearly walked straight into Nik.

"What are you doing back here?" I whispered frantically, pushing past him to check if my father's limo was in the parking lot yet. "He's coming any minute!"

"I know," Nik said. "That's why I rushed." He grabbed my hand and shoved something into it. "Here."

I looked down in confusion. Nik had thrust an envelope into my hand, one of those yellow bank envelopes no one used anymore. The kind they put cash in.

"What's this?"

"A loan," he said, staring at me intently. "I'm loaning you ten thousand dollars."

I jumped so hard I almost dropped the envelope. "*What?*"

"I'm loaning you ten thousand dollars," Nik repeated. "Now you can pay your dad."

"You can't do that!" I cried.

He shrugged. "Why not? You already cost me millions of dollars tonight. What's ten thousand more?"

"I can't accept this," I said, thrusting the envelope back at him. "You can't just give me ten thousand dollars!"

"I'm not giving it to you," he said, his voice growing annoyed. "I already told you, it's a loan. You can just pay it back later."

"No, I *can't*," I said desperately. "If I could just 'pay back' ten thousand dollars, I wouldn't be in this mess! But there's no chance. I'm cursed."

Nik smiled at me. "You're not cursed."

"No, I mean I'm *literally* cursed with dragon magic," I explained. "That's why I've had such a horrible five months. I found out from the dragoness who took the cockatrices that my dad cursed me to have bad luck."

"Oh," Nik said. Then he shrugged. "Doesn't matter."

"How does that not matter?" I cried.

"Because *I'm* not cursed," he said, giving me a smirk. "How about this? You've always been a better Cleaner than I am, and I've always been jealous of your ability to look at a place and see the hidden money. Now you need someone to make bids who isn't magically doomed, so what if we worked together? You can tell me which units are good buys, and I'll handle all the actual transactions that your bad luck would hurt. That way, we can finally stop wasting cash bidding against each other. We'll piss everyone else off, make a ton of money, and you can pay me back out of our earnings. Everyone wins! We'll split everything sixty-forty. It'll be great."

I scowled at the envelope of money in my hands. "Fifty-fifty."

"Deal," he said immediately, sticking out his hand.

I took it at once, wrapping my fingers tight around his as we shook. "Thank you."

"You act like I'm the one giving charity," he said, grinning at me. "But I just got my number-one competitor working on my side, so who's ahead now?" He rubbed his palms together. "I'm finally going to get my hands on those jackpot auctions you're always winning."

"Don't count your money yet," I warned him. "I still don't know how this curse works, and—"

I cut off when my ears caught the sound of footsteps on the stairs. Very familiar footsteps. From the look on his face, Nik heard them, too, and he bolted for the door. "Tomorrow morning," he whispered over his shoulder as he raced down the open hall. "Six a.m. auction. I'll pick you up."

I nodded, shooing him away with my hands just in time as my father rounded the opposite corner.

There was no pretty accessory mortal this time. He was alone, and he looked strangely tired, his beautiful face pinched. His eyes flicked past me to the open-air corridor Nik had just vanished down, but while I was sure he could smell that I'd had a visitor, my father didn't comment. He just held out his hand.

"Come."

I scowled at his extended palm, and then I slapped Nik's envelope down on top of it.

My father's upswept brows furrowed slightly. "What's this?"

"My payment."

His yellow-green eyes flicked down as he tore the envelope open, and then his jaw tightened. "Cash?" he said scornfully, pulling out the bills. "Who still uses *cash*, aside from criminals?"

"Me," I said, crossing my arms over my chest. "Sorry it's not a bank transfer, but it's still legal tender, and you have to take what you can get when there's a curse on your head."

He didn't even try to deny it. "I suppose you're going to demand that I remove it?" he said, crossing his arms over his chest.

"Nope," I said, shaking my head. "You're not going to, so I'm not going to waste my breath. I just wanted you to know that *I* know and that it doesn't matter. Curse or no curse, I'm not giving up. I'm going to pay you back in full, and then we never have to see each other again."

My father's hand clenched, his pale, elegant, claw-like nails shredding the money I'd handed him into confetti. I flinched at the soft sound of ripping paper, but when I looked up again, he wasn't staring down at me in fury. He just looked sad. So, so sad, like that money had been his heart, and I, not him, was the one who'd torn it to shreds.

"Why are you doing this, Opal?" he asked quietly. "Why will you not come home?"

"Because I don't want to come home."

"Why?" he demanded, throwing the shredded money on the ground. "Have I not been a good provider? Have I not given you *everything* you could want?"

"You never gave me what I wanted," I told him bitterly. "You gave me what *you* wanted. You gave me a handcrafted Steinway baby grand piano for my twelfth birthday. I don't even play!"

"You could have learned," he said, the horrible sadness falling off his face as the much more familiar anger pushed its way to the fore. "I will not apologize for being generous. And as to your *wants*, I have done nothing but cater to them for the last four years. I have let you run positively wild, and you have made an absolute mess of it. I just had a call from the *Peacemaker*—the insane Dragon of Detroit himself!—that my daughter was running around in the Gnarls with injuries. Do you have any concept of how badly that reflects on me?"

"On *you?*" I cried. "I was the one who was hurt!"

"Because of your recklessness!" he yelled back. "You care more for the well-being of the *criminal* who was just here than you do for your own. But you are *my* Opal! My treasure! I would never allow anyone to treat my property as shoddily as you have treated yourself."

"Then stop making me!" I shouted, not caring that my neighbors were starting to poke their heads out. "If I wasn't trying to pay your debt and struggling under your curse, I wouldn't have had to do any of this!"

"The debt was *your* idea," he snarled. "Not mine! If you can't pay it, that's not my fault. But if you think for one moment I will allow you to walk away without a fight, you have not been paying attention."

"Believe me," I said in a deadly voice. "I've been paying attention. I know *exactly* how dirty you're willing to fight now, but you should know better than anyone that I will never give up. Curses, debts, hacking my AI, that's just you showing how desperate you're getting, which means I must be closer to winning than ever. And I *will* win, even if I have to break everything to do it."

By the time I finished, my dad was staring at me like he'd never seen me before. "You selfish, foolish child," he whispered, reaching out to touch my face. "You don't even know what you're stomping on."

"Neither do you," I said, ducking away from his touch. "If you want me to stop taking risks, stop putting my back against the wall. Just leave me be!"

"*Never,*" he swore. "Where do you think you learned not to quit? I will *never* stop chasing you, little dog girl. Not until you are safely back at my feet where you belong."

"Then I guess we'll be doing this again next month," I said stubbornly. "Because this month is mine. Now." I pushed the pile of shredded money he'd dropped on the ground toward him with my foot. "Here's your payment, so kindly get off my porch."

He grabbed the money in a motion so fast my eyes couldn't follow it. Clutching the ruined bills, he bared his sharpening teeth at me and whirled away, stomping down the stairs with such force, the whole apartment block shook. I shook, too, my body trembling as I watched him get into his limo and drive away.

When I was certain he wasn't coming back, I went back inside and started moving the bigger pieces of debris to block my broken door. Not to block him—I'd learned ages ago there was no stopping my father when he wanted in—but it was impossible to relax when you didn't have a door. I couldn't fix it tonight, but I could make a barrier, so I piled the wreckage high. When I felt comfortable that any would-be intruders would trip and break their necks before they reached me, I curled up in the shreds of my bed and went to sleep. After all, I had an early work day tomorrow, and there was no way Nik was letting me sleep in.

And when I dreamed, I dreamed of the brief, happy time when I'd been young enough to confuse presents with love and my father had been my world.

THANK YOU FOR READING!

Thank you for reading *Minimum Wage Magic*! If you enjoyed the story, I hope you'll consider leaving a review. Reviews, good and bad, are vital to every author's career, and I would be very grateful if you'd consider writing one for me.

Need more DFZ? The next book, *Part-Time Gods,* is out **right now**! You can get your copy from Amazon.com or Audible.

Want to know when I release a new book? Sign up for my New Release Mailing List (at rachelaaron.net). List members are always first in line for everything I do, *and* they get exclusive bonus content like the list-only Heartstriker short story, *Mother of the Year.* Signing up is free, and I promise never to spam you, so come join us!

Still need more to read? Why not try one of my already completed series? Visit www.rachelaaron.net to see the full list. You can also follow me on Twitter @Rachel_Aaron or like my Facebook page at facebook.com/RachelAaronAuthor for updates on my books, blog posts, and appearances.

Again, thank you so *so* much for reading! I couldn't do any of this without you!

Yours always,
Rachel Aaron

ENJOYED *MINIMUM WAGE MAGIC?* YOU'LL LOVE

Life in the magical mess of the Detroit Free Zone is never easy. When you're laboring under the curse of a certain prideful, overbearing dragon, it can be downright impossible.

My name is Opal Yong-ae, and I'm a Cleaner. At least, I used to be. Thanks to the magical bad luck that turns everything I do against me these days I'm more of a walking disaster. Getting rid of this curse is the only way to get my life back, but dragon magic is every bit as sneaky and scaly as the monsters behind it, and just as hard to beat. A more sensible mortal would give up and go home, but I've never been one to take her doom at face value, and in an awakened city that rules herself, dragons are no longer the biggest powers around…

Available in ebook, Kindle Unlimited, print, and audio!

NEED A NEW BOOK RIGHT NOW?

Try one of Rachel's other completed series! Just keep reading to see the list of my other books. Or go to
www.rachelaaron.net
for full sample chapters, links to reviews, and lovely covers in high resolution!

As the smallest dragon in the Heartstriker clan, Julius survives by a simple code: stay quiet, don't cause trouble, and keep out of the way of bigger dragons. But this meek behavior doesn't cut it in a family of ambitious predators, and his mother, Bethesda the Heartstriker, has finally reached the end of her patience.

Now, sealed in human form and banished to the DFZ--a vertical metropolis built on the ruins of Old Detroit--Julius has one month to prove to his mother that he can be a ruthless dragon or lose his true shape forever. But in a city of modern mages and vengeful spirits where dragons are seen as monsters to be exterminated, he's going to need some serious help to survive this test.

He just hopes humans are more trustworthy than dragons.

"Super fun, fast paced, urban fantasy full of heart, and plenty of magic, charm and humor to spare, this self published gem was one of my favorite discoveries this year!" - **The Midnight Garden**

"A deliriously smart and funny beginning to a new urban fantasy series about dragons in the ruins of Detroit...inventive, uproariously clever, and completely un-put-down-able!" - **SF Signal**

THE LEGEND OF ELI MONPRESS

Eli Monpress is talented. He's charming. And he's the greatest thief in the world.

He's also a wizard, and with the help of his partners in crime--a swordsman with the world's most powerful magic sword (but no magical ability of his own) and a demonseed who can step through shadows and punch through walls-- he's getting ready to pull off the heist of his career. To start, though, he'll just steal something small. Something no one will miss. Something like... a king.

"I cannot be less than 110% in love with this book. I loved it. I love it still. Already I sort of want to read it again. Considering my fairly epic Godzilla-sized To Read list, that's just about the highest compliment I can give a book" - **CSI: Librarian**

"Fast and fun, The Spirit Thief introduces a fascinating new world and a complex magical system based on cooperation with the spirits who reside in all living objects. Aaron's characters are fully fleshed and possess complex personalities, motivations, and backstories that are only gradually revealed. Fans of Scott Lynch's Lies of Locke Lamora (2006) will be thrilled with Eli Monpress. Highly recommended for all fantasy readers." - **Booklist, Starred Review**

THE PARADOX TRILOGY
(written as Rachel Bach)

Devi Morris isn't your average mercenary. She has plans. Big ones. And a ton of ambition. It's a combination that's going to get her killed one day - but not just yet.

That is, until she just gets a job on a tiny trade ship with a nasty reputation for surprises. The Glorious Fool isn't misnamed: it likes to get into trouble, so much so that one year of security work under its captain is equal to five years everywhere else. With odds like that, Devi knows she's found the perfect way to get the jump on the next part of her Plan. But the Fool doesn't give up its secrets without a fight, and one year on this ship might be more than even Devi can handle.

"*Firefly-esque in its concept of a rogue-ish spaceship family... The narrative never quite goes where you expect it to, in a good way... Devi is a badass with a heart.*" - **Locus Magazine**

"*If you liked* Star Wars, *if you like our books, and if you are waiting for* Guardians of the Galaxy *to hit the theaters, this is your book.*" - **Ilona Andrews**

"*I JUST LOVED IT! Perfect light sci-fi. If you like space stuff that isn't that complicated but highly entertaining, I give two thumbs up!*" - **Felicia Day**

FOREVER FANTASY ONLINE

In the real world, twenty-one-year-old library sciences student Tina Anderson is invisible and under-appreciated, but in the VR-game Forever Fantasy Online she's Roxxy--the respected leader and main tank of a top-tier raiding guild. In the real world, her brother James Anderson is a college drop-out struggling under debt, but in FFO he's famous--an explorer who's gotten every achievement, done every quest, and collected all the rarest items.

Both Tina and James need the game more than they'd like to admit, but their favorite escape turns into a trap when FFO becomes a living world. Wounds are no longer virtual, stupid monsters become cunning, NPCs start acting like actual people, and death might be forever.

In the real world, everyone said being good at video games was a waste of time. Now, stranded and separated across thousands of miles of new, deadly terrain, Tina and James's skill at FFO is the only thing keeping them alive. It's going to take every bit of their expertise--and hoarded loot--to find each other and get back home, but as the stakes get higher and the damage adds up, being the best in the game may no longer be enough.

"Rachel Aaron and Travis Bach have written an amazing story and a realistic LitRPG." - **The Fantasy Inn**

"Excellent characters, an engaging story, and geek humor. What more can one ask for?" - **TS Chan**

The first in a new gamer/fantasy collaboration from Rachel Aaron and Travis Bach!

2,000 TO 10,000: WRITING BETTER, WRITING FASTER, AND WRITING MORE OF WHAT YOU LOVE
(nonfiction)

"Have you ever wanted to double your daily word counts? Do you sometimes feel like you're crawling through your story? Do you want to write more every day without increasing the time you spend writing or sacrificing quality? It's not impossible; it's not even that hard. This is the book explaining how, with a few simple changes, I boosted my daily writing from 2000 words to over 10k a day, and how you can too."

Expanding on Rachel's viral blog post about how she doubled her daily word counts, this book offers practical writing advice for anyone who's ever longed to increase their daily writing output. In addition to updated information for the popular 2k to 10k writing efficiency process, 5 step plotting method, and easy editing tips, the book includes all new chapters on creating characters who write their own stories, plot structure, and learning to love your daily writing. Full of easy to follow, practical advice from a professional author who doesn't eat if she doesn't produce good books on a regular basis, 2k to 10k focuses not just on writing faster, but writing better, and having more fun while you do it!

"I loved this book! So helpful!" - **Courtney Milan, NYT Bestselling Author**

"This. Is. Amazing. You are telling my story RIGHT NOW. Book is due in 2 weeks, and I'm behind--woefully, painfully behind--because I've been stuck...writing in circles and unenthused. Yet here here is a FANTASTIC solution. I am printing this post out, and I'm setting out to make my triangle. Thank you, thank you, THANK YOU!" - **Bestselling YA Author Susan Dennard**

ABOUT THE AUTHOR

Rachel Aaron is the author of sixteen novels and the bestselling nonfiction writing book, *2k to 10k: Writing Faster, Writing Better, and Writing More of What You Love,* which has helped thousands of authors double their daily word counts. When she's not holed up in her writing cave, Rachel lives a nerdy, bookish life in Broomfield, CO, with her perpetual-motion son, long-suffering husband, and grumpy old lady dog. To learn more about Rachel, read samples of all her books, or to find a complete list of her interviews and podcasts, please visit rachelaaron.net!

Cover Illustration by Tia Rambaran
Cover Design by Rachel Aaron
Editing provided by Red Adept Editing

As always, this book would not have been nearly as good without my amazing beta readers. Thank you so, so much to Michele Fry, Jodie Martin, Eva Bunge, Beth Bisgaard, Christina Vlinder, Judith Smith, Rob Aaron, Hisham El-far, and the ever amazing Laligin.

Y'all are the BEST!